Anne Cameron

Child Of Her People

Anne Cameron

Child Of Her People

spinsters / *aunt lute*

San Francisco

First Edition
10-9-8-7-6-5-4-3-2

Spinsters/Aunt Lute Book Company
P.O. Box 410687
San Francisco, CA 94141

Cover and Text Design: Pamela Wilson Design Studio
Cover Art: Kristen Throop
Typesetting: Grace Harwood and Comp-Type, Fort Bragg, CA
Production: Raquel Cion   Kayla Sussel
                   Martha Davis   Kathleen Wilkinson
                   Debra DeBondt   Joey Xanders
                   Lorraine Grassano

Publication of this book was made possible in part through a grant
from the California Arts Council.

Spinsters/Aunt Lute is an educational project of the Capp Street
Foundation.

Printed in the U.S.A.

Library of Congress Catalog Card Number: 87-062315

ISBN: 0-933216-28-9

For my children   *Alex*
                     Erin
                     Pierre
                     Marianne
                     Tara

For Eleanor, with love

and for everyone who read The Journey *and asked for "more"*

For a story to be told, it must be told properly, and to tell a story properly, it must be told with respect. A story properly told will contain an old story, a new story, a message, and an example from the past for those who will come in the future.

This does not mean a properly told story will contain what the European dominant ideology would refer to as a *moral!*

The history of this continent has not been told properly, and what has been told improperly has been told without respect, and without truth. The history of this continent, improperly and untruthfully told, has become a lie, and on that lie a society has been based which yearns for something most of us have never known in our lifetimes.

We like to convince ourselves our society is peaceful, built of principles of liberty and justice and kindhearted liberal concern for our neighbours. We like to convince ourselves and our children we are a peace-loving people who have never oppressed or invaded any other nation—and yet how else did we get here if not by invading, oppressing, and exterminating our indigenous cousins?

"Oh," we say, "why bring up all those mistakes of the past? What's done is done and can't be undone, so let us move forward and put behind us all the sorrow." Easy to say when it isn't *your* sorrow. Easy to say when it wasn't *your* great-grandmother who became the last of what had once been a numerous, healthy, and happy family! A society which does not remember and learn from the mistakes of the past is a society which takes no responsibility and thus will repeat those mistakes of the past.

History, as it has been taught to us, is the lie the conquerors force down the throats of the children of the dispossessed. So if lies must be told, let them at least be told with love, let them at least contain some magic. After all, what is a story but a magic lie?

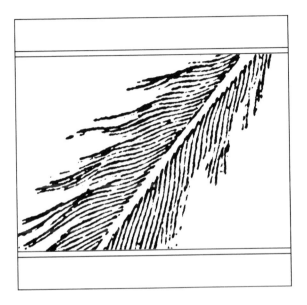

The ridiculous contraption had been sitting there for at least two days and the poor horses harnessed to it were more dead than alive. They had eaten as much of the rich prairie grass as they could reach, but had not quenched their thirst. They had tried to continue pulling the cart in search of water; there were gouges in the earth, deep raw patches where the large rocks placed in front and in back of the wheels had dug in and shifted. The ground under the horses' feet was scuffled and churned, they had pawed and heaved, but to no avail. The brake block was set against the wheel, jammed in place, and tied tight.

Ravens and crows circled, waiting patiently, making that strange threatening growl deep in their throats, the sound that says they know the heat of the day will do its work and they will soon feast. If not today, tomorrow; if not tomorrow, the day after, but soon. The horses knew what the carrion birds knew and waited with resignation.

Woman Walks Softly had followed the tracks for most of the day, trying to press back into the earth the clumps of grass cut loose or uprooted by the wobbling metal-rimmed wheels, knowing, even as she stubbornly tried to repair the damage, that too much time had passed; the roots had been exposed too long to the hot summer sun. Then, there it was, the foolish thing she had been tracking.

She hunkered in the meagre shade of a dwarfed bush, trying to read the scene, looking for any hint of danger, any trap for the unwary. Two days, at least, the bizarre thing had been sitting there. Sitting there miles from any of the settlements placed on the face of the grasslands by the Newcomers, stopped as if waiting for something important, waiting in the knee-deep curly grass, waiting under the hot sun.

The bent and flattened grass showed where a rider had raced away at full gallop, either chased by enemies or in frantic, mindless search of friends. But there was no sign of enemies—no signs of threat, or danger. Only the carrion birds, waiting and croaking, only the hawks circling high in the sky.

The horses were looking at her, not yet daring to hope, just looking with patient dark eyes. Strongboned, too heavy for racing, but more powerful than range ponies, they were fit for Chief's horses. If they could endure what they had already been put through, surely they would easily endure anything the Good People would expect of them. Mares, both of them, just old enough to start welcoming and allowing the stallions. Either of them, put with the spotted-rump stud she had traded four good ponies for, would have foals which would grow into horses others would look at with envy. Her mother, Strong Heart Woman would ride such a horse with pride, her warrior trophies displayed for all to see.

A person didn't have to know very much to know the Newcomers were all basically crazy. All a person had to do was look at how the Newcomers lived, how they behaved, how they reacted in times of crisis, how they fulfilled their obligations to each other and to the Mother Of All, and their craziness was exposed.

The Human Beings had always considered crazy people to be holy; people caught halfway between two separate and distinct realities, people whose souls had been in such a hurry to return to this life, this reality, that they had not properly severed their ties with that other place. The Human Beings had always tried to treat their Crazies as gently and kindly as possible; one might be judged in the spirit world by one's actions toward a Crazy in this world: indeed one might, oneself, return to this reality as a Crazy in a future life.

The Human Beings studied the Crazies for clues to the behaviour of those who were not themselves crazy, but who might perhaps be given to strange responses or strange ways of behaving. Even the most bizarre behaviour of the Crazies was often no more than an exaggeration of what was considered appropriate and therefore acceptable behaviour. The People were not always sure what "normal" behaviour was; what worked for one person did not always work for others, what was normal for a badger made no sense at all for a wolf. Watching the Crazies one could sometimes learn what did not work, what was not appropriate.

The most interesting of the Crazies were the Berdache and the Inverted. The Berdache loved only those most resembling themselves. The Inverts took every human action, turned it back on itself, and then did exactly the opposite from most people: walking or riding backwards; seeing where they had gone rather than where they were going, living always in their own immediate past, ignoring their present, ignoring and unconcerned about their future; washing with dirt, drying with dust, painting and decorating themselves with dung and offal; eating only that food which they found by accident and to which they made no gestures of preparation.

Woman Walks Softly sometimes wondered if there was something lacking in her own make-up, some understanding she had not developed properly. The first time she had seen an Invert gnawing at the carcass of a prairie dog, slavering and chomping like a hungry fox, straining to bite through the very skin and fur of the rodent, her stomach had heaved and she had almost lost her own most recent meal. She had wanted to yell at the Invert to at least skin the fly-blown corpse before beginning to eat, to at least gut the creature and bury the entrails, or leave them for the ants and hawks. Thank the spirits she had kept her mouth closed, as much to keep the sour bile from spilling out of her mouth as to keep the improper words from issuing. Later, she thought about the incident and searched for the lesson the wise women said was hidden in every experience in life. Finally, she had taken her puzzlement and disgust with her and gone on a Vision Quest, segregating herself to ponder better in private. On the third day of her Quest she realized the Invert was an example to teach her how terrible it was not to observe properly the laws of food preparation and personal cleanliness. From that time of realization, Woman Walks Softly had been more careful than most about the preparation of food; and she never had failed to give thanks to the Voice Which Must Be Obeyed, the Creator, the Provider, who gave the world all it needed to survive.

But this abomination was really too much. Hard enough to try to find an understanding of the behaviour and actions of the Crazies when you at least spoke the same language, but what was a Human Being to make of the ways and lives of the Newcomer Crazies, who resembled Human Beings, but whose language was impossible to understand or even listen to for very long without getting confused by all the strange sounds and lifeless rhythms? People whose clothing was impractical and whose ways of behaviour were incomprehensible. Crazies who seemed to have no purpose except to spread chaos. Crazies who came with guns and knives and who insisted there was a line running across the grassland, and that the territory below the line was Long Knife territory, and the territory above it belonged to a woman chief no one had ever seen. It made no sense, and no matter how long she pondered there was no reason of any kind that she could find. She could hunker and ponder for the rest of her life and nothing would come of it.

She rose, and moved toward the cart. Crazy. Just crazy. No matter how many horses a Human Being had, she wouldn't leave them tied like this in the hot sun, leave them at the mercy of wolves and coyotes. Dying of thirst was no way for any child of the Mother Of All to leave this life and the horse had always been the cousin of the Good People.

Well, she would take them back to the Human Beings, take them and that stupid cart, take whatever the hysterically fleeing Crazy had left inside the cart, and it would all be hers. The cart and what was inside she would share with the other Human Beings, but the horses she would keep for herself. She would stake them by the river, let them drink the life-giving fluids of the Mother, she would gather arm loads of curly grass for them, and when they knew her voice and associated her with safety, food, and comfort, she would start the business of training them properly. Strong Heart Woman would ride one, and Woman Walks Softly would ride the other. She would braid into its mane protective charms, and hang little bells there, too. Running Quickly had bells and would trade; even if it cost one of Woman Walks Softly's treasured pale-eyes' knives, she would have bells for her Chief's Horse.

"Ooooh Cousin," she crooned, stroking the dust from their muzzles. "Oooh, ssssh, all will be as it should be," and she aimed her breath at their nostrils, to accustom them to her scent. Then she poured water from the bladderskin she always carried and caught it in her other cupped hand and held the water against the bristly lower lip of the dehydrated mare and the animal licked. Again and again she gave the animals water to drink and explained to them what wild ponies knew and tame horses did not, that too much water would cramp their bellies, perhaps even kill them. And all the time she talked to the horses, she was aware of the smell coming from inside the canvas-covered cart. A smell that told her she would not take the stupid thing with her after all, but would leave it and would leave the goods packed inside. No Human Being would casually take the possessions of the dead. War trophies were one thing; if you had defeated an enemy in life you had power over the spirit, but if you took things to which you had no claim, if you took from the dead, the ghost might follow the things that had been his, might haunt the one who had the belongings. If it was a mean ghost, or an angry ghost, it might reach out at night with a fogwisp hand and twist the face of the person who had taken the goods, twist the features to one side or the other and freeze them there, leaving that person marked for life, unable to form words clearly, unable to eat properly, sometimes unable to keep the saliva from drooling from the paralyzed mouth.

Then she heard the weak mewling from inside the cart. She moved quickly, soundlessly, and pulled open the canvas covering that lay loose and untidy on the rough-shaped ribs arching above the cart. A woman was lying in the stifling hot half-light inside the cart, and Woman Walks Softly didn't even have to look to know the woman was already dead. Dead, and swelling in the heat, almost obscured by a cloud of disgustingly bloated flies.

Between the legs of the poor dead woman, who was little older than a child herself, lay an infant girl, covered with dried blood and birthfluids, a newborn more dead than alive, too weak to cry, able only to mewl and whimper like a newborn puppy, unable to brush away the flies that swarmed over her face, over the dry-crusted mess of her own umbilicus.

Newcomer Crazies. This was the proof. Who but a Crazy would leave a woman alone in labour, especially a woman in labour with her first child? Who but a Crazy would race off at such speed? Who but a Crazy would suppose a newborn girl could look after herself?

Where were the aunties, the older sisters, the mothers, the grandmothers to assist with the birth and instruct the mother? Where was the waiting house, the necessaries, the proper things? Didn't the Crazies know anything at all? There are proper ways of doing things, proper things in the proper places, proper words to be spoken, proper rituals to be observed. Coming into this world is not something to be treated lightly or without respect. Crazies, and worse than Crazies. Newcomer Crazies, who had to be the Craziest of all!

"Oh-ai-ya," she crooned, lifting the bladderskin and drinking a few drops. "Oh-ai-ya," and then she filled her mouth with water, holding the water, warming it while she cut through the dry-crusted cord and brushed the worst of the flaking blood from the flaccid little body. She held the child almost upright, inserted her finger in the tiny mouth, and, when it was open, she spit a few drops of water down the scrawny throat.

She prayed to the Mother Of All for the child's life. With the Mother's help, she would most certainly not allow this child to die! She would take her with her, back to the Human Beings. The newborn soul deserved its chance to live, and to live properly, not live like the Crazies who could not even reproduce themselves properly. And what else in the world cannot reproduce? Rabbits manage. Rats manage. Prairie dogs manage. Even the fool hen manages to raise her chicks. But the Crazies send their women out onto the grasslands in ridiculous wagons, to bleed to death; the person who went there with the woman had raced off, doubtless to tell the other Newcomer Crazies . . . something. Whatever it could be.

The child stirred, her tongue moved, and Woman Walks Softly dribbled more water into the back of her throat. The child opened her eyes, and looked into the eyes of the Cree woman. "Greetings," Woman Walks Softly crooned. "Yo, future woman, your timing was inappropriate."

She tucked the still-filthy little body under her own loose-fitting summer shirt and tied a piece of rawhide cord around her waist, holding the child safe. Then she gave the horses another little drink of water, and with her knife, slashed them free of the harness. They could smell the water in the bladderskin and would follow her; if not her, they would follow the water.

"Are you possessed by ghosts, future woman?" She talked softly to the child, who had spent so much time in the belly of another woman, hearing another voice. If the child did not learn to trust the new voice, if she did not associate Woman Walks Softly with safety and love, how could she grow in beauty?

"We will welcome you properly, future woman. We will bathe you in warm water with mint and sage leaves steeped in it. We will rub you with clarified oil to ease the dryness of your skin. We will pray over you and for you and purify you with sage smoke, with sweetgrass smoke, even with the precious cedar our Git-k-skan cousins bring for us from the other side of the mountains."

The child squirmed, her tiny fingers stroking the firm muscled belly, and Woman Walks Softly stood still, understanding suddenly the look on the faces of women who carry happiness, the look of wonder when a living person moves inside them. If this child was not inside the body of Woman Walks Softly, she was against it, and only three fingers-width of soft skin and muscle separated her from the inner cradle.

"You will not be a Crazy," she assured her daughter. "Perhaps the Newcomers are Crazies because they are new to a land they do not know, a land which has always been home to the Good People. This land belongs to us," she explained, "only because we belong to it, and we keep it in trust for our grandchildren. We love it and care for it because one day our grandchildren will turn to us and ask, 'How did you care for this, the land I hold in trust for my grandchildren?' We are answerable." She shifted the child's weight slightly. "Answerable and accountable for all our actions."

She stopped at a small waterhole, letting the near-frantic horses drink, but not much, just enough to refresh them, not enough to cramp them. "You will have a proper name," she told the baby. "You will be one of the People who have always been welcomed by this land. And though you grew in the belly of a Newcomer Crazy, you will not feel yourself an outcast or a stranger, for the stories of all the women in my family and clan will be told to you. You will not feel lost, small person, and therefore, you will have no reason to feel Crazy." Woman Walks Softly decided right then and there, walking through the rich curly grass followed by two unusual horses, that the child she had found and whose life she had saved, the child for whom she was now fully responsible, would be known as and called Child Of Her People.

Her mother, Strong Heart Woman, watched with disbelieving eyes as Woman Walks Softly took the infant from her shirt and laid it on the dirt floor near the firepit, where it was warm.

"What have you done?" her mother asked quietly.

Woman Walks Softly explained how it was she had found the child and what she had decided. Then watched as her mother lifted the infant, breathed softly into the small nostrils and smiled, then tsk'ed her tongue against her teeth and shook her head at the stupidity of the Newcomer Crazies.

"Blue Quail has said she is ready to wean her son, and she is a reasonable woman, always ready to exchange services. I will go to her and ask her if she will be milk mother to this poor thing."

"What service could we exchange?"

"Food for food. You will hunt for both lodges for as long as this nameless future woman needs milk. That will free the other members of the family and allow them to teach the son of Blue Quail the things he would ordinarily be taught by his mother, who will, of course, be too busy with this child to be able to spend all her time with her son."

"I will help with the care of Blue Quail's son," Woman Walks Softly promised. "And I will teach the younger sister of Blue Quail how to ride. I will—" she had thought she would be unwilling to do the next, but found herself eager—"I will give them two good ponies, one for the younger sister, one for the son."

"I hope," Strong Heart Woman rose easily in spite of her years and moved to the entrance flap of her lodge, "I hope my granddaughter lives. You show no interest in providing me with children to warm my heart."

"If I had been at home with a husband," Woman Walks Softly said calmly, "I would not have been hunting; had I not been hunting, I would not have found this Child Of Her People."

"An answer for everything," her mother grunted, leaving before anything else could be said.

Woman Walks Softly rubbed the infant with warm oil and wrapped her loosely, padding her with soft moss just in case there was enough fluid in the tiny body to allow the child to urinate. Then she held her daughter close, humming a song to her, a song that promised the taste of sweet berries, the pleasure of cool water, the joy of running freely through soft spring sunlight, if only the child would live. When Blue Quail arrived, smiling and eager, and took the child, and held her to her breast, Woman Walks Softly watched, almost envious, as the little girl tasted warm milk, made her decision, and slurped greedily at the fountain of life.

When Child Of Her People was asleep, Woman Walks Softly tethered the strangely proportioned horses near the creek, with more rich grass than they could possibly eat. Then she explained to them what had been decided, blowing gently in their nostrils again so they would remember her smell and associate it with food, with water, with comfort and safety, and when they were settled for the night, she went back to the lodge of her mother and lay down beside her sleeping daughter, and considered all that had happened and tried to understand what it all meant.

For the first four years of her life, Child Of Her People lived as any infant. Nothing was demanded of her and very little was expected of her. She learned early that she was not to cry; at the first sign of a wail, Woman Walks Softly would place her hand over the baby's mouth, and with her fingers, pinch shut the nostrils. It only had to happen a few times, and the baby knew certain actions brought only unpleasant results. This was something every child of the Human Beings had to learn; in a world full of danger, any betraying noise was a potential threat.

The child was fed when she was hungry; she was rocked; she was cuddled; she slept warm whenever she was tired and not once was she slapped, hit or spanked. She learned to talk the language of children, and all the games she played were preparation for the training she would need to become one of the adults. When she was four, without anyone saying anything, her life shifted. Her games became lessons in the skills and duties of a woman. She learned to run, jump, and wrestle; she learned to set traps for small animals; she learned to skin her catch and bring back food for the cooking pot, to prepare hides for clothing, for blankets, and for teepee covers. She learned by doing, by watching, and by playing.

Woman Walks Softly taught her how to track animals and set snares so cunningly even the fox could not find them— before it was too late. Blue Quail, her milk mother, taught her how to stitch designs into the clothing she made and how to decorate even the simplest thing and turn it into an article of beauty. Strong Heart Woman, who had been a warrior woman of skill and daring, taught her how to defend herself; how to use the edge of her palm as a weapon, how to direct a strong kick to the knee and topple an enemy, how to throw a knife, how to fashion a spear, how to ride, and how to run. And always she was taught how to enjoy the endless blessings of the land that was her home.

Strong Heart Woman focused on the child all the love she had, and their lesson times were times of joy and laughter. The little girl was quick and strong, and learned easily and well.

"Stop," Strong Heart Woman said quietly.

Child Of Her People stopped struggling and waited, her grandmother's strong hands pressing on her shoulders, keeping her too far away to be able to touch the firmly muscled body. She was supposed to be learning how to protect herself, but what could she do when her grandmother's arms were so much longer?

"Think," the old woman whispered. "I have my hands on your shoulders, pressing down and pushing you away. Your arms are short. I am stronger. What would happen if you were to drop to your hands and knees? What would happen if you were to dart like a rabbit, between my legs? What if, in the darting, you were to grab my ankle and topple me to the ground?"

"There is a rock," Child Of Her People panted, face wet with sweat. "As big as my head. I could lift it. I could drop it on your head."

"Slowly," the warrior woman laughed proudly. "Slowly, now, we are just trying to find out what would happen . . . and do not really drop a rock on the head of your poor old grandmother!"

Child Of Her People dropped, shot forward, rolling and kicking. Strong Heart Woman obligingly fell to the grass. Instead of reaching for the rock and pretending to lift and drop it, Child Of Her People flung herself carefully onto her grandmother, arms hugging, face nuzzling.

"I am chewing out your throat!" She laughed, "I am ripping you open like the coyote does!"

"Well, then," her grandmother gasped, hugging her tightly, "here I am, defeated, and there you are, with another feather to tie to your war pony's mane. They will change your name from Child Of Her People to something else, Drinks Blood, perhaps, or Chewed Her Grandmother. Or maybe," she rolled, laying the child on the grass, tickling her, blowing in her ear. "Maybe they will call you Who Pees When She Laughs Too Much!"

"Peace! Peace!" Child Of Her People squealed, giggling and twisting. "You win, no, no more!"

Woman Walks Softly had to go further and further in search of meat, and the animals were warier than they had been. Strange stories were spreading from the south, from below the line no Human Being could see, from the land the Newcomer Crazies said was Long Knife territory. Stories of a huge monster some said was made of the same metal as knives and axes, but others said was the old Wit'igo, the cannibalistic spirit whose cry brought terror and who warned of disaster. This new monster had one round eye that glittered in the daylight and shone a bright light along the things on which it rode at night.

Every description of those strange things differed. Some said they were like knife blades, but not sharp. Others said if the Human Beings were to think of the shaft of a spear, flattened and made of metal, they would have some idea of these things laid on slabs of wood across the prairie.

In any event, the Wit'igo screeched and belched smoke and allowed Newcomer Crazies to ride it. Not on it, inside it. And these Newcomer Crazies fired guns from inside the monster, shooting buffalo by the uncountable numbers, shooting them, killing them, and leaving them dead on the prairie.

The Southern cousins spoke of how the scavenger birds and the wolves feasted on the carcasses until the birds were so fat they could barely fly and the four-legged made so unnatural that all the bitch wolves whelped instead of just the senior bitch. The litters grew and thrived, spreading along the trail of the Wit'igo and even beyond it, upsetting the balance of things and with the balance gone, nothing behaved as it once had.

Newcomer Crazies were flooding into the territory of the Good People, the families, tribes, and clans of the Cree nation. Newcomers who built strange dwellings of poles and sod, who dug wells where none had been intended by the Creator to be, who were such incomprehensible people as to eat horse meat and set fire to the grass. What kind of person would eat her cousin or burn her mother's hair?

The Newcomer Crazies had guns, and a gun could bring down meat the hunter could never get with a spear or an arrow. They had knives and axes, they had cooking pots that could sit in the fire and neither burn nor break. Stupid people would never be able to design such pots. And yet, for all their cunning, they ate horse meat. It had been seen. It had been witnessed and reported. They could walk up to a horse and shoot it in the head, or slit its throat so that it bled to death, then actually cook and eat the meat of their cousin. But they gagged and even puked when they saw the Human Beings eating dog.

Blue Quail was no longer milk mother to Woman Walks Softly's daughter but the obligations are never cancelled, the debts of life are never paid. Without the milk, the child would have died. So now, each time the child laughed or wept, each time she knew joy or the angers of childhood, the gift of milk was remembered. Hunting for two lodges kept Woman Walks Softly away from home more than she wanted to be, but what gift is more precious than a child's life?

Woman Walks Softly stood still, her single-shot rifle loaded and ready. The wind blew the musk of the male deer to her. She nodded, hearing inside her head the words of thanks to the departed ancestors who had guided her to this food.

"Grandmothers and Grandfathers," she prayed, "there is one who thanks you for your help. Oh male deer, your life is completed, your purpose fulfilled. A family will honour you, a family will make full use of you, a family will tell others of you, and will give praise to your spirit."

Child Of Her People had as many years as there were fingers on both hands and was starting to show signs of becoming a woman. The moon circle around her nipples was spreading, her nipples no longer tiny nubs. The big-bellied look of babyhood was gone, her abdomen was flat, her pelvic arch showing. When she turned or twisted, when she bent over or reached up for something, the line of her muscles was evident, and there was a firming of jaw and chin that gave glimpses of who she would be when she was a grown woman.

She did not resemble the Human Beings, and yet she was built exactly the same way. Her hair was dark, her eyes dark, but her skin, however darkly she tanned, was not the same colour. There was an obvious difference in the shape of her eyes and nose, a less definable difference in her top lip. Her feet were so differently shaped that anyone would notice: narrower at the toe, higher in the arch under the foot but not as high in the arch on top of the foot; wider at the heel, and something in the ankle seemed different. Her hands were large and strong but her wrists were smaller and Strong Heart Woman had made her practise lifting rocks, holding them on her palm, balanced carefully, until the tears stood trembling on her lashes and the thin muscles from arm to hand were tight with strain.

An adult man who ought to have known better began to take notice of her, even approached her, smiling. After talking to her briefly, he went to Woman Walks Softly and suggested that when Child Of Her People was the proper age he would be interested in having her for his wife. Woman Walks Softly answered sharply, briefly, reminding him he was probably older than the child's natural father, reminding him that not long ago, before the Newcomer Crazies arrived and too many things changed, no man approached any woman, but waited until the woman noticed him and honoured him by inviting him to father her child.

"Things are changing," the man growled, his eyes cold.

"Things always change," Woman Walks Softly agreed, "but that doesn't mean I have to change with them. When the trees lose their leaves, I don't lose my hair. When the snow-shoe rabbit turns from brown to white for the winter I do not have to change colour, too. And just because this country is infested with Crazies does not mean I have to become a Crazy!"

"A woman who dares talk like that to a man needs to be taught a lesson!" he flared.

"And are you the one who will try to teach me?" She met his stare, and returned it until he dropped his eyes. He knew how much success he would have if he tried. But she knew she could never again trust him behind her back. Another change.

Woman Walks Softly scooped the brains from the skull, placed them in the carefully hollowed log, then drained the urine from the bladder of the deer and put that, too, in with the reeking mixture. Child Of Her People wrinkled her nose but began to pulp and pound the brains gently, stirring the acidic mix carefully.

Woman Walks Softly checked the deer skin for any over-looked bits of fat or meat; then, satisfied it was as clean as it could be, she placed it in the foul mixture to soak. Child Of Her People carefully pushed the hide down to the bottom of the trough, smoothing it with her heavy stick, easing out air bubbles, her eyes watering slightly in the stink.

When Woman Walks Softly was satisfied, they left the hide-curing area and went to where the other women were sitting with their curved slate and bone blades, rubbing the fur from other deer and elk hides which had already soaked in the mix of brains, urine, and wood ash. The hides were stretched tight on frames made from what once had been travois poles and, before that, teepee poles.

Carefully, with gentle strength, the tanned hands worked curved blades over the hides, stretching and softening the skin, while removing the hair. Their soft voices exchanged the news of the families, the happenings of the various lodges, and Child Of Her People sat listening, her own small hands busy.

"You would be welcome to visit me," the Old Woman said quietly, smiling at the girl who was so carefully trying to do as her mother had showed her. "It seems to be time to start your first training in preparation for womanhood." They all smiled knowingly as the girl blushed, then beamed with joy.

"And when it is time," Woman Walks Softly assured her, "we will build you a small hut, and you will live there while you learn the things a woman must know. Each of your mothers will spend time with you and each of your aunties, and you will learn the prayers and the ways of doing things, learn the protections and the responsibilities, and when you come back from your time of learning, you will have your Vision Quest. And then," she smiled again, nodding for emphasis, "then your grandmother and I will hold a Sun Dance and you will be introduced as a woman."

Blue Quail's daughter, Rides Proudly, looked sideways at Child Of Her People and smiled, then nodded encouragement. "I will be your Older Sister," she promised, "and you can bring your complaints to me." The Old Woman chuckled knowingly, and Rides Proudly winked at Child Of Her People. "They make it sound as if it is a wonderful, peaceful time," she teased, "but it all seems more wonderful when you're looking back at it than it does at the time you have to endure it."

"That's right," Woman Walks Softly said. "Scare her now so that the reality seems easy compared to what she imagined."

"And who heard my complaints?" Rides Proudly asked. "Who listened while I talked away my childhood and began to think like a woman?"

"I thought I did," Blue Quail teased.

"You?" the Old Woman snorted with pretended anger. "It was me listened to her as she learned to braid her own hair properly!"

"No," Woman Walks Softly laughed. "It was my ears were worn thin, and my hands that wiped her tears."

"Don't worry," Rides Proudly leaned over, hugging Child Of Her People. "You already know most of what you need to know. You just don't know that you know it."

"And when you are a woman," Woman Walks Softly promised, "you can look around at the young men and choose one to invite to a private place. And then," she smiled, "you will know why you were given your strong and healthy body."

"Pick one who has already been chosen several times," Rides Proudly suggested. "The more he knows, the more you will enjoy yourself."

"And if you choose an older man," the Old Woman said, "you will not be as apt to want to fall in love with him. It is not good," she said stubbornly, "for a woman to want to marry her first man. Especially if he is a young man. If you choose an older man, he will be more skilled and you will think two or three times about being second or third wife."

"There is nothing wrong in being second or third wife," a young woman said quietly. "I enjoy my life, and my sisters-by-marriage are my friends."

"Of course," the Old Woman agreed, "but you didn't choose him to be your first friend. I seem to remember quite a few who strutted proudly for a few nights."

"Some people," Strong Heart Woman muttered, "have never decided to stop sampling." Woman Walks Softly laughed easily. "Some People," the older woman chided, "give no thought to their obligations."

"Some people have mothers who had so many husbands," Woman Walks Softly teased, "that a person learned men were temporary things." She leaned over, pulling her mother's hair, gently. "Who would I choose for a husband?" She laughed. "Half the men I know have at one time or another been my father." Even Strong Heart Woman laughed at what was only slight exaggeration.

Child Of Her People sat with the other girls in the lodge of the Old Woman, hearing the stories and learning the language of women. When her first blood moon came on her she would be expected to stop using the language of children and to speak to other women in their own language. Only to children would she ever again speak the child's language. To men, she would speak the other language she was learning, the language of adult people.

"The world is shaped like an egg," the Old Woman told them, "and if you were able to throw a rock hard enough, it would travel around the egg and come back to you. We know that." The Old Woman nodded, and the girls nodded their reply and acceptance. "We have always known there were people who were not the same colour as ourselves. We have always known there were people with white skin and other people with black skin, and some of you have seen these people in and around the Newcomers' settlements. There are also," she told them firmly, "people with skin of a light yellow-brown colour." The girls gasped, their eyes wide with amazement. "And there are people who are shades of these four colours, children whose parents were of different nations. And we are all cousins."

"Then why do the Newcomers act as they do?"

"I do not know," the Old Woman admitted. "Who can understand it?" She stared at the fire for long moments, then resumed her lesson. "The yellow-skinned people live so far to the West of us that it has become the East. Think of an egg, and think of heading always West, and you will understand how it is the West becomes, finally, the East. And the yellow-skinned people know the secrets of the wind. They are able to travel wherever the wind blows, and they can control their breathing to such an extent you would think them dead, and yet they live. And yellow is the colour of the East. The black-skinned people know the secrets of the West, the secrets of water and of calm thought, and those secrets heal both the body and the mind. The colour of the West is, therefore, the colour black. The white skins come from the Northland, and they know the importance of fire because in their land it is always cold, and around the fire the family gathers, and so at one time they knew the importance of family. Now," she hesitated, then shrugged, "now it appears their dream has been lost, or broken, or stolen. Or something." She sighed and waved her hand to signal her own confusion. "And we, the red-skinned people, we are of the South, and we know the Earth and the secrets of the Earth."

The girls waited for the Old Woman to continue her story and, while waiting, thought over what she had already said. It did no good to ask too many questions, anybody who needed to have each and every aspect of creation explained to her was probably unable to truly learn anything anyway. Asking questions all the time was a sign of infancy. Why is grass green, why is the sky blue, why do fish feel slippery and can they talk to each other? Questions are the way a child learns the language of children, but these girls were here to learn the language of adults and the language of women. To learn either or both, they first had to learn how to consider what had been said and find for themselves what it was they needed to know.

"It is important to remember that First Woman, who became First Mother, was created here, by the Voice Which Must Be Obeyed. Created here in this land, and created from the very dirt and rocks and soil and earth of this land. She did not come here from some other place. She was not made of materials that are not found here. She was made from this homeland of ours, and in her veins the water became blood, but it was the same as the water in our rivers and streams. Her breath is the breeze, and that breeze is from this place, which the orators say is held in the palm of the hand of the Creator. First Woman, who became First Mother, did not fly here on the winds from the East, nor come on the water from the West; she did not come here from the North nor yet from the South. She was made here and made to live here, and she is our Mother, and that is why we are here and not somewhere else. That is our tie to this place. We belong to this land. We are born from it and when we die our bodies return to it, and that is our bond with it. If ever the day comes when this land dies, we will die. If ever the day comes when all the People die, this land will die. We cannot live without her and she cannot live without us because we are joined, and that is how it was intended to be."

"But the Newcomers crowd into our land, and take it from us, and treat it differently," Child Of Her People observed, frowning, worried.

"They do not know how to behave or how to be," the Old Woman answered, smiling gently. "They have come from somewhere else. And they treat everything badly. But you are proof they are not intended to be without the knowledge of the proper way. And if we do as the land does, and endure, the time will come when they will learn, as you have learned, and then they will belong here, and when that happens, they will stop acting as they do."

"In which case they will be of the People as well?"

"Perhaps. Or perhaps not. When it is Time, we will know, and until it is Time, we cannot know. There is frustration in that," the Old Woman admitted. "But since we can do nothing to change it, we might as well learn to accept it."

Later, Child Of Her People cuddled close to her mother and whispered her confusion. "Nothing really gets explained," she confided, "Old Woman just keeps saying Endure, Endure, Endure, and then she says Accept. That isn't really very much help."

"It doesn't seem like it," her mother agreed, "but how can anyone know each and every thing that will happen in a lifetime? And so, to protect you, she tells you the things that will be useful no matter what circumstance should occur."

"Have you ever had to . . . endure?"

"Yes," Woman Walks Softly smiled gently. "Yes, and I was not sure I would be able to do it, but when everything seemed to be as bad as it possibly could be, I heard the voice of the one who was Old Woman before this one," she laughed, "nagging me, just as she had done when I was your age. Endure, Accept, Endure, Accept, Endure, Endure, Endure, and I did."

"If we accept . . . if we do not resist . . . ," the child groped for the idea, but it ran away from her attempt to form it in words.

"You will learn," her mother pulled her closer, "that accepting is another way of waiting. When you cannot see any way to go or any thing to do, you accept that. And you wait. However long it takes, you wait. And then one day you will see what you are to do, where you are to go, how you are to get there, and you can make your move. You will have accepted the need to wait and have endured the period of waiting and you will not have exhausted yourself in futility."

"There was a time, long ago, when the grandmother of my grandmother was a small girl, that it happened a young woman went into the mountains for her Vision Quest." The Old Woman dropped the precious Kinnickinick leaves into the water boiling in a metal trading kettle and the listening children smiled, knowing they would soon drink the special tea. "This young woman was walking along a path and suddenly she heard a whimpering sound. Looking down, she saw a wolf cub, a very little wolf cub, lying on a ledge not far below the path. How it had strayed from its den, where its mother and the rest of the pack had gone, none of this was known, but the girl knew the cub was close to death. It was easy for her to swing her legs over the edge and slide down to where the cub was lying, easy for her to lift the nearly dead wolf and place it up on the path, and easy for her to pull herself back up to the path. But for the little wolf, all chance of climbing or jumping was denied it because it was so small. A grown wolf, or even a half-grown wolf, could have jumped to the path, but for a baby wolf, the small drop might as well have been the height of the moon itself."

The Old Woman poured tea into a small bowl, passed it to her left to a girl who passed it to the girl on her left, who passed it again until the bowl came back to the girl to the right of the Old Woman. Another bowl and another, until the Old Woman poured Kinnickinick for herself. The girls waited until the Old Woman had sipped and nodded her approval before they too sipped, and felt warmed by more than the special tea.

"So this girl took her wolf cub home with her, she gave it water, and she gave it the juice from the stew in the family pot, and the wolf cub decided to live. Soon people were quite used to seeing the young woman accompanied by a wolf cub, and later, they were quite used to seeing the young woman accompanied by an adult bitch wolf. And the bitch wolf was as tame as any dog, as loyal as any dog, and as gentle as any dog. In fact some people began to think of it as a dog.

"The young woman was by a stream picking berries when a man not of our people suddenly appeared. He stared at her and made a move as if to reach out and take hold of her. Then the bitch wolf was growling and the man went away, but the young woman knew that man intended trouble. Sooner or later.

"She began to notice a young wolf following them, a young male wolf who was not tame, not kind, not gentle, and had no loyalty to people. She thought for a long time and decided it was part of the life of her wolf and the business only of her wolf. And the wild wolf followed them everywhere, right to the very borders of the village.

"The stranger appeared inside the village and began to try to court the young woman. But she could never forget the look on his face when he had thought her alone and helpless. Every time he smiled she remembered how he had stared at her, and no matter how soft his words, she remembered the glittering in his eyes.

"When being nice and saying pleasant things did not get him what he wanted, he began to follow her, hoping to find her alone. By now, of course, he knew her wolf was as tame as a dog. And because his attention was fixed on the young woman, he did not notice that other wolf, the wild one, the savage one.

"Picking berries by the stream one day, with only the wolves for company, the young woman turned and saw the man standing right behind her. He reached for her arm but she jumped out of his way and then the two wolves moved between them, two very large wolves. 'Which of those is yours?' the man of bad intentions asked. 'The gentle one,' the young woman laughed. 'And which one is the gentle one?' he asked, thinking she did not know what he intended. 'Well,' the young woman said, 'all you have to do to find that out for yourself is pick either one, and put your head in its mouth. If you can remove your head, you have chosen my wolf.'

"And she walked away, making a gesture of disdain with her hand, and the stranger knew he might just as well leave and go back to his own people because the young woman knew he was danger, while he did not know which wolf would eat his head."

The Old Woman finished her bowl of tea, nodded her head, then looked at each little girl individually. "And since that time, we have been the women of the wolf. We do not need to be taught each individual danger, we do not have to learn all the do this and do not do this of other people. We learned from our many times great-grandmother and her sister, the tame wolf, that we must always be careful; for though the world is a wonderful and magical place, not all the people on it are as we are."

"What do the dangerous people look like?" one of the girls asked.

"If we knew what they looked like," the Old Woman smiled, "they would not be dangerous. It is not the outside of a person that can tell us if that person is a good person or a dangerous person; it is what is inside. And we can only know what is inside by getting to know how that person handles individual responsibility. So, since we do not know for sure and certain that we are dealing with one of the Good People . . . we must always be careful."

"Now," Strong Heart Woman said quietly, standing beside the imitation person—two strong poles, buried in the earth, leaning toward each other, and tied at the top with strong lashing. "Think of these as the legs of an enemy, a man who wishes to do you harm." She took a small grass-stuffed pouch and tied it to the lashings at the juncture of the poles. "You are to dive to the earth, face down, to trip him." She spoke slowly and clearly. "And as you land, roll your body in whichever direction you like, to avoid any blow he may aim at you. And as you roll, reach up, and grab this bag. Squeeze as hard as you can and pull it toward your chest while rolling out from underneath him. You should," she grinned, "wind up behind him with his bag in your hand."

They practised until they were bruised and sore, the skin of their arms and legs abraded by the tough grass, the hard earth, the pebbles, and grit. Still the old Warrior Woman insisted they try again.

"Good," she said finally, "and now that you know how to do it, you must practise control. Tomorrow the boys will come and you will practise with them." The old fighter laughed happily. "So you must be sure only to touch them, not to grab and pull or there will be no husbands for you and no fathers to give you children."

At first the boys only stood nervously, wincing as the girls raced at them, fell to the ground, rolling between their legs and reaching upwards.

"No!" Strong Heart Woman called. "No! You did not touch him, you must touch him, and touch him gently. It is in gentleness you learn one of the limits of your strength. May you never need to know the other limit, but if you do, you must know exactly what to expect."

And so they practised some more, and some more.

"Now," she laughed, "now, I want the boys to try to attack these girls."

"Attack the girls?" A young man turned slowly and stared at Strong Heart Woman. "If I was to attack my cousin, her mother and my mother would throw my things from their lodge and leave me without family."

"No," Strong Heart Woman promised, "not this time. How else will they learn that no matter how much they know or think they know, it is not enough when the threat is sure to come from someone bigger and stronger?"

"You never met anyone bigger and stronger!" one of the girls challenged.

"Yes, I did," Strong Heart Woman corrected. "But I was smarter!" She beckoned one of the senior boys. "Come," she invited, "demonstrate what you have learned."

"Promise not to hurt me," he teased.

"Oh, of course not," she promised. As he smiled and reached for her hand, she reached out, and before anyone knew she was going to do anything, she had done it. The young man was lying on his back in the grass, staring up at her in total surprise. "Your father," the gray-haired woman laughed, "made that same mistake. Do not watch my hand," she helped him up. "Watch my eyes."

He nodded, and she held out her hand. He reached for it, his eyes fixed on hers. She swung her leg, knocked him behind the knee, and dumped him again.

"Never do the same thing twice in a row," she chided.

Again she helped him up, again she held out her hand, again he watched her eyes, and again she kicked his knee and dumped him. He lay in the grass laughing, pointing at her and laughing. "Twice in a row," he accused.

"Yes," she agreed, "and now you have learned something. Never trust anybody, not even an old woman who is losing her teeth!"

"Cross your arms between elbow and wrist. That gives you lots of room to slip the thong over his head. Now grip the thong as tight as you can and straighten your arms. Keep pulling sideways, that's the way. Now sink to your knees, place your head in the middle of his back, push forward with your head and keep pulling."

Child Of Her People tried to do everything at once, straining against the figure made of sticks and dry grass. The figure was an enemy, he would hurt her mother and grandmother, steal their horses, steal their food, kill them. She strained and then felt her grandmother's hand on her shoulder.

"Good," the older woman laughed. "You have just pulled his head right off his body."

"Clench your fist. Now think of the back of his head. You are going to hit him on the back of his head. But you are going to punch through his face to do it. You will always hit only that which you aim for; if you aim for his chin, you will only hit his chin. If you hit through his chin to his brain, you will hit his brain. And, if you hit through his nose to the back of his head, you can be sure he will know he has met one of our women."

"My mother was told that the reason the Newcomers have such wonderful things, like the trading-kettle, is because the men have learned to make all decisions and to run the world the way they want it run," a girl hazarded, her eyes welling with tears. "The men told my mother that the New-comer women do not ride free as we do, and do not make their own decisions, as we do, and that is why the Newcomer women have sewing needles and bright beads and mirrors and all manner of wonderful things."

"Any time the buffalo passes hot wind," the Old Woman snorted, "you can be sure he will very soon also pass shit!" and she laughed. "When the first of the Newcomers arrived here, they had treasures but were starving. We had no treasures, but we had all the food we needed. They froze in their houses while we were warm in our winter lodges. And when the first Newcomers came, both men and women of the People were Bundle Guardians, both men and women were

Pipe Carriers, both men and women were the Keepers of the Way. But many men threw down their bundles, cast aside their pipes and forgot the Way, in their haste to rush forward and grasp greedily for the strange treasures. It was the women who picked up the discarded bundles; it was the women who lifted from the dirt the calumets; and it is the women who still guard the Way. In the wintertime, the marten changes colour and seems to imitate the snow. It may happen that we, too, must learn how to pretend to be what we are not. But even in disguise, the marten is who she always really was, and the ways and secrets of the marten are still strong in her heart. If we have to pretend to be who we are not, we will do that, but we will still be the Guardians of the Bundles, the Keepers of the Pipe, and we will teach the Way and always be who we have always been. Children of the Good People."

"Why are things changing?"

"How else would you know how true a thing can be if you never saw the lie? Things change. But they can always change back again. All you have to do is Endure and keep your faith."

And things were changing. Definitely changing. Changing because the Crazies were causing changes almost guaranteed to make even the Human Beings crazy. Some of the Crazies wanted buffalo hides and were willing to trade strange treasures for them. All along the migration routes of the enormous herds of slow-moving creatures, Newcomer hunters fired, dropping uncounted thousands of animals; paying no attention to the old rules; shooting pregnant cows as well as young bulls; shooting and killing without regard for the herds' ability to reproduce; shooting until their guns were too hot to shoot any more, then getting other guns and shooting again. They stripped the skins off the dead animals and left the carcasses to rot on the prairie. The slaughter went on so long and so stupidly that the Human Beings were forced to forbid any more hunting by outsiders on the land the Human Beings had always claimed as their homeland. They told the Crazies, and their cousins the half-breed Metis, they could no longer hunt on the Good People's land and would not even be allowed to travel on it.

And still the slaughter continued—beyond the borders of the Human Beings, to be sure—but the animal killed miles from the land of the People does not arrive when expected, does not provide food, does not provide the robes to keep the Human Beings from freezing to death in the wintertime.

And so, finally, the Human Beings began to move, to move West, into the area traditionally considered to be a neutral zone between them and the Blackfoot nation; into the Cypress Hills where there was still game, where the valleys were rich and sheltered from the worst of the winter blizzards. The Blackfoot, facing hunger and privation for the same reasons as the Human Beings, resented the move, and the violent incidents increased. Then the Blackfoot suggested a peace meeting. Maskepetoon The Elder, the diplomat who had negotiated several truces, went with his young son and a few other negotiators, to meet with the Blackfoot.

The tribes and lodges of the Human Beings were dispersed across the face of the Mother, along the route usually taken by the Great Herds, each group grimly searching for the food they would need to survive the time of cold. Each individual required the meat and skin of thirty animals each year, and they had always been able to fill their needs by hunting the fringes of the migrating buffalo.

The huge animals ordinarily moved northward in the early spring, small herds meeting other small herds and combining into larger herds which met other merged herds and combined until vast miles of prairie were covered with dark shaggy creatures. They spread out across the open grass, feeding, breeding, nursing their calves; their hooves turned the sod, spreading and burying the grass seed, fertilizing it with their own droppings; when the dry heat of summer turned the grass yellow, the seed was protected from the drought by an insulating layer of earth and manure. The huge beasts responded to the drought by gathering at or near the water holes, simplifying the hunting, until they gradually turned and headed south again, to the warmer winters where they would split up into small herds and seek shelter in the valleys and canyons of the broken, hilly country. They passed the winter there, surviving on the fat layered on their bodies, then, when the snow and ice began to melt, they once again headed northward in small herds.

But the Long Knives were at war with the tribes and to starve them into surrender, had set fire to hundreds of miles of grass, turning the herds, baffling the dumb animals, stopping the migration. Trapped, the animals had no choice but to overgraze the range, adding to the barren swath blocking their movement.

The exposed soil became dust and was blown by the wind. Erosion caused the banks of the waterholes to collapse. Thirst and hunger sent thousands of animals mad, they thundered desperately in any direction at all, running until they fell and died. Others were slaughtered from the comfort and safety of the railway cars, still others were butchered only for their tongues and hides.

The few who made it past this wasteland of horror to the traditional hunting grounds of the Human Beings were thin and desperate, wild-eyed and easily spooked. Even Woman Walks Softly, one of the best hunters in the entire Cree nation, was hard pressed to find food.

When she did find meat, it was no guarantee she, her mother, and her daughter would survive the winter. What a hunter brought back to the camp was food for the entire camp. No Cree would stockpile food while another Cree went hungry; no Cree had piles of robes while children of the Human Beings shivered with cold; no Cree hoarded anything at the expense of others.

And the food the hunters brought back was needed. The Good People were hungry in what ought to have been the fattest time of the year. Child Of Her People was busy from first light to last, setting snares in the prairie dog colonies. She even strung nets made from the inner fibres of the water rushes, catching fish in the streams and rivers, although the Good People were not accustomed to eating fish and considered it mainly food for dogs.

But there were few dogs left in the Cree nation. They had been killed and fed to the children in the worst days of winter.

Anything that moved was fair game for the desperate hunters. Snakes and lizards, even carrion birds became food, and, inevitably, the Good People looked at the homesteads of the Newcomers who had caused this famine, and steers, goats, pigs, and even watchdogs disappeared without a trace.

Maskepetoon The Elder and his son went with negotiators from the main body of the Cree to meet with the Blackfoot to try to find a way for everyone to survive. He wanted the two nations to combine their hunting forces to head south, and cross over the invisible line the Newcomers had drawn on the face of the Mother, protected by the most fanatical and suicidal of the warrior society, the Ghost Dancers. Defying the blue-coated Long Knife soldiers, they could find the herd and either hunt it there, bringing back the meat, or herd the buffalo the way the Newcomers herded their disgusting steers, driving them across the wasteland, across the line no sane person could see into the land of the white-skinned woman chief, where there was grass in plenty, but no animals to feed upon it and grow fat.

The Cree waited for the negotiators to return; waited hoping for word of a successful agreement with the Blackfoot. But each day followed the other, and there was no word. Finally, it was Woman Walks Softly who headed out, alone, to track the old chief and his party.

She made no attempt to hide her purpose, no attempt to cross the miles of open grassland unseen. She just rode quietly and steadily to the Cypress Hills, which jut out of the dry plains of the southwestern prairie, an oasis of grass, water, and protected valleys almost halfway between the Missouri and South Saskatchewan rivers. Here the animals wintered, protected from the killing cold; the hills for centuries had been an unofficial buffering zone between the fierce Blackfoot and the Cree, and the Assiniboine, their Southern neighbours who shared the same wintering grounds but whose territory went below that border line the Crazies had imposed, into Long Knife country.

She watched carefully for any sign of the Crazies, especially the Long Knife traders from Fort Benton who supplied the outposts of Soloman and Farwell. These two had set up rival trading posts on opposite banks of a stream deep in the Cypress Hills, rough log palisades enclosing two or three log shacks. Woman Walks Softly deliberately avoided the area;

there was too much whiskey in Soloman's post, too many quarrelsome people at Farwell's post.

She moved out of the protection of the broken country and started across the flatland at night, guiding her progress by the stars, stopping when the sky began to pale. She found a secluded cutbank where she could spend the day, and waited. She had water, she had food, there was some shade for her horses, and one more day would make little difference.

She saw the smoke rising from Blackfoot territory, columns of it, four, six, more than she could count. Black columns of smoke rose from greasewood fires deliberately banked with sod; the fires dampened regularly to keep the smoke billowing, to call back the Blackfoot hunters, to reassemble the warriors of the Blackfoot nation.

She moved at night and made her way to where she knew there was a small gully forbidden to the Blackfoot by religious custom. She left her horses there, where they had plenty of water and grass and would wait for her return. She had no time to worry about Blackfoot ghosts, and could depend only on her spirits to protect her.

She ran all night, keeping her position by the pattern of stars. When the sun began to show Her face, Woman Walks Softly found a safe place to hide, to chew wild onion root and drink warm water from her bladderskin. Then she slept all day, and wakened, refreshed and eager, at nightfall. She moved forward quickly, guided now by the sound of drums, and, eventually, by the glow from the great fires.

The Blackfoot had sentries posted, but, like the Cree, they had been forced to eat most of their dogs. The few who had been spared were nursing puppies, and the Elders had not named her Woman Walks Softly without reason.

She saw the sentry and flattened herself against the ground, waiting quietly and patiently. She could not see his face, but his body was slender and he walked carefully, tense and wary. He turned, his back to her, and began to walk away, and it was easy to rise, move forward silently and crack her palm edge against the back of his neck. He fell as if boneless. A male dog barked, and Woman Walks Softly dropped to lie next to the fallen sentry. She saw several warriors rise to their feet, outlined against the glow from the great fires. Then a bitch dog with several puppies dragging at her teats snarled at the male dog and it slunk away. The warriors settled back, convinced it was a quarrel between the dogs, and nothing to worry about; the sentries had made no sound.

She walked carefully away, the unconscious young sentry draped over her shoulder, and made her way to the banks of the small river. She walked into the water and lowered the still unconscious guard; then, with one hand clamped over his throat ready to squeeze off his breath and voice at the first hint of movement, she floated him on his back, swimming with the current, moving swiftly away from the Blackfoot outpost. When the young man stirred, she squeezed his throat tightly. He struggled weakly, then let his hand rise and fall again, a gesture of submission, and she eased her grip, allowing him to breathe.

When she was well out of hearing distance, well beyond the perimeter of any roving sentry, she pulled the groggy youth from the water. He was young, no more than a boy, and in ordinary times he would not yet have finished his manhood training. But the Blackfoot, like the Cree, were not in ordinary times.

She thumped him on the back of the neck, stunning him again, and lashed him to a tree. Then she waited until he could once more focus his eyes, and she took her knife from its sheath and drew the back of it, the dull side, along his throat.

"Do you understand?" She questioned him in halting Blackfoot.

"Yo."

"You are mine, now," she continued, "I am as your second mother, for you are alive only because I have given you life."

"Yo," he gritted, his face flushed, his eyes welling with tears of rage and shame. "You are my second mother," he forced himself to agree.

"Tell me of Maskepetoon," she said quietly, her eyes narrowed as she smiled the cold smile of the hunting wolf-mother.

Woman Walks Softly rode into the camp with two horses loaded with meat, followed by a young man who walked as proudly as he could, trying with admirable courage to hide his uneasiness. He was in the camp of the enemy and had no reason to suppose the People would decide to spare his life. The woman who had defeated him could claim him as family or could hand him over to the others to kill. In other times, times of peace and full bellies, she might feast him, recount the story of his capture, claim him as cousin, then shower him with gifts, give him a good pony to ride and send him back to his own people to be living proof of her skill and status. But the chances of that happening were slimmer than the buffalo they had chanced upon during their return. He expected he would die. He hoped he would die with dignity. And die quickly.

"Maskepetoon the Elder and the Younger," Woman Walks Softly told them, "will not be returning." The People gathered around the evening council fire sucked in their breath sharply, their worst fears realized.

"This person I have taken," she said in a deliberately level voice, "and to whom I have given second life, was there. He told me, and I believe him, for there is no profit for him that would encourage him to lie. The truth puts him in danger. A lie might have saved him and allowed him to return to his mother."

She waited a moment, pushing down the emotions that tried to rise, then continued. "Maskepetoon and his son led the way to the council fire and took their place in the circle followed by the other negotiators. They were unarmed and so were the men of the Blackfoot who formed a circle with them. They waited for the pipe to be offered and passed among them. Instead, hot-blooded young warriors moved in behind them, and struck them dead, smashing their heads and spilling blood in the council circle. This newborn one saw it. He was not sitting in the council circle; he is too young. He was not one of the hot-bloods; he follows his senior instructor's orders and his senior instructor is a follower of the chief of the Blackfoot."

"But now," she looked up and saw the angry faces of the young men, "now the Blackfoot are caught. They know we now know we have been betrayed. They know that only if they kill their own young men and deliver the bodies to us can war be averted; and they will not kill their young men. They know we can demand that even the brothers and cousins of the offenders be executed and delivered to us, and they will not do that. A few young hot-bloods disobeyed their instructors and their chief and now, the Blackfoot have lit the war fires."

She looked around the circle, her face sad. "I personally believe we would be insane to do anything except mourn the death of those brave men. We do not need a war, we need hunters out gathering food. And Maskepetoon The Elder would prefer we go to the Blackfoot and make an alliance in spite of this. The death of these men and the risk we all run because of their deaths could be the example we all need to ensure a strong alliance. Our enemy is not the Blackfoot. Our enemy is hunger. Our enemy is starvation. Our enemy is the death of our People this coming winter!" Her words had no effect.

In almost no time at all, the Cree war fires were lit. The young men began dancing and the war drum throbbed insistently. Warriors gathered their weapons and caught up their swiftest ponies and rode off to tell other bands of Cree what had happened, or to find the main band of the People and offer themselves for the war that was already as good as declared.

"I do not want my daughter to be part of this," Woman Walks Softly said firmly. "It is suicide that two starving nations should fight instead of hunt. It is madness that hunters should hunt other hunters instead of hunting for meat. My daughter and I go North, and we will hunt. Perhaps some of the Human Beings will survive this war, and if they do, perhaps we will have found some food to keep them alive."

"I go with my daughter and granddaughter," Strong Heart Woman said.

"And I," the Old Woman agreed. "I want my students to know about life before they learn about death."

There were no recriminations from the warriors, some of whom even sent their children with the Old Woman, away from the disputed territory, perhaps even safely away from the war.

They travelled light and they travelled fast, their few necessaries lashed to travois dragged by tough little ponies. North and west, up to the neutral zone, hunting each day for the remnants of the Great Herd. When they found no trace of it, they turned westward, dangerously close to the Blackfoot hunting grounds.

"Newborn one," Woman Walks Softly said quietly, "this pony is yours, and this knife is yours. This rifle is yours, a gift from my daughter. Your name in this family will always be Life Saved And Precious, and when we pray to the spirits of our ancestors we will ask them to watch over you. Go back to your first mother and her family, tell your uncles what has happened; tell them this is not a war party. Tell them we are hunters with children who ought to be fat and are, instead, very lean. Tell them if they wish to kill us, they can, but all we intend to do is hunt meat and go to the Great Pillar that guards the mountains, so that our children may see this one magic wonder before they die."

"Second mother," the young man said. "I want no part of this war! You have treated me well; your people gave me a fair share of food even when the children were hungry. It seems wrong to me that we should all fight and die because of a few who defied the will of many."

"Life Saved And Precious," she smiled, "tell your first mother that I, your second mother, give her son back to her on one condition: he must never lift his weapons against his other family."

He smiled then. "Yo. I will tell her. And I will tell my people this is a hunting party, a survival camp, and not a war party."

They had only fool hens and prairie dogs to eat for days. The children could only trust in the Old Woman and mix dirt with water, then drink the mixture to stop the cramping of their bellies. They were in rich grass, the ponies could feast, but where were the animals who ought to be grazing here?

Then they were staring in awe at the massive pillar of rock that stood at the entrance to the pass into the mountains, the pass through which the Git-k-skan and Wet'sulwitain came to trade the dried fish that in no way resembled the freshwater fish the Human Beings did not like to eat. The coastal cousins brought smoked salmon and oolichan, brought dried mountain goat and rich fish oil, brought dentalia shells and puffin beaks for decorations, brought fragrant cedar pitch for sacred ceremonies. And when they came, they came past this massive pillar.

It reached so far up to the sky that a grown person had to bend her head back to see the top. The women and children joined hands and reached and still could not circle it, and from the bottom to as far up as the eye could see, it was carved with symbols.

"Years ago," the Old Woman told them, "the ice of the North began to spread, and all the animals fled before it. Summer disappeared, and winter ruled increasing amounts of the land. And when the People had no idea what to do, the Elders came through the mountains to this place and told us that their land was also affected by ice and snow, and that they had been told to move South and East, away from the endless winter, to a place where they would be safe until the new springtime came to the land. They stopped here and they did magic. They drummed and sang, they played six-holed flutes and shook instruments made of deer hooves and the shells of a creature that lives in the sea. They danced, and the huge wooden masks they wore changed shapes, one moment being a supernatural bird, the next moment a wolf or a coyote or a deer. Then their women began to sing, and they invited our forefathers and foremothers to sing with them. Our drums joined the prayer, our flutes were played, and our young women and men did the thong dance and there was a sound that was unlike any sound we had ever heard, a sound louder than thunder; and the earth trembled. An entire piece of the mountain pulled itself away and floated on the power of that wonderful song our combined people made! Floated across the grassland without leaving any trace of its passing, and then it lowered to the ground here, and the ground rumbled, shifted, and made room for the Great Pillar, and we all knew the Elders knew magic beyond belief.

"And the singing and dancing continued all night until the next day. Continued until the sun was right overhead and burning hot. And then the Elders brought forth deerhide pouches; from inside the pouches they brought forth glittering red rocks set into the bones of a creature they said lived in the salt sea but which gave birth to living young and fed its young with milk. Then they held these glittering red rocks in a particular pattern so the light of the sun was caught in each one and, somehow, all the gleams of light became one—like a stick no one could see. And, just as a stick can make marks in the sand, the magic stick no one could see made marks right in the stone.

"They stayed here for many moons. We showed them how we hunted the animals and made jerky and pemmican. They had none of our hunting skills for, of course, their land was different so their skills were different. And while we hunted together and laughed together, their holy people continued this great project.

"They told us they were making a map of their journey through the mountains. They told us they knew they would never again see their homeland, or see us again after they left. They told us the day would come when the children of their children's children many generations to come would want to return, and that this map would guide them through the mountains. For stories told can be altered or forgotten, but what is marked into living rock will not disappear.

"And we escorted them to the very edges of our territory and asked our cousins to take care of them and escort them safely. Some of their young people stayed here because they had made family attachments with us, and some of our young people went with them for the same reason.

"And the ice continued to press forward. We, too, had to move South, into the land where the strange fruit grows and birds of bright colours fly. And we stayed there some generations, then started back again. As the ice retreated, we continued back into our own land, saving this story and coming to this marvel to make contact with the spirits and to re-affirm that which we have always known."

The small band of survivors rested beside the huge graven Pillar, wondering what the symbols meant, trying to imagine the stories locked in the rows of what looked like dogs, what might be waves, what might be breasts, what might be almost anything at all. The Old Woman waited until their young curiosity began to falter, then she called them together to tell them the little she knew.

"This row that goes all around the rock and which looks like eggs or the stones made smooth and round on the bottom of a stream, this is a root that grows in their land. From it grows a flower that is sometimes yellow, sometimes white, and which smells slightly the same as the wax in a beehive. These roots are good to eat. And this row, which looks almost the same, but which is made up of less regularly-shaped eggs, this is another root that these people eat, the flesh is yellow. See these strange figures? That is a thing they made from trees; it floats and in it they went to a southern land and traded furs and oil for these roots and the knowledge of how to grow them. These breasts are not only breasts but also represent the mountain that spits fire. That mountain also spits a kind of rock that can be pounded into a thin sheet, and used for decoration, and it is magic; it comes in five colours, some of which are almost the same colour as our skin. And this is corn, which we know of because we have traded for it with our southern cousins; how the Elders knew of it, I do not know. And that is all I know of the markings."

They paid their respects to the Pillar, smudged it with sweetgrass smoke and sat staring at it. They could all see and read the directional signs; they could recognize markings they had seen all their lives on their own teepees. They knew what those signs meant and knew, too, that the Pillar pointed the direction to safety.

"Perhaps," the Old Woman warned them, "the day will come when you will have to enter the crack in the mountains and go to the land of the Elders and seek refuge there as they sought refuge here. If that day comes, remember, we are one people, and our needs and wants are the same."

"Are we one people with the Blackfoot?" a small boy asked.

"Yes," the Old Woman sighed.

"With the Newcomers?" Child Of Her People dared.

"Yes," the Old Woman assured her. "Obviously. For your birth mother, your dead mother, was a Newcomer, and yet here you are, and you drank the milk of one of us and did not sicken. And you are," she teased, "most certainly the daughter of your true mother. You even chew grass like her and lace your fingers together the way she does, and hold your head to one side when you smile. Of course we are cousins to the Newcomers. It is not our fault they do not know that."

They found buffalo in a valley and blocked their escape. Woman Walks Softly and Strong Heart Woman organized the others and planned the hunt. It was not a hunt that they liked. There was no excitement, no thrill, no daring race along the edges of the herd, no courageous riding. They simply placed themselves around the herd, their single-shot rifles resting on supports, and they fired, one after the other, reloading and aiming carefully, then firing again and again until their rifles were hot and the valley floor was littered with animals.

When Woman Walks Softly signalled, the shooting stopped. The children moved away from the valley entrance, taking their blankets and sleeping robes with them, and as soon as the flapping and yelling stopped, the surviving animals moved to the exit and raced out of the valley.

"Follow them," Strong Heart Woman told several of the older children. "Watch where they go. Sleep away from us two nights, then return. We may need to find these animals again." She looked at the other children and nodded. "We have work to do."

They worked swiftly, stripping off the hides, sprinkling the raw sides with ash, putting them aside for later, not able to take the time to start curing them. They cut the meat into strips and hung it over racks made of small sticks, in the smoke of the fires. They hung meat to dry in the sun. They spread meat on hot rocks to dry and cure. They cut meat, they sliced meat, they ate raw meat, and wished there were more of them to do the work.

Child Of Her People dug a pit and lined it with rocks, then covered the rocks with a layer of animal dung, then a layer of dry wood, then more dung, and more wood. She and several others went to the stream and scooped thick mud, smeared it onto the haunches of two young bulls, put the mud-smeared heap of meat on the wood in the pit, covered the meat with more mud, added more wood, then started the fire. While the fire burned and the meat cooked, they cut more strips for drying, replenished the smoking fires, and hung fresh buffalo tongue on green sticks to cook over the smoking fires.

When only bones were left, the haunches were taken from the firepit and again smeared thickly with mud. When the mud was half-dry, a layer of grass and leaves was pressed into it, each overlapping the other. Then more mud was spread, more overlapping leaves, and a final layer of mud. The meat was sealed in its own cooked juices and with any kind of luck except bad luck would remain good until they could rejoin their small band.

The scouts returned with news of the location of the herd, and again, it was not a hunt, but slaughter. They worked frantically to dry, smoke, and cure the meat and when that was done, there were hides to preserve for the scraping and soaking that would happen later.

They found the rest of the survivor camp on the flatland and led them to where the meat was cached. The main body of the Cree were at war, but the foragers stayed out of the battles. Someone had to hunt, someone had to try to put aside food for the winter, someone had to keep the children safe as long as possible. They knew the Blackfoot had similar camps trying to ensure a tomorrow when the turmoil of the present was finished and the Assiniboines had made it clear they were neutral and determined to stay clear of the disputes of the others.

Woman Walks Softly was lean and her eyes always tired. She moved as swiftly and quietly as ever, but seldom smiled. She rode her ponies until they were tired, then borrowed others to ride while her own rested; she brought not only food and news of the locations of small herds, she brought, also, news of the on-going skirmishes.

Then, when the first frost signalled the beginning of winter, she brought news of sickness. Sickness that caused a membrane to grow across the throat and suffocated the ailing. Sickness that caused strong men to shake with chills and burn with fever. Sickness that covered the body with raw sores and sickness that set people to coughing until blood came from their mouths and they died.

The foraging band passed the winter in the Cypress Hills, their teepee liners lashed in place, the space between liner and outer wall stuffed with insulating prairie grass. They survived, but only marginally. As soon as the thaw started, Woman Walks Softly was off to check on her ponies, to ride into the high country looking for deer and elk. She had her mother and daughter to feed, she had her cousins and their children; and where she went, Blue Quail's daughter, Rides Proudly, went too.

"The sickness is among the Blackfoot, too," Woman Walks Softly reported. "They suffer even worse than the Cree. Blankets were given them by the Long Knife soldiers and those who had the blankets were the first to die. Even after they burned the cursed blankets, people continued to fall sick. Big Bear, Piapot, Little Pine, and almost a thousand warriors of the Cree decided to attack the Blackfoot and stop the war by winning it." She paused, shaking her head, and Child Of Her People was shocked to see her mother's hands were trembling.

"The Blackfoot also got repeating rifles from the Long Knife pony soldiers. Rifles," she explained, "which do not have to be loaded, fired, and then loaded again, but which can fire many times without reloading." She reached for a charred stick, rubbed the soot and charcoal onto her hand, then put her hand on the side of her face and pressed firmly, leaving her own handprint in black on her tired face. "One out of every three of our warriors is dead," she said quietly. "There are so many dead the survivors cannot even recite the names. The Battle of Oldman River has ended the war, but no one has won it. Except, perhaps, the Newcomer Crazies who provided the blankets, guns, and bullets, and who can now move onto more of our land."

The Old Woman sat cross-legged in front of her fire, her eyes peering out from the wrinkled folds of her face. The young women who had finished their training and spent their time isolated in the purification lodges, were now ready to be introduced to their people as fully adult women and sat across from the fire. Behind them, the younger girls sat quietly, awed at being allowed to be present—behind the Old Woman, the adult women, the aunties, mothers, grandmothers. In another lodge, the Old Man was addressing the combined group of boys and men of all ages. Everyone was very aware that this was a most unusual ceremony, one not done in the memory of anyone of them, not even the Old Woman.

"When it is Time for a thing or person to change, it is Time, and nothing we do can change that," the Old Woman said. "Changes have come on us one after the other, faster than any person can believe. Our entire nation is reduced in size, not only by war, but by Change. Men and women are leaving our way of life to sit waiting for food at the Newcomers' forts and hamlets. Men who should know better watch the Crazies and think they do not suffer so terribly, even if what a Crazy knows about hunting is less than a child once needed to know. Men who should know better try to live the Crazy way; trading with Newcomers instead of hunting for the People, slaughtering what the Crazies tell them to slaughter, leading the Crazies across the grassland to rich valleys where they can start new settlements. Men who should know better imitate the way the Crazies live, and do as the Crazies do. They beat their wives and daughters, trade the use of the women of their People to the Crazies in return for a little food, in return for whiskey to drink. Men who once had a clear awareness of how things ought to be look at young girls and think of them as women. And so for some of us, obviously, a time of change is at hand.

"There is not enough food in this land. If half our people had not died of war and sickness, we would all have starved. But those who died have saved our lives and the spring is upon us again. It is time for the young adults to make the move of courage. It is time for the strongest among us to pack their goods on travois, take the best ponies from the combined herds, and go North to where the Great Pillar guards the entrance to the mountains and the Grease Trail of the Git-k-skan. To follow the trail to the Cave Of The Wind, and to meet there with the Lil'wat and ask for haven in the grasslands of the coastal country."

They breathed as one, a gasp of total disbelief, and the Old Woman held her hand up for silence.

"There are those of our cousins the Metis who are going to this other place, and some of them speak a language the coastal people can understand. You are to go with them. The Lil'wat will teach you what you need to know to survive in the land they will allow you to use.

"And when you arrive at the Cave Of The Wind, go there prepared as you would be for a Sun Dance. This is the cave where the Elders learned their secrets and mysteries. It is bigger than I can describe to you. In this cave are hot pools which keep the air warm all the year, even in wintertime. And there are other pools which are warm, and still others which are less warm, and some which are cold. When the ice covered the face of the earth, the Elders took their young adults there and told them to live there; told them the fish in the pools and the lichen which grows on the walls would keep them alive. Told them the ice could not possibly cover every valley, that there would always be some places where a few people could find food to survive. The people who stayed in the Cave Of The Wind will help you. You will take to them a map, a copy of part of the carvings on the Great Pillar, and this will tell them that you are of the People who helped look after their Elders, and you will be safe."

Child Of Her People felt confused and tormented. She was shocked at her conflicting emotions. Hunger, sickness, and war were terrible things, and she mourned because of them, but the same series of horrors were the reasons her own womanhood training had been interrupted; if her puberty training had continued, she, too, might have been one of the young adults being sent to the far-off land. And yet, if there had been no war, no starvation, no epidemics, there would have been no need for anyone to leave the land they had been created to live in and honour. She tried to talk to her mother about her feelings and could not find the words she needed, could not even begin to distinguish between her sadness and her relief, her mourning and her joy that she had not learned what she needed to know to survive properly. The one thing she knew and knew clearly was that she was glad she did not have to do as so many of the others did. She did not have to pack up her life and say last farewells to her family, heading out into the first spring air to meet with the Metis and travel through the mountains to the land of the Git-k-skan and Lil'wat.

Rides Proudly was one of those being sent to the land none of them had ever seen. For days Woman Walks Softly moved like one whose spirit has been damaged; then, with an obvious and deliberate self-discipline, she began to talk of the move as an honour rather than a tragedy.

"You will be one of the first of the People to go there," she tried to smile and managed a slight, bitter grin. "And so you must go properly, as befits a woman of the Human Beings. The war-horse I found when I found my daughter has had daughters who have themselves had daughters. They will go with you. You will certainly Ride Proudly, and it honours me to know that our horse-cousins will also go to the land of the Lil'wat. You have been a second daughter to me, I have taught you all I can. You are," she vowed, "a better hunter, a better stalker, a better warrior and a better woman than I ever dreamed I would be. You honour us."

Woman Walks Softly danced and she sang, she laughed and promised them all great adventures and many honours. When they left camp, she rode with them for half a day, then returned alone. She went straight to her teepee, lay down on her sleeping robes and cried like a baby.

More than 700 lives had been lost in the time of war, and no one knew how many had died because of the epidemics. The defeat at Oldman River, near the whiskey post at Fort Whoop-Up was the last significant battle; and in the spring following the near-massacre, the Cree sent tobacco to the combined Bloods and Piegans of the Blackfoot nation. The Blackfoot accepted the tobacco, and the peace saw all the tribes hunting without worrying about traditional territory; the tribes were all exhausted by war, by sickness, and by the increasing presence of whiskey.

The Human Beings were camped in the Cypress Hills, in a deep cut in the earth, protected from the wind. Winter had come early and stayed long, and the People had suffered. But now the animals were moving again, the first small shoots of green were showing through the rotten snow and thick mud, and the snares and traps of the women were once again providing meat.

The trading posts of Soloman and Farwell sat on opposite banks of the stream and the People had survived the winter because of that. When hunger was at its worst, the People had traded pelts, skins, and robes for food. Then, when the good pelts were gone, the Crazies had demanded the use of the women, and one does what one must do to feed the children. There was whiskey in the posts, and many of the men acquired a taste for it. They even began to demand that their wives and daughters visit the Crazies and stay with them to ensure a steady supply of the poison that warmed the belly.

The Assiniboines were camped there, too. Chief Manipupotis with thirty-three lodges of followers and Chief Inihan-Kinyen with ten lodges were almost ready to break camp and move into the hills. The hunting and trapping were sure to be better there, if only because the Crazies would not be there with their noise, their smell, and their strange habit of digging into the earth and leaving great patches of it unfit for the nibblers and grazers. The Old Woman was convinced the animals knew how important it was to stay clear of the Crazy Newcomers and lectured the young on the idiocy of staying in one place too long.

"We move often," she said stubbornly, "so the animals will not abandon us. These others sit in one place, exhausting the food supply so that they have to go ever further in search of berries and plants."

"But they had food when we were hungry," a child protested.

"They had unnatural food," the Old Woman answered. "And it is this very unnatural food which makes us hungry. They move their cattle onto the land and the animals trample the grass, eat it too close to the ground, then trample it again and again. And when the natural animals, the natural food tries to feed, there is nothing there. So it moves away and we are left where we have always wintered, but there is no food. So we must try to endure, and to adapt, to trade with the Newcomers and to survive the long cold. But we move," she said firmly, "and next winter we will not camp where the Newcomers have built their shelters."

"Still, they had food," the girl insisted. "My father says we should learn from them, and do as they do, with herds of cattle to feed us."

"And when the beef have ruined the grassland?" the Old Woman probed gently. "When the grass can no longer keep the soil from blowing away on the wind? What of those years when the chinook blows all winter, when the snowpack has no chance to form and there is no water stored in the peaks? The land dries in the summer heat, the water holes disappear, and even the Great Herds suffer. What will happen then, if already the grass is weakened and over-grazed?"

"That has never happened in my lifetime," the girl grumbled. "My father says it is a rare thing, and he says we could have enough food saved from the beef herds."

"When the Newcomers arrived," the Old Woman shook her head firmly, "they were starving. Obviously, something had happened in their own land or they would never have come here! Without the Good People they would have died. And that must be remembered. It is proof their ways did not work. The Good People fed them, it is only right they now feed us."

"My sister," the girl said defiantly, "has eaten well all winter. She has many fine and beautiful things. The men with whom she lives vie with each other to please her. She does not have to pack all her things on travois and travel through the mud and cold to try to find food."

"Ah," the Old Woman corrected, "but your sister does not enjoy what she must do with these men to have those things. If the inside is not happy, one tries to pleasure the outside. She braids strips of coloured cloth in her hair, she wears decoration every day and not just on special days, she spends most of her time obsessed with her appearance because there is no joy for her body in what she allows these men to do."

Nobody was surprised when the young woman left the camp and went to live with her sister. Old Woman sighed, and retreated into her small winter lodge, to pray and to intercede with the spirits on behalf of the two young women.

Then the wolf hunters arrived. They ignored both of the Crazies' settlements and made camp by themselves, across the stream from the Good People. Every morning the wolf hunters left early, spreading poison bait on the prairie. The wolves, starving after the cruel winter, ate the poisoned meat and died.

The wolf hunters stripped the agony-contorted bodies of their thick winter pelts and left the poisoned meat where it lay, not caring that the coyotes and the scavenger birds, intended by the Mother Of All to keep the grasslands clean, would eat the poisoned corpses and themselves die.

The Good People watched the slaughter and could neither understand nor believe what they were seeing.

"We must leave immediately," the Old Woman said. "Those who stay close to what they know is evil expose themselves to evil."

"We are not yet ready to leave," others protested. "We need several more days to be quit of this place."

"There was a time," the Old Woman accused, "when the People could be packed and gone in less time than it takes a mother to give suck to her newborn! Now, we are slowed and made pathetic by the metal pots, the heavy axes, the noisy guns and the heaps of totally unnecessary and useless things the Crazies have introduced to our lives! The longer we sit here, the longer some of you seem determined to sit! Will we still be here sitting in our own mess when summer is on us and the stream goes dry?"

With that, she went back to her small lodge, packed her few belongings, and sat waiting where everyone could see her.

Some of the People grumbled, but the example of the Old Woman prodded them. The packing began and the excuses dwindled. Those who had been most unwilling to leave began to wander toward the encampments of the Crazies, where they added their shelters and belongings to the ever-growing litter of confusion.

"Horses have been stolen," the leader of the wolf hunters shouted angrily, sitting high in the saddle, waving his rifle, and glaring at the unarmed Manipupotis. "More than forty of our horses have been stolen." He looked past the winter lodges to where the herd of the Good People grazed on the exposed curly grass.

"Those are not your horses," Manipupotis said, flushing with anger. "Those are our horses."

"Half of them are ours," the wolf hunter insisted. "Either you pay for them, or you give them back."

"You never had forty good horses," Manipupotis sneered. "What you ride are skinny poor excuses. If horses were stolen, they were stolen by others, not by us. And I, for one, do not believe horses were stolen from you. I believe your horses are exhausted and you want fresh, rested horses. Rather than trade for them, or pay for them, you try this lie."

"No horses were stolen," Inihan-Kinyen laughed. "I have never known Crazies to have forty horses worth stealing."

The Old Woman moved away from her winter lodge, calling the children to her, herding them toward the brush growing on the sides of the ravine.

"If we had left here when we were supposed to," she chided, "we would not have even been here when these insane ones arrived. There would have been no quarrel over horses and life would not be so complicated."

Men hurried to stand with their chiefs and join their voices to the growing argument. Harsh words were followed by harsher words; then, suddenly, without warning, the wolf hunters opened fire with repeating rifles.

"Run for the thicket!" Woman Walks Softly grabbed Child Of Her People by the shoulders, spun her in the direction of the brush, and gave her a push to start her on her way.

A shot sounded, Woman Walks Softly grunted explosively, blood sprayed from her shattered arm, splashing on Child Of Her People's arm.

"Run!" her mother screamed, staggering sideways, off-balance, and suddenly very pale. Child Of Her People streaked for the protection of the brush. A boy not yet old enough for his manhood ceremony fell in front of her, his head blossoming red. She jumped over his twitching body, attention fixed on the safety she was so desperately trying to reach.

Hooves thundered to one side. She whirled in time to see one of the wolf hunters raise his rifle, bringing it down butt-first on the skull of the Old Woman. As the old body fell, the children she had tried to save scattered like quail, but not all of them made it to safety. The wolf hunters were deliberately riding them down, trampling their horses over the bodies while firing their repeating rifles into the trapped and frantic People.

Child Of Her People leaped up the bank, her fingers grabbing branches, her feet scrabbling frantically. She threw herself flat in the underbrush, behind the protecting bulk of a log, and watched in disbelief as the Human Beings were slaughtered. She caught a glimpse of her mother, smeared with blood, one arm hanging uselessly, running toward a wolf hunter who was clubbing a crumpled body, and Child Of Her People gasped with horror at the realization her grandmother, Strong Heart Woman, was dead. Woman Walks Softly screamed with fury, threw her hatchet one-handed, and had the satisfaction of seeing it split the head of the wolf hunter. Then Woman Walks Softly was herself spinning and falling, seemingly boneless.

The wolf hunters were clubbing the wounded, beating them to death with their rifle butts, setting fire to the lodges and teepees of the People, capturing and stealing the horses, stealing anything they thought might be of value; acting more viciously than the wolves they slaughtered for profit ever did. And not one person rode out from the settlements of the Crazies; not one person came to offer aid.

Child Of Her People pressed herself against the soggy ground, unable to watch over the rim of the log and witness the butchery. The noise from the repeating rifles was overpowering. She could smell the scorched wind coming from the burning hide lodges, and no matter how tightly she squeezed shut her eyes she saw over and over again the rifle butt smashing into the skull of the Old Woman, saw the bearded wolf hunter clubbing Strong Heart Woman, saw Woman Walks Softly fling her hatchet, then fall, twisting like a leaf in the wind.

Child Of Her People clenched the muscles in her jaws, locking in the wails threatening to burst from her body, and then a filthy hand was closing on her shoulder, yanking at her, turning her face toward his. She smelled whiskey and stale sweat, the stench of chewing tobacco and rotted teeth, and she knew by the grin splitting his beard what he had in mind. She struggled, trying to keep her back from touching the ground, trying to drive her knee into his belly, knowing her struggles were futile. Worse, they were exciting him, inflaming his determination.

Woman Walks Softly and the aunties had taught her what to do when threatened with sexual attack. If there was any chance at all of fighting, fight like a fury. But if there was no way to avoid the act and still live, then send her spirit far from the atrocity being performed on her meat and bones, send her Self somewhere else and leave the Crazy with nothing that would give him pleasure.

There was no chance of winning this fight. She saw the other Crazies hurrying forward, attracted by the wolf hunter's yells of triumph. They were laughing, and she knew continued resistance would bring death. Why die unprepared? Her duty was to live! She took a deep breath, pulling air desperately, filling her lungs. As they dragged her away from the feeble protection of the log, her head was already spinning; her spirit gathering itself for its flight. She hardly saw the wolf hunter who lowered himself on her, and before he had entered her she was gone from her shell. Her spirit, her soul, her very Self was far above the Cypress Hills, untouched and unscarred.

When her spirit returned, she was tied belly-down to a horse, her wrists lashed tightly, a thong passing under the horse knotting her hands to her own ankles. She ached and knew she was bruised, knew patches of skin had been left behind when they dragged her from where she had been lying to where they had hoisted her onto the horse. She lifted her head and saw the Crazies' outposts burning, smoke billowing, flames dancing. Impaled on a lodgepole near the outpost, she saw the severed head of a Human Being, the face so badly battered she could not recognize who he had once been; she knew he was male only by his hair. She let her head drop again and began to recite the proper words of farewell to the spirit of the dead man, the spirit of her grandmother, the spirit of her mother, and the spirits of all the People who had been killed.

Her prayers were interrupted by the questions her confused mind kept repeating and she was unable to comprehend most of what she had just seen and experienced. She wondered about the Crazies who had thought themselves safe in their outposts, wondered what they had thought when the wolf hunters had raced across the flatland, then torched the soddies and cabins. Had any of them had time to remember that the wolf hunters would not want witnesses to their work of slaughter? Had any one of the ones who had once been People but had chosen to live with and like Crazies, who had left the encampment and done nothing to defend it, felt shock and betrayal when the wolf hunters had turned on them? Had they wished then that they had stayed with their own people, died surrounded by those who had loved them?

The wolf hunters were no more than twenty men, but they had repeating rifles and had known in advance what they intended to do. Even so, how could twenty men slaughter so many of the Human Beings? Forty lodges, men, women, and children, and the adults all trained to defend themselves. Yet, in a time-frozen nightmare of noise and terror, the ground was blood-stained mud, churned and roiled by the hooves of the panic-stricken horses.

Even so, the wolf hunters had not escaped unscathed. There were less than a dozen left, herding more horses than they would ever need or be able to guard effectively. She peered carefully, pretending to still be in that other place and tried to count how many others rode with her. But her head was aching, her mouth dry, and the sound of the blood pounding in her lowered head smothered all thought.

The wolf hunters stopped several miles from the burning outposts and set up camp hurriedly and sloppily. They ate hugely of the food they had stolen, washing it down with whiskey, guffawing often, seemingly uncaring of the deaths of those who had ridden with them. They gloated over the number of horses they now had, the extra rifles and gear they had taken. Then, drunk and laughing, they set about repeatedly raping Child Of Her People and the four other women they had kidnapped.

She saw them coming toward her, saw the ugly dark splashes on their clothing where blood had mixed with dust and dirt, then dried. One of them had a broken front tooth, she could only hope it ached fiercely at night, depriving him of sleep. She was again faced with the choice to fight and die, or to send her spirit somewhere else divorced from her meat and bones, leaving nothing of her Self for them to use, depriving the men who assaulted her of whatever pleasure it was they got from using unwilling flesh. Tied as she was she could not fight properly, and who can follow the teaching of the dead Old Woman and "endure" if the Old Woman has been shot in the head? No one can endure a bullet in the brain! Even as she thought these thoughts, her mind scrambling like a mouse in the long grass, her body recoiling from the touch of the laughing men, she knew her decision had been made. There was no heat from the late afternoon sun, she was slipping into that other place where everything is cold as mid-winter, and the only colours are pale green and light blue. Then she was floating peacefully, at home in that comfortable chill, looking down on her own body, face pale, eyes rolled back, mouth slack. Looking down on the frustrated wolf hunters as they beat and kicked her senseless flesh, trying to force her spirit to return to her body. She could hear their curses, see their faces clearly, even smell their whiskey stink and sweat, but she felt nothing. She did not feel anything even when they left her body alone, drank more whiskey, then moved to amuse themselves with one of the other women.

She watched them from that other place. Watched and wished she could find some way to speak to the frantic woman. Child Of Her People wanted to remind this woman of the teachings of the Old Women, but the woman was so frightened there was nothing to be done, no way to visit her. She was not one of the family, and the words she shrilled were Assiniboine, not Cree, but the accent was not pure, there was a sound of another tongue to the words, a tongue Child Of Her People did not recognize.

When the men were finally finished with her, the foreign-born woman crept away, weeping, and curled herself into a ball of misery. The wolf hunters laughed at her, and in a language whose words the woman did not understand, they told her what they intended to do to her next, and she understood their intent. She found a sharp-pointed stone and dug it repeatedly into her arm, ripping the vein open from wrist to inner elbow. When they went back to her, she was dying, staring at them with fever-bright eyes, cursing them with the last breath of her body, her spirit already joining the departed ones, moving past that chill blue and green haven where Child Of Her People's spirit was waiting, moving past the place of limbo to that other place the living can only imagine.

Child Of Her People watched the wolf hunters drag the dead woman's body behind some bushes, dump it, and leave it there. They swore and raged, cursing loudly to mask their own uneasiness. They drank some more whiskey, then moved to a second woman, a follower of Manipupotis, also called Little Soldier, an older woman who had seen her two children killed. The Assiniboine woman grinned at them, her decision made, and the quality of her grin enraged them. As one of the men kicked at her, she grabbed his booted foot with her tightly-bound hands, jerked it, and dumped him on his ass in the dust while his companions laughed. He got to his feet yelling and fell on the woman, trying to beat her, shame her, subdue her, and rape her all at one time. She rolled and struggled in spite of her bonds, and several other men moved in to help the first.

They managed to grab and hold her, thinking her sudden slumped passivity meant they had taught her the futility of resistance. To more easily gain access to her body, they cut the lashings holding her ankles. She kicked with all the force she had left in her body, her foot catching one of the men in exactly the right place. He fell to his knees, clutching himself and groaning, and the woman was on her feet, fighting so skillfully and so viciously that in their attempts to subdue and use her, they beat her to death. Her spirit rose from her body like a scarlet spear and flashed triumphantly toward that warm bright place where her children were waiting for her.

The wolf hunters moved away from the dead Assiniboine mother, approached the two surviving conscious women more carefully, and with as much planning as they could manage, drunk as they were, tied the women spread-eagled to bushes. Child Of Her People's spirit turned away, ignoring the abominable acts being done to the two women who lay as if bored, ignoring as best they could the grunting and humping of the drunken men. The chill other-world beckoned, her freed spirit wanted to explore, to move past mountains of glittering crystal ice, over seas of deep blue water where islands of snow shimmered and there was no smell of sweat, rotting teeth, and rotgut whiskey.

She would have stayed there forever but she became so entranced by the strange, magical other-place her control faltered. Unwillingly, she returned to her cramped, stiff body. It felt cold, even where the bruises throbbed, her arms and legs swollen, heavy, and unfamiliar, as if she had outgrown them and was now held prisoner by flesh she knew to be a burden.

She lay unmoving, listening to their voices, trying to discover where each of them was, what they were doing.

A hand grabbed her hair, raised her head, poured water on her face. She opened her mouth, drinking thirstily. The man laughed, pouring the canteen on her until it was empty. She reached for it, watching his face, willing him to watch hers, willing him not to notice she was not supporting the container at all, but holding the thong on her wrists in the splash of spilled water. He was the one with the broken front tooth, and now that he was close to her she could see his lip was cut, his face bruised. He was saying something to her, his breath foul. The words meant nothing to her, but she understood what he meant. When he released her hair she fell back to the ground bonelessly, her wrist thong landing in the small puddle of spilled water.

She turned her head and her attention was caught by the approving look the older Assiniboine woman gave her. Child Of Her People tried to smile, to give encouragement, to offer what she could to console and encourage the woman. The muscles in her face moved as if she had never moved them before, the grimace she made felt strange, but the woman nodded. Child Of Her People had seen this woman before, but had never spoken to her. She wished now that she had, wished she knew her name, the name of her mother, whether or not she had children. The other woman, the younger, was one of Inihan-Kinyen's people. She lay quietly, preserving her strength, apparently unconcerned by the behaviour of the wolf hunters. Child Of Her People hoped that she, herself, was demonstrating the same degree of courage as these two women. The Assiniboine had long been allies of the Human Beings, and the behaviour of these two women demonstrated why it was that the Cree, who had always considered themselves as occupying the centre of the universe, had wanted friendship bonds with their southern neighbours.

Twice during the night Child Of Her People sent her spirit to the other place, each time returning to her body unwillingly, returning to an increasingly numb and bruised body, to a brain that seemed disinterested in what was happening to her, or to those around her.

Four men hauled her from the ground, tossed her on a horse and sat her upright. They ran a rope from one ankle to the other, tying her securely to the horse, then brought the rope up and looped it around her neck, fastening the free end of it to the saddle of the one who rode beside her. If her horse ran away or was spooked, she would die, either strangled or beheaded. She knew that, but she did not care. The two Assiniboine women were similarly tied and they rode off in the early morning paleness, leaving two dead women behind for the animals.

Child Of Her People whispered a brief prayer for the souls she knew had gone with honour, but even prayer did not seem to matter any more. She tried to focus her eyes, tried to sit proud and upright like the Assiniboine women, but she was so tired, so terribly tired and her eyelids drooped in spite of her best efforts to stay awake.

She dozed and jerked awake, then dozed again, slumped forward, her body resting against the sweaty back of the horse. Time had no meaning, no shape, no flow, there was no continuity to anything. Fragmented images pushed through the fog of exhaustion, disembodied voices pierced the protective blanket of shock, when her eyes were open, she saw the sweaty front flank of the horse, the prairie stubble, the rocks and sand, but none of it seemed to have anything to do with her.

The men stopped in the heat of the day, untied her ankles, dragged her from the horse, dumped her on the ground and re-tied her ankles. Everything she saw seemed to have a black line around it; the sun in the sky seemed to hover just beyond her nose and even when her eyes were shut the light hurt them.

She heard faintly the sounds and rough voices of the wolf hunters as they lit a fire and warmed food; then the reek of whiskey assailed her nostrils and her stomach churned. The younger Assiniboine woman rolled onto her side, arched her body, and inched forward, paying no attention to anybody else, not even to her tribal sister. She pushed with her legs, reached as far as she could with her bound hands, pulled herself another few painful inches, and drew her feet up to her buttocks, digging, straining, pushing herself forward.

"Lookit," one of the men laughed. "She's tryin' to get away!"

Child Of Her People did not understand his words, but she knew what he was saying. She watched the wolf hunters drinking whiskey and watching the Assiniboine woman, laughing at her. When the woman had almost made it beyond the camp area, one of the men walked over, grabbed her by one arm, and dragged her back to where she had been.

The woman made no attempt to hide what she was doing. She lay a few minutes where she had been dragged, resting, catching her breath, then she started again, crawling away from the camp. Child Of Her People cringed in sympathy when she saw the raw bleeding patches on the woman's arms and legs where the rocks and sticks had abraded her skin.

Again the men watched, laughing, mocking. Again they waited until the woman was almost beyond the camp area, then went to her, and dragged her back to her place. The woman's eyes glittered like those of an enraged, trapped animal, but she made no move to struggle or fight. She waited. She rested. Then started crawling again, following the marks made by her previous attempts.

It wasn't as much fun this time to haul her back to her place with the other two women. Child Of Her People watched the wolf hunters drinking their whiskey, their humour turning to annoyance, their annoyance becoming boredom, their boredom becoming frustration. When their frustration turned to anger, they kicked the woman, punched her repeatedly, then, as if to prove they had at least one kind of control over her, they raped her again. The woman ignored them, as she had done before, which enraged them further. When they were finished with her, they tied her to a tree and shouted insults.

The older woman quietly began to chant, the sound seeming more like a moan than a song. One of the wolf hunters yelled something, threw a clod of earth, then turned away, determined to ignore her. Child Of Her People listened to the faint sound of the chant and was both consoled and encouraged. Not the death chant, but the chant of determination and endurance, a chant of faith and courage. The bound woman licked the blood from her lips, sat as straight as she could against the stunted tree, and nodded weakly.

The wolf hunters fed the women some kind of sour stew that tasted too disgusting for words, but Child Of Her People ate it and managed to let them know she was thirsty. She drank what they brought her, gulping desperately, swallowing convulsively. She would have slept then, but the short fat one began fumbling with the cords around her ankles. She knew what he had in mind and deepened her breathing. When he started to pull her to where they could force her to lie down, she took that last deep breath, felt the welcome sensation of falling, slipped her Self from her body, and went elsewhere.

By evening the wolf hunters were in particularly foul moods, arguing with each other and scowling. One of them went behind a bush, vomited repeatedly, then staggered away from his own stench and collapsed on the ground, snoring and sodden.

The younger Assiniboine woman continued to defy them, openly trying to chew her bonds with her teeth, lips bleeding from the coarse ropes. The older woman watched, eyes fiercely proud. Child Of Her People could see nothing that suggested the older woman was trying to escape, and yet she knew the woman was not passively accepting captivity.

Twilight was softening the outlines of the rocks and stunted trees, brightening the glow of the campfire, pushing her eyelids shut. She drifted off into a welcome healing sleep, different from the exhausting attempt to stay in the blue and green safety of that world.

When she wakened, it was nighttime, the campfire had burned down to a large bed of coals. The wolf hunters had eaten and were drinking the last of their whiskey, each of them guzzling greedily, trying to make sure they got their fair share before it was all gone and they were forced into unwilling sobriety. Even the one who had been so violently nauseated was once again swilling eagerly.

The one with the broken front tooth approached her with a bowl of food, and put it on the ground next to her, glaring. She licked her lips, her breathing ragged, her movements slow. He walked away sniffling often, cursing what could only be the start of a bad head cold. She looked at the mess in the bowl, bits of meat floating in a watery sauce where yesterday's overcooked beans sogged with today's halfcooked beans. She flicked a glance at the fire. None of them were looking at her, they were arguing, passing the whiskey jugs, their movements jerky and drunken.

Child Of Her People pulled the bowl toward her, bent her head over it as if trying to lap food like a dog, but instead of eating any of the mess, she slid her wrists into the bowl.

The salt they used in excess stung her raw flesh; the smell of the half-fermented over-cooked beans made her throat tighten, then flood with sour bile. But the leather thongs on her wrists were in the stew, soaking up the moisture, and already she could feel them softening.

She ached from head to foot, especially in the lowest part of her belly. She could feel dried blood on her inner thighs; knew she was swollen and torn. She also knew that only the hate burning deep inside her kept her from sending her spirit so far away that her body would perish. She could feel the hate, just below her navel but above the pain in her lower belly, a hard, hot lump of fury that kept her heart beating, her lungs filling and emptying.

The wolf hunters weren't even interested in rape tonight. They, too, were tired and the fun was gone for them. She knew that within the next day or so they would casually shoot all three women, leaving their bodies for the scavengers, then ride off in search of more poison with which to kill more wolves. Kill more wolves so they could strip off and sell the skins. Then with the money buy more ammunition, more liquor, more poison to kill more wolves. She knew, too, that if they encountered any Human Beings they would kill, burn, rape all over again, until they again needed more supplies to continue their crazed assault on all life.

The rawhide thongs were softer. When she flexed her wrists there was undeniable stretching. She lay still, waiting, watching the wolf hunters as they readied themselves for sleep, rolling themselves in their filthy blankets, coughing and hacking, snorting and spitting.

She watched carefully, ensuring she knew where each of them was. Waiting. Waiting as the Old Woman had taught her to wait. Planning, mentally practicing her every move, seeing it as if it was actually happening, doing what her grandmother and mother had taught her to do, pulling energy from the ground beneath her, the sky above her, the grass around her. One by one they stopped talking. One by one they fell asleep. Then only the night guard was awake, his back turned to the three women whose staring eyes made him so uncomfortable and angry.

Child Of Her People twisted, wriggling quietly, pulling her wrists over her upthrust knees, then rolling to an awkward position, back bowed, hands cramped beneath her, the thong trapped under her body. When she released her bladder, almost gasping with relief, the urine soaked her long-tailed doeskin shirt, and fell on the rawhide thong. The scalding flood burned her where she was bruised and torn; she gritted her teeth together to silence her gasp of shock and pain. Then she lay down again, carefully twisting her body so the thong lay against the sodden doeskin, deliberately lying in her own pool of urine, softening the rawhide.

She had been so long with her legs bent that her knees felt as if there was fire in them, but she thought of all the good things she had known in her life, promising herself she would not let these men take those pleasant memories from her. "Accept," the Old Woman had said. Child Of Her People had accepted. She had known what her choice to live would entail. She had accepted that; rather than fighting to the death, she had endured. Now she had to accept that she was not yet free, and endure the pain in her legs as she prayed there had been enough fluid in her body to loosen the imprisoning thong.

She twisted her hands, pulling, pulling, feeling the hot blood dribble from her raw wrists, and still she pulled. The knots stretched; they tightened; they resisted. But the thong itself was stretching, enough that she could get her hands near her face, enough that she could begin to gnaw the thong. Ignoring the knots, now pulled small and hard, she concentrated on stretching the thong as long and as thin as possible. When her wrists were in front of her face, she bent her head, stretching her back, almost shouting with triumph as her teeth closed on the cord.

Then one hand was free. She wanted to wave her fist at them and laugh. But what good would that do? This was not a game for children to play; this was her life. She picked, being careful not to change position or in any way betray her slight measure of freedom. Picked and picked and then her other hand was free. She could roll onto her side, pulling her knees up to her chest, working on the lashing around her ankles.

Her fingers were swollen, her hands stiff, and everything seemed to take such a long time. Her breathing sounded like thunder, she expected the night guard to hear the blood pounding in her head. And then her ankles, too, were free. She flexed her toes, wiggling her feet, willing her blood to return to them. She couldn't just leap up and charge the guard, her legs probably wouldn't hold her. Even if they did, he would hear her coming, would turn and calmly shoot her dead. She would die laughing if she knew she could take even one of them with her, but she had no intention of dying for no reason at all, not now, not after having survived this long. She waited. Waited until her skin was itching and her muscles screamed for the chance to stretch and propel her at the night guard, sitting near the fire, his back to her, nodding in the glow from the campfire coals.

He rose, she stiffened, afraid he had heard her thoughts, but he ignored her as he stretched, then moved a few steps to piss against a rock. Time changed, then, the pounding in her head stopped, she felt calmer than she had ever felt in her life. All her training had been for this one moment. She was moving, her legs weak, but they obeyed her. She was dizzy; she knew she was moving awkwardly and far more noisily than she had been taught, but she was moving and he was half asleep, the sound of his water splashing on the rock hiding the sound of her approach. The thong which had held her wrists and ankles for so many days was gripped in her hands. She crossed her arms, as she had been taught. A brief shadow before his half-asleep eyes, then her arms straightened. She pulled tightly, all her rage focused on this one wolf hunter.

He reached desperately for the cord, but it was buried in the flesh of his throat, and his grabbing only scratched his own skin. He sagged to his knees and she dropped with him, her head pushing between his shoulder blades, forcing his spine and chest forward as his head was pulled backward and down, the cord stopping any sound, however desperate. Child Of Her People pulled as hard and as tightly as she could. She thought of her mother, of her grandmother, and of Blue Quail her other-mother, she thought of the children trampled, the blood spilled, and she dedicated the death of this abomination to those who had died.

She thought of the Old Woman, clubbed from behind and knocked to the ground, trampled by horses until there was no recognizing the blood-soaked heap. She remembered how Woman Walks Softly had lifted her to the back of her own horse, ridden with her, holding her safe with a strong tanned arm, taken her to where the birds had their nests hidden in the long grass and had shown her the downy chicks. Child Of Her People could hear again the shocked gasp, feel the blood of her mother again hot on her own arm, hear again her mother's voice urging her to run to safety.

Then the guard was dead, his body no longer straining. She let him drop, reaching across his body, taking his knife from its sheath, then slitting his throat to be sure he was dead, now and forever. She didn't know if Crazies went to that other place after death, but just in case they did, she slashed his nose to mark him there as one who left this world in shame.

She moved quietly to where the other two women were tied, and cut them free, neither receiving nor expecting any thanks from them. They were as weak and as poorly coordinated as she was, but knew what needed to be done. The wolf hunters slept on, sodden with whiskey and the fatigue of the past days. It was no great challenge to carefully slide a repeating rifle from its scabbard, lever a shell in place.

She was never really sure if they killed the wolf hunters outright, or if any of them lived through the fusillade of shots, but it didn't matter if they lived a minute or two, an hour or two, or even a day or two longer; they would die, die certainly and surely, from wounds, from thirst, from hunger, or from the vengeance of the spirits of the slaughtered.

The horses were panicked by the gunfire, and it was harder than it had ever been in her life to get up on the back of one of them. The other two women were already mounted and riding away, but Child Of Her People took the time to cut the picket line, not wanting the other horses to perish tied, as she had been tied. She chased them off, certain they would keep running until they were far from the place that smelled so strongly of blood, gunpowder, and death. Any of the wolf hunters who survived the rain of bullets would be in no shape to walk, certainly not to walk far enough to get help. Without help, the ghosts of the dead would avenge themselves.

She held onto the mane of the horse, wincing from the pain as her bruised body was banged and pounded. There was no strength in her legs to grip with her knees and ride properly, she could only hang on and bounce like a lifeless sack. She had known how to ride better than this before her milk teeth were loose, but there was nobody to watch her, nobody to shake a disappointed head, and even if there had been, she wouldn't have cared.

She fell from the horse at some point during the night and it was only the pelting of rain that brought her back to consciousness. She was lying in mud, the horse she had been riding was standing nearby, under the meagre shelter of a thorny bush. The cold mud felt so good on her raw flesh she longed just to stay there, closing her eyes, going back to sleep, perhaps forever. But her lessons had not saved her simply to die in the mud; she had not accepted and endured so much just to give in now, just to kill herself by inaction and defeat. She crawled to the bush, grabbing a branch, pulling herself upright.

"Yo, cousin," she gasped, trying to control her voice, trying to soothe the uneasy animal. "I am not a ghost." She leaned against it, needing the warmth of its body. Its hide rippled under her face, the large head nuzzled at her shoulder, and she forced her desperately tired body to get up on the horse's back, where she could lie with her belly against the animal's body warmth.

The horse wakened her, stamping his feet, snorting uneasily, shifting his weight restlessly. The rain had stopped, the soft morning light was clear, and the terrible pounding was gone from behind her eyes.

She rode in a large circle, looking for the tracks of the Assiniboine women, but the rain had washed the land thoroughly, removing every trace. She had no idea where she was, no idea which direction to take. Given time to rest, given food and something hot to drink, she would orient herself by stars and moon, by sun and the length of shadows. But there was no food and nothing warm; she was too weak to hunt, and her fever was mounting.

She knew the Assiniboine women had their first duty to their own families and would not spend much time looking for the one who had been unable to keep up with them. It was as it should be; they owed her nothing. She was the one who had chosen to take the time to cut loose the extra horses.

She was unable to hold any thought in her head for any length of time. All she could seem to do was sit on the horse and mourn her mother's death, sit on the horse and shake with sickness and shock. When the horse finally stopped to drink at a small creek, she slipped from its back and drank of the clear water. Then she lay down and decided she did not care what happened to her. If the ghosts wanted her to join them, they would come to her and she would go, if only to be with her mother and grandmother again.

At some point she opened her eyes and saw blurred figures moving toward her, figures outlined against a hot afternoon sun, figures she thought in her delirium might be the ghosts. She tried to sit up to greet them. She tried to raise her arm to wave to them. But they weren't ghosts come to take her to a good and peaceful place; they were the Queen's soldier-police.

Painfully thin, still covered with bruises and half-healed sores, her lips raw from broken fever blisters, she tried to explain to them, but, of course, not one of them spoke the language of the Human Beings.

When they moved to her, took her by the arm and tried to lead her away from the stream she remembered the wolf hunters. Her eyes rolled back into her head and she collapsed.

When her spirit came back to her, she was in a Crazy's bed and knew she had been there for days. Her bruises had faded, her wrists and ankles were scabbed and healing, and the terrible aching in her bones was gone. A woman, covered with Crazy cloth, only her hands and face showing, was bent over her, talking in a soft voice, repeating words Child Of Her People could not yet understand.

"You are safe," the nun said. "Do not be frightened, child. Here, drink some of this, then you'll feel better."

The bowl was held to her mouth, and Child Of Her People recognized the smell of soup, she drank eagerly, her eyes welling with tears of weakness and gratitude.

"What is your name, dear?" the nun asked her, and Child Of Her People smiled, understanding not one syllable.

Sister Mary Joseph thought for the first week that the girl was simply in shock and unable to communicate because of the horror of what she had obviously had to endure. But when she heard the girl talking to a puppy, talking in a language the gentle sister did not recognize, she knew it was more than, or, perhaps mercifully, less than a fear reaction that kept the child from speaking. It was Marie-Berthe who solved the minor riddle, Marie-Berthe who was of mixed blood and could speak several dialects of the savage tongue.

"No," Child Of Her People protested, "it was not the Human Beings who burned the settlements, it was wolf hunters." She told, in detail, what she had seen and heard. But the Crazies had their own version of events, and if what they had only imagined was not true, it still suited them to believe it. "We were preparing to leave and go in search of meat," she insisted, "and then the wolf hunters accused us of stealing their horses, and they began shooting."

"Ask her," the Queen's soldier-police man ordered, "why white men would attack other white men and kill them?"

"I do not know white men," Child Of Her People answered, "and I cannot explain why they would do anything. It was wolf hunters did the killing."

"Ask her why we found savages dead right inside the settlement," he demanded. "How did they get there if not shot when attacking?"

"There were some who had decided to stay with the Crazies," she blurted, "And what safety was there for them there? Ask this man why so many of the Human Beings were killed near the stream if they were attacking the settlements? Why were pregnant women, and children unable to walk, slaughtered in their camp? Does he think they too were attacking the settlements? Those people in those dirty settlements did nothing to help us, and then the wolf hunters went after them too, so there would be no tongue to tell the truth!"

But the Queen's soldier-police man shook his head, dismissing her story, preferring to believe what he already knew, that savages were savages and not to be trusted. "They sent people into the encampment," he growled, "to pretend friendship. And when the others attacked, there were traitors already there, betraying the settlers. That's why," he decided, "so many of them were shot in the back."

When she told Marie-Berthe it was not the People who had abused her, Marie-Berthe believed her, but nobody else did. They had all heard stories of what happened to white women who were taken captive by the savages, they had all heard of the fate of captive children.

"I cannot understand," Sister Mary Joseph mourned, her eyes flooded with tears, "why she clings to her belief that she was well treated. One only has to look at her to know what was done to her!"

"Sister," Marie-Berthe hazarded, "it is not the way of the Good People to use girls as if they were grown women. She says the encampments were the first whites she had seen. If she was raised by a band which, until now, had avoided whites, she would be raised in the traditions. It is only those who have been exposed to whiskey traders who behave the way the stories would have us believe all of them behave."

"Ask her what she knows of her real parents," the nun said, ignoring Marie-Berthe's attempted defense of the natives. After all, Marie-Berthe herself had aunts and uncles, cousins and even in-laws who were, themselves, savages.

"She knows nothing of any mother except her Indian mother," Marie-Berthe replied evenly. "The only family she has ever known was Indian. Murdered, she says, by white wolf hunters."

The nun sighed, and left the room. She would find out more when the child could speak English. One could not always trust everything Marie-Berthe said, especially these past months. Marie-Berthe wanted to leave the residence and go back to her family, the way almost all of the mixed-bloods wanted to leave. She seemed to think she was being kept here against her will, next thing to a slave, and would not believe it was for her own good.

But the young woman brought by the Mounted Police was white, not mixed, and once she learned to communicate, the truth would reveal itself. Her face, arms, hands, and legs were tanned as dark as any Indian's, her hair was dark and straight, her eyes almost as dark as Marie-Berthe's, but where her skin wasn't tanned dark brown, it was pale, as pale as any white child's. The only part of the story told thus far that the good sister believed was that the child was white and had been raised by savages. They had probably murdered her poor parents and stolen her. It was a familiar story, and unfortunately, the only unusual part of it was that God had delivered the stolen child back to her own. Usually the stolen children were never seen again. Sister Mary Joseph went to the chapel to pray for all the lost children, and to give thanks for the return of the girl she had decided to call Mary.

Child Of Her People was fed and clothed; she was warm and had a comfortable place to sleep, but none of her skills were of any use to her. She had no idea where she was and didn't even take the time and trouble to find out; she was too busy learning to speak the strange language, too busy learning how to wash clothes, hang them over the lines in the back yard, bring them in when they were dry, fold them, iron them, put them in their proper places. Too busy learning the prayers, learning the strange customs of these strange women, too busy learning how to cook food the way they liked it cooked, learning how to wash dishes, how to keep the kitchen clean and tidy, how to dress herself the way they wanted her to dress.

Spring moved into summer and summer into autumn, and then it was winter and the world was covered with snow and ice. She got used to answering to the name she knew would never really be hers, and she could say the prayers the way they wanted them said. She could even sing their sacred songs and answer the questions they asked her in catechism study, but she understood very little of their religion.

It made sense to her that the Christ was born of a virgin mother; that was one of the signs of a supernatural, that he or she be born of different and particular circumstances. One supernatural boy was born after his mother swallowed a pine needle with her drinking water; another when his mother laughed and inadvertently sucked in a fly. Of course, the pine needle was no ordinary pine needle and the fly no ordinary fly, but rather the spirits of the children who wanted to be born. So of course the Christ would be born of an unmarried woman. And of course the unmarried woman would be the daughter of a saintly woman. The eager spirit would not choose a family of low morals. But Child Of Her People could not understand why so much fuss was made over the mother of the Christ, whose name had been give to her. She was the mother, true, but she did not seem to know, herself, who or what her son was or why he had chosen to be born. The one Child Of Her People most understood was Saint Anne, mother of Mary, grandmother of the Christ. She was easily understood! She was Old Woman, the first mother, the grandmother, the crone, the aged one, and anybody would have known that. Everybody honoured *her.* Every time a baby was born to the Good People, they gave thanks to the Old

Woman. If some people wanted to call her Saint Anne, what difference did that make? She was still the Grandmother, whatever her name, just as Child Of Her People was still who she had always been, even if they did call her Mary.

She learned not to discuss any of her thoughts with Sister Mary Joseph, because the corrections and explanations only confused her further. She could understand why it was that the Christ had not saved himself with magic but rather allowed himself to be sacrificed. Supernaturals did not always behave the way people did. By their very nature, they were apt to do things in very strange ways. And if he had flown away on the wings of magic he might not have demonstrated to his people that death was not a thing to fear. People cannot fly from death, and so he had done as a person would have had to do. He died without fear, setting an example, and that was understandable. He came back to demonstrate that death was not final, although it was amazing how little of that the sisters themselves understood. They thought they would go to heaven, and perhaps they would, but the re-birth, the return, the coming back Christ had so clearly shown, did not mean to Child Of Her People that she would have to stay forever in the heaven of the supernatural people, but rather that she, as Christ had done, could choose to return to this earth another time.

"Oh no!" Sister Mary Joseph gasped, her face paling. "No, dear, that is not what is meant at all. You will go to Heaven, and be an angel." She pointed to the sky and once again described the place she called Heaven.

Child Of Her People nodded, as if she suddenly understood something; she had begun then to realize how little good came of asking questions. The matter of baptism puzzled her, but not so much she didn't answer all the questions the way they wanted them answered. When even the priest who came at irregular intervals was satisfied that she had learned her catechism, she was baptized and chose for herself a second name. That name was written in the records as Mary Anne, but there was no family name chosen.

She wanted to ask if the wolf hunters had been Christians too, but she suspected the answer she would be given would satisfy nothing inside her. The men who sold whiskey were

Christians, some of them even wore the sign of the cross on a chain around their necks. The men who fed tainted beef to hungry children were Christians, the men who plowed the grassland and slaughtered buffalo they could not eat were Christians, the men who set fire to the long grass to turn away the herds and drive the last of the Human Beings into the hills were Christian, but she knew their Christ would never bless them.

Learning to read helped her enlarge her vocabulary, and enlarging vocabulary helped her improve her reading. At first the marks Sister Mary Joseph demonstrated meant nothing, Child Of Her People just stared at them, eyes wide, waiting for something to happen, waiting for an explanation. Day after day, for one or two hours at a time, the nun worked patiently, writing words on a slate, saying them aloud. One afternoon, without warning, the marks were no longer marks; Child Of Her People looked at them and saw what they meant: dog. She saw the dog, saw it sitting with its head cocked to one side, one ear lifted, tongue lolling.

"Dog," she said hesitantly. Mary Joseph smiled. "Dog!" Child Of Her People repeated happily.

"And this?"

"Cat. Cat!"

Child Of Her People read the Bible often, puzzling over the stories, not daring to ask why nobody taught her the story of Deborah the warrior woman. She wondered why, instead, she was told repeatedly that fighting was a sin, that one should turn the other cheek and forgive those who had done harm. Deborah had turned no cheek, Deborah forgave nothing. Even the Christ, when pushed too far, had lifted the tables and thrown them from the temple, using his strong carpenter's muscles to chase out the money lenders. He did not turn his other cheek and forgive them.

But she kept these thoughts to herself because Sister Mary Joseph got so upset when the wrong questions were asked or the wrong answers given. Child Of Her People just did her work and learned not to look at the priest when he spoke to her, but to look down, at the ground, because that was proper. It was ladylike. It showed respect. That's what they told her, and that's what she did, because, after all, this was part of something she must accept and endure until she knew what else she was supposed to do.

When her first blood moon was on her, she told Marie-Berthe and asked where the seclusion and meditation hut was for these women. Marie-Berthe laughed and told her there was none, that the women stayed in their rooms, or pretended nothing at all was happening.

"They are shamed by it," she said.

"But it is the most holy of times!" Child Of Her People blurted.

"They do not think so," Marie-Berthe shrugged. "I was told that before Eve tempted Adam and they both sinned, there was no blood moon time for Eve. After the Sin, their God cursed her, and every month the woman bleeds, to remind her of her sin."

"Do you believe that?" Child Of Her People asked carefully.

"Do I look a fool?" Marie-Berthe asked, and then they were both laughing happily, but Child Of Her People knew she would keep her secret to herself, let them think her still a little girl. Moss was easily collected; there was no need to ask anybody for cloths or any of the other gear Marie-Berthe told her the white women used.

Marie-Berthe went home to her family for Christmas and did not return after New Year, as had been planned. Sister Mary Joseph waited anxiously, counting the days, her eyes often red-rimmed from solitary weeping. One day she accepted what Child Of Her People had known all along, and from that day forward, she refused to mention Marie-Berthe by name. Child Of Her People wondered what had happened to the idea of forgiveness and understanding, but she said nothing.

The priest arrived to celebrate Easter with them, which meant Child Of Her People was busier than ever, cooking, baking, and cleaning. The priest heard her confession, although there were no real sins to confess, and blessed her. He called her "Mary" and patted her head as if she were still a little girl, complimenting the sisters on her progress.

"We must find a good Christian home for her," he said, smiling.

"She has a home here," Sister Mary Joseph protested quietly. "Sometimes I feel as if she were sent here by God. Sometimes, I think she may be one with a calling."

"If she is, she will be called as quickly with a family as she will here," he answered.

Three weeks later, a man and a woman in their early forties, both of them looking tired and more than a bit uneasy, arrived at the residence.

"There's too much work for just the three of us," the man explained, "and there's no hired help to be found for love or money. Everyone wants a place of their own. They no more than learn what needs done and how to do it than they're off and filing for a homestead."

"We've only got one child," the woman added, her voice soft, "our son Joseph. He's a good boy, and he's willing, but . . . ." She smiled, and shrugged slightly. "We need someone else, as well."

"A child?" Mary Joseph asked hopefully, thinking of the eight- and nine-year olds who were in need of a real home.

"Well," the woman answered hesitantly, "not a little one." Her face flushed, she tried to smile. "The priest said . . . I suppose it sounds selfish, but . . . I'm just not up to the demands a small child makes. Perhaps a few years ago, but . . . we were still hoping for our own and . . . the priest said you had an older girl. Someone who would be company for me and . . . ." She smiled hopefully.

Sister Mary Joseph sighed, but nodded. Poverty, chastity, and obedience, she had vowed.

There wasn't much to pack. A change of clothing, a hairbrush, her Bible, her rosary. Child Of Her People left with the settlers, riding the horse the soldier-police had found with her at the creek, the horse Mary Joseph said was her own property.

"It's a start of a new life," Mary Joseph said, "a family of your own."

Child Of Her People was certain Sister Mary Joseph believed that, but nobody else did, least of all Child Of Her People.

The homestead was small, but sturdily built. A three-room cabin, with a wide front porch protected from sun, rain, and snow by an extended roofline. A roomy barn, a hen house, and an open-front shed stacked full of dry firewood. Some hens scratched and picked in the grass, a few horses grazed on the prairie grass, their front legs hobbled to keep them from straying. Child Of Her People controlled her facial expression carefully, but inwardly she was both shocked and horrified that anyone would hobble horses and make them so vulnerable to injury or attack. One snake buzzing her rattles and the horse would panic, try to run, stumble in the hobbles, fall and probably break one, if not both, front legs. Hungry wolves could race in, kill the horse, rip it apart, fill their bellies and be gone before anybody even knew they were in the area.

Within moments of her arrival, she knew they didn't want a daughter, they wanted someone to help with the work. A daughter would have been given a room in the house, but Child Of Her People was given a room in the barn, a small area partitioned off from the rest of the space by a half-height wall. She had a small bed, some wooden pegs in the wall to hold her clothes, a rough board shelf, and a stand with a small candle she was told not to leave burning untended.

She was allowed to eat her meals with them, at least, and it was at supper she met their son Joseph. His mother had talked of him to Sister Mary Joseph as if he were still a boy, but Child Of Her People was startled to find he was a grown man, a grown man who stared at her in such a way she knew she was the only woman for miles. His mother, introduced to Child Of Her People as Mrs. Grainger, looked from her son to Child Of Her People with hopeful expectation, obviously eager for the two young people to become friends.

"How'd you get away from the Indians?" Joseph asked bluntly.

"Soldier-police," she answered, knowing there was no place in this house for truth.

"Were you married?" He grinned. "I hear tell they marry their girls early."

"No," she said coldly. "You heard wrong."

"Was it awful?" the woman asked. "Living with them, I mean."

"They saved my life," she said, as gently as she could. "I didn't know before what it was they were trying to tell me, but I think, now, that my parents were heading West for free land and . . . something happened. My father rode for help, but my mother died in childbirth."

"What happened to him?" the woman asked.

"I don't know." Child Of Her People shook her head. "My mother found me and took me back to the Good People." She ignored the snort of derision from one of the men, and continued addressing the woman. "They never made me feel . . . different. I was one of the children, treated like all the others."

"Have you tried to contact your real family?"

"No," she smiled widely. "I don't have any other family."

"But somewhere there might be grandparents," the woman urged, "and they might be wondering what happened, they might be grieving and desperate."

"I don't know them," she shrugged, "and I don't think they would . . . like me . . . if they found me." She laughed softly. "And anyway, what does it matter? They must know by now their children are dead."

"No," the woman shook her head firmly. "No, they would never give up hope."

Her little room pleased her; she was glad she had more privacy than she would have had in the small cabin. She could fix things up the way she wanted; she could retire there as soon as the evening chores were done and be away from the eyes she felt were always watching her. She picked the long grass and reeds growing beside the shallow stream and around the edges of the small pond, soaking them in a washtub half full of water. When they were properly softened, she wove a mat for the floor beside her bed.

"I could show you how to make a rag rug," Mrs. Grainger offered hesitantly. "I've been saving rags for nearly three years now."

They sat together ripping shirts and old sheets into strips, rolling the strips and braiding them into two long strands. Then they sewed the ends of the two strands together, making one very long one and began to coil it carefully, stitching the edges tightly. Every afternoon for almost two weeks they sat on the porch, shaded by the extended roof, working together companionably. When the large multi-coloured oval was finished, they sewed it to a backing made of feed sacks they had washed and hung on the line to dry. Finally, they trimmed off the excess sacking and sewed down the outer edge of the braided rug.

"You can have it for your room," the woman offered.

"It should go in the kitchen," Child Of Her People answered, "where everybody can enjoy it." For a moment she forgot she was a stranger here; for a moment the smile on Mrs. Grainger's face made Child Of Her People think she was included in the family.

She helped shovel manure from the huge pile behind the barn onto a heavy wagon, spreading the pungent mess evenly on the rough boards. The workhorse hauled the wagonload of fertilizer easily and stood, tail swishing idly, as the two women shovelled the composted mess onto the garden space, spreading it thickly. Load after load until the pile was gone from behind the barn, and then they dug it all into the garden, mixing it with the soil, breaking it into small pieces, and after it had been rained upon, they planted vegetable seeds.

It was after the garden was planted that Mrs. Grainger hesitantly suggested Child Of Her People should call her "mother."

"Mrs. Grainger sounds so . . . stiff," she smiled shyly. "And we all live much too closely together here to be so formal."

"Yes, ma'am," Child Of Her People nodded. But she couldn't make herself say the word. Even in a foreign tongue, it meant Woman Walks Softly, not this other woman.

"Do you know a family named Morrisette?" Child Of Her People asked during supper that night. "I met a girl named Marie-Berthe at the church school, but . . . ."

"We know no Frenchies!" Mr. Grainger said harshly.

"Their name is not Frenchie," she answered innocently. "It is Morrisette."

Joseph laughed; his mother smiled, then all three Graingers contributed to the lecture. Child Of Her People was told about Frenchies, warned not to trust them, told how filthy dirty they were, how untrustworthy and dishonest.

"Nothing but a bunch of troublemakers," Joseph decided.

Child Of Her People almost made the mistake of voicing her puzzlement, but wisely said nothing. Their anger was too evident, their disapproval too strongly felt. She knew Marie-Berthe was none of the things the Graingers insisted she was, insisted she had to be if only because she was a Frenchie. But it would do Marie-Berthe no good to defend her in this kitchen, to these people. She dismissed any idea she might have had of being able to learn where her friend lived, possibly even some day to visit with her.

She had freedom here she hadn't had at the residence, and life was more enjoyable than at any other time in the year she had spent away from the People. Once the morning chores were done she could whistle up the horse she had brought from the residence, the horse she had taken when she escaped from the wolf hunters, and could ride off for several hours of precious solitude.

The flatland stretched in every direction, and her eyes stopped looking long before there was even a hint of the mountains she knew lay to the west. The grass was thick and yellowing, but there were flowers, too, and a prairie-dog colony where she could sit and try to imitate their whistle, coax them from their burrows, then watch their busy scurrying to find seeds to store for the winter. There were ground-dwelling birds and fast-moving rabbits, and the hawks circled and drifted overhead, riding the air currents. Willows grew wherever there was water and when she tired of watching, she could ride the horse, the wind soft on her skin, her body moving easily with the rhythm of the heavily muscled animal.

"But what do you do when you're out there alone? What do you find to look at?" Mrs. Grainger asked.

"It's alive," she tried to explain, "it's like a friend I've known all my life."

"There's nothing out there but grass and more miles of nothing at all!"

"There is everything out there," she protested. But the woman was not born here. The family had arrived only a few years ago and the ocean of grass was foreign to them, something to be tamed, not loved; something to be subdued, a place to impose their presence. They wanted to wrench from the land a life they wanted to live on their own terms.

"If you must go," the woman sighed, shoving the repeating rifle at Child Of Her People and almost forcing her to take it, "at least take the gun with you. It's dangerous out there without one."

Child Of Her People didn't want to take the gun, but didn't want an argument either. She had little experience with guns, her hunting had been done with a bow or a spear. She knew only that rifles could kill. She had seen them kill, had used one to kill, and having the gun with her seemed foolish. She had nothing to fear from the prairie.

But when she saw the fat buck drinking at the waterhole, the rifle became a tool, not something to be distrusted. It was reflex to shoulder it, to peer down the sights and to pull the trigger.

It wasn't an expert shot, it wasn't a clean headshot, and it was nothing any hunter would brag about, but it struck home. The buck crashed to the dirt, then struggled back to his feet, chest heaving, eyes wide with shock. She raced her horse forward, jumped from its back, landed lightly, knees flexed. As the buck tried to run, she raised the rifle again, and her second shot dropped the animal to the ground.

She gave thanks to the ever-watching spirits for their help, whispered words of honour to the animal, then pulled her knife and quickly, expertly, slit the throat and gave the blood back to the Mother Of All. She gutted it quickly, leaving the steaming heap for the scavengers, and rode home dragging her kill behind her.

"Two shots," Joseph grunted, "that's one more than you ought to need." But then he grinned at her. "Help me hang it in the barn," he said easily, "and after supper I'll show you how to use that rifle properly. No use wasting the entire front shoulder every time you get one," he teased.

"Thank you," she managed, surprised to see a different side of him.

He tied an old piece of board so it hung from a strong branch, with an X marked on the board in whitewash.

"Put your feet solid," he said gruffly. "Set yourself steady. Now lift it and tuck it into your shoulder." He laughed and shook his head gently. "Naw, now," he corrected, "don't ram it against yourself like you were trying to make a hole through to your back. Just pretend it's a kitty-cat and you're cuddlin' it. Now look through the back sight and line up the front one so's you can see it. It oughta fit in the middle with nothing showing on either side."

"It isn't as easy as it looks," she admitted.

"It isn't hard," he encouraged. "Some of the biggest fools in the world learn how, so you shouldn't have no trouble." He smiled. "After all, you already got your first kill."

She almost said the wrong thing. She almost told him the buck wasn't the first thing she had killed with a gun, but she drew in a sharp breath and shoved the words back down her throat. No need to tell anyone about the wolf hunters, about standing shaking with uncontrolled fury and just firing and firing and firing until there were no more bullets left to fire.

"What's wrong?" he asked as she hesitated.

"Nothing." She pressed the trigger, the gun kicked against her shoulder, the board spun at the end of the rope and Joseph laughed freely.

"You don't need lessons," he told her. "You just need some practice."

He was a puzzle to her. He was like several different people living inside the same skin. Sometimes he seemed surly and wore a heavy frown for days on end, other times he seemed like the boy his mother had made him out to be at the residence. When he glowered, Child Of Her People stayed well clear of him, but when he was in a good mood, he did friendly, even endearing things.

He sat for most of one hour cracking corn small enough for the newly-hatched chicks to be able to swallow it and laughed softly when they clustered at his feet, cheeping steadily.

"They look like bits of dandelion fluff," he admitted, his face red, blushing with shyness. "Every spring that old hen comes out from under the barn with anywhere from ten to a dozen-and-a-half of these little things. And she's still bossin' them around come autumn, when they're as big as she is."

A younger hen walked around the corner of the barn, and the rooster rushed to her, dancing excitedly, wings spread. The hen ignored him, scuttling sideways, as the rooster jumped, grabbing her by the feathers on her head, beating her with his wings, forcing her to squat in the dust. Still hanging onto her head feathers, still flapping his wings the rooster climbed on her back, ignoring her shrieks of protest. It was finished in mere seconds, and the hen rushed off, flapping and squawking. The rooster pranced and crowed repeatedly.

Joseph laughed happily. "See?" he teased, "that old rooster doesn't take not interested for an answer. He gets what he wants."

"I'm not a chicken," she answered flatly. "And I'd hope we all had more brains than a rooster has."

"Were you so unfriendly to the redskin bucks?" he asked coldly, all sign of the laughter and gentleness he had shown to the chicks gone, now. "From what I hear you wouldn't get away with it for long. Not with them! They got some pretty direct ideas of courtship from what I hear."

"You hear wrong," she said, not for the first time. "Most of what you've heard about the People is made up in the minds of those who don't know any better. A man waits until a woman expresses her interest."

"How long does he wait?" Joseph said shortly, rising quickly, dumping the chicks from his lap to the dust.

That afternoon, instead of going riding by herself, Child Of Her People stayed to visit with Mrs. Grainger, sharing a cup of tea and trying to explain her uneasiness.

"Oh, I'm sure you misunderstood," the woman insisted gently. "Mary, dear, really, I know Joseph didn't mean what you thought he meant. I know my son! He's a good boy, a good man. You have to remember, you've only been talking

English a little more than a year, and sometimes people think other people mean one thing when they really mean something else. I'm sure he only wanted to be friendly."

At suppertime, the mother brought up the subject of Mary's uneasiness. Joseph glared, his father glowered, and Child Of Her People wished she had kept her worries to herself.

"How's a person to know what's true and what isn't if a person doesn't ask someone who's most apt to know?" Joseph glared. "I was just tryin' to find out why she's so proddy some of the time, is all."

"Those who think evil always find evil to think about," the father snapped. "If she looks for something else, she'll find it."

She was in the scrub house, doing the family laundry, pulling clothes from the blistering hot water, spreading them on the plank table, rubbing them briskly with a brush, concentrating on grass stains and the dirt-discoloured knees.

"Why'd you say that to my mother?" he asked from the doorway.

"Because sometimes you act . . . strange," she said calmly.

"I try to be nice," he accused her, "and you act like I'm nothin' but dirt!"

"I don't think you're dirt," she said, suddenly angry. "But I don't like the way you watch me, sometimes, and I don't like the way you talk, as if it's all just a matter of time before you win the right to give orders."

"Listen," he grabbed her arm holding tightly. "I can be nice or I can be—" he was staring at her, fear pulling the colour from his cheeks, as she pressed the point of her knife against the front of his pants.

"Leave me alone," she said clearly. "You don't have my permission to touch me. You don't have my permission to even so much as think about me." When he released his grip and stepped backward, she stood her ground, the knife still held ready.

There was a fuss about that. "I'll be damned if any savage, no matter how pale-skinned she might be, is going to pull a knife on my son! By God, this is his home, and when we're gone it'll be his place. Nobody around here uses knives on people!"

"Tell him," Child Of Her People shouted, "to keep his hands to himself! I don't grab him by the arm and leave marks. I don't grab you, and I don't grab her. So why should he think he can grab me?"

"Mary, dear," the mother wept. "It wasn't what you thought."

"My name isn't Mary," she answered, suddenly tired of all the uproar, "and I know what it means to be grabbed by the arm."

"Never mind your goddamned arm!" the father roared. "What we're talking here is you and your knife!"

"He doesn't know about courtship is all," the woman pleaded. "He hasn't had any chance to learn."

"Courtship?" Child Of Her People shook her head scornfully. "You made no mention of courtship when you talked to Sister Mary Joseph."

"You should consider yourself lucky!" Joseph shouted. "Lots of women would. You'd have security and one day . . . ."

"If lots of women would," she said coldly, "then why bother me? Go try your courtship on all those other women." She looked at the three of them and knew they could not understand her attitude. "I am not interested," she said, wishing her voice wasn't shaking. "I am not interested at all. I will not lie with him, I will not be touched by him, and I will never marry him."

"Stop it!" Mrs. Grainger screamed, her face pallid, her lips blanched. "My son isn't like that! You don't know what he really meant, you don't want to know the truth, you see everything the wrong way!"

She stepped between Child Of Her People and Joseph, as if trying to protect him. He towered over her, he could have lifted her with one hand, but she was his mother, and to her he would always be her little boy. Child Of Her People knew the only chance she had ever had of gaining an ally here was gone.

"I'm leaving," she said, shrugging, and suddenly tired of the tension and uneasiness that seemed to follow her everywhere. "First thing tomorrow morning, I'm leaving."

"Leave and be damned to you," the father answered. "You'll find out fast enough just how good you had it here. You'll find out what you've turned down. And don't bother coming back to apologize. Won't do you no good to change your mind. You leave, you're gone."

She went to her partitioned-off room and packed her few things, rolling them in the reed matting, then climbed into bed, certain she was too upset to be able to sleep. But she had made a decision. The time of accepting was over, and her body felt relaxed and safe. She was sound asleep in minutes.

She awakened in the dark, wondering what it was she had heard, or if she had even heard anything. She sat up in bed, listening, the warm early summer breeze soft on her shoulders. The cows were shifting sleepily, snuffling and calm, the barn cat was purring in the hay loft above her, and outside the barn the frogs down by the pond were croaking steadily.

She yawned, shifting her weight, ready to lie down and sleep again, when the loop of rope slipped over her shoulders, tightened, and pinned her arms to her sides. She tried to leap away, but she wasn't sleeping on a bed of loose furs. There were sheets, tucked in at the bottom and part way up the sides, and a blanket which tangled in her legs. Then his arms were around her, his weight forcing her to her back. She butted her head into his face as hard as she could. He swore, blood from his nose dripping onto her face, then his fist slammed the side of her head. She was cursing herself for all kinds of a fool, cursing herself for not having remembered, for not having a tame wolf to help protect her.

She didn't send her spirit anywhere; she just waited for him to be finished. When he was, he lay beside her, one leg pinning hers, one arm under her, the other holding her firmly.

"See," he whispered, his voice soft. "See, it wasn't so bad. You were scared, is all. But it's settled, now, and there's no reason for you to be scared any more. Tomorrow, I'll move your stuff into my room. When the priest comes by we'll have him marry us." He kissed her cheek and nuzzled her ear, his hands stroking her belly. "We'll be happy," he promised, raising himself to roll onto her again. She squirmed, inching the rope up and over her shoulders. It lay across her throat, and she shuddered, remembering the long mindless hours tied to a horse. His pleasure seemed to increase as she rolled her head repeatedly, and he moved the rope up over her face, misinterpreting when she heaved shoulders and head from the bed, and pressed her face briefly against his chest.

As he placed his hands on the thin mattress, one on either side of her head and lowered his face to kiss her, she slammed with both hands, the edges of her palms hard against the sides of his neck. He stared, eyes wide with disbelief as she rammed her knee upward, butting with her head the way her grandmother had taught her. He sagged and she rolled him off the bed and onto the floor.

She didn't kill him. She would gladly have killed him but she knew what the Crazies did about that. They put a rope around your neck and choked the life out of you; killing people who killed to prove killing was wrong. And she did not want to swing from the end of a rope simply because nobody would want to believe what he had done and why she had killed him.

But she did use her knife. Used it on him the way the Human Beings used a knife on young stallions they didn't want as breeding stock. He tried to speak and couldn't, then his eyes rolled back in his head and he fainted with the pain.

She pulled on her clothes, snatched up her roll of belongings and was running, whistling for her horse. Never mind the saddle, never mind the bridle, never mind anything. She knew he would be conscious soon, staggering for the house, holding himself and bleeding, screaming the parents awake, and the father would be after her with the rifle.

She grasped the horse's mane and jumped, landing belly down across his strong back. A quick wriggle and she was sitting, her knees gripping tightly, the bedroll under her arm. She clucked and the horse was moving into the night, away from the homestead, away from the sleeping parents, away from the barn where Joseph was beginning to stir.

Day after day, calling on all her training, doing everything she could to get the most out of her horse without exhausting it, she hurried toward the chance of safety, the salvation promised by the Old Woman, by the Elders, and by the generations of faith and belief.

When she found it, she stared in numb horror, slid from her tired horse and felt her legs collapse. She sat in the grass, her eyes wide with uncomprehending grief. A feeling of hopelessness came over her, numbing her, and driving her deep into her own mind.

The twin rails moved toward the crack in the mountains; from somewhere in the pass, she could hear the steady sound of heavy hammers on steel spikes. The Pillar which had stood for thousands of years was gone, its graven message smashed forever by the explosive force of the dynamite the construction crew had used so freely. The twin rails sat firm on crossties that rested on a railbed of crushed rock, crushed rock still bearing the markings of the Elders, crushed and broken rock which had once been the Pillar of Promise.

There was no place of safety, and no chance of peace. She was alone and without hope. She looked at the twin tracks, at the track bed of broken, sharp-edged and pointed rubble, and thought seriously of opening the veins in her arm and dying, there under the afternoon sky. She would have done it, done it and welcomed the spreading numbness, but her moon time was late, and she knew what that meant.

She rose, finally, and led her horse to water, sat watching the tired beast chewing the rich, restorative grass. Her brain absolutely refused to work properly, and she could only depend on her reflexes. She had half a cooked rabbit, left from last night's hunting and cooking. She had water. She had what she had been taught by two different cultures, and she had growing inside her a child she had not wanted from a man she hated.

She blinked repeatedly, trying to focus her spirit, trying to make her numb brain work. She felt as she had when she wakened in a Crazy's bed, and a woman covered with Crazy cloth was bending over her, talking softly to her.

Sister Mary Joseph wasn't much of a chance, but it was a slight one. And even a slight chance was better than no chance at all. She lifted the cold cooked meat to her mouth and made herself eat.

"Oh, dear God," Sister Mary Joseph gasped, but Child Of Her People knew the nun believed her, believed every word. "He was here," the nun said, "the father. He said you had left . . . said he thought you were . . . not well."

"Crazy," Child Of Her People guessed.

"But he said his wife wanted you back, wanted to . . . help you."

"Did he mention his son?"

"No." The nun turned away, struggling with her own emotions. Then in a flat and colourless voice she added, "They won't tell anybody about that. It will be . . . the family secret. But if he ever finds out where you are . . . he'll kill you."

"I need clothes," Child Of Her People answered, deliberately ignoring the threat the father presented. "Nobody will give me a job looking the way I do. And I can't live the life of the Good People." She felt as if her eyes were so dry they were turning to stones. "There is no life left for the Good People. It may be there are no Good People left alive."

Sister Mary Joseph heated water for a bath and brought clean clothes, but was too modest to enter the washroom with them. She reached around the almost-closed door, put the clothing on the floor and retreated silently.

Child Of Her People scrubbed herself carefully, concentrating on what she was doing so that she would not have to think. She did not want to think. She wanted to never have to think again in her life. She did not want to remember, either. What use to remember the Good People when remembering would only bring the image of the shattered Pillar, the ruined bodies blasted by wolf hunter bullets, the sight of Woman Walks Softly falling. What use to try to think of the future when there probably was no future, not for her, not for the Good People, not even for this unfortunate she carried inside herself.

With no past and no future and no hope for either, she could only live one day at a time. Enough days and she would have finished her life and be able to die.

She finished her bath, dressed in the clean clothes, had a meal and was off again, with a letter from Sister Mary Joseph tucked safely against her skin. Two days later, she was at the Mother House, where she stayed until a place was found for her, doing kitchen work for a family in town.

Child Of Her People made no friends and did not want friends. She did her work as if it was the most important work in the world, and when the work was done she went to her little room in the attic and sat on a straight-backed chair in front of the one small window, staring out at the shingled roofs of other houses and the few businesses. She prepared and cooked meals, she washed dishes and scrubbed pots, she even uncomplainingly did more than just kitchen work and, when asked, helped with housework and laundry. But she said nothing of her past and made no overtures of friendship. That job lasted three months, but she had known from the start it wasn't a permanent placement.

Her next job was in a boardinghouse, and she liked that better. There was more work to do, less time to sit trying to stifle the images that pressed against her consciousness, trying to demand her attention. There were floors to wash, wax, and polish on her knees, the work establishing its own rhythm. She particularly liked the polishing, and the boarders all said the floors had never looked so good. She had a big pad of sheepskin and would place it, fleece down, on the dull waxed floor. Onto the soft tanned inner hide she put a large heavy brick. Kneeling, both hands on the brick, she swayed from the knees, side to side, side to side, until the floorboards gleamed. Then Child Of Her People moved her legs, backing up slightly, and started again, rocking side to side, pushing the brick, side to side, and even she knew she was not entirely sane. But the brick demanded nothing. It did not ask her questions about her family; it did not ask her where she had grown up; it did not ask her where she had learned to read; it did not ask her why she seldom spoke except to answer direct questions. The brick just warmed under her hands and allowed itself to be moved side to side, side to side, while the layer of wax went from dull to shiny and the rocking helped flatten the world. It didn't matter that the flattening removed the peaks of joy she had once known; they were gone, anyway. What did matter was that the holes of horror could be ignored. As long as she was rocking, swaying, sliding the brick and buffer across the wood-plank floor, she was in control of something, even if it was only a piece of sheepskin, a brick and her own hands.

She kept the knowledge of her child a secret for as long as she could, but in the end, of course, everybody knew. They thought she was a whore because of it. The boardinghouse became another part of her past, the job gone because of her growing belly.

She packed her things and walked from the huge weathered gray house full of bedrooms, her moccasined feet making no sound on the board sidewalk. She wanted to defend herself, wanted to explain to them how it had happened, but if she said one word about that, they would know what else she had done. Then what would happen to her? What would happen to the child? She remembered the look on Mrs. Grainger's face when she had questioned Child Of Her People about her dead birth mother, about her unknown white grandparents.

"No," she had said, "no, they would never give up hope."

Child Of Her People knew as surely as she knew her own name, if Mrs. Grainger ever suspected there was a grandchild, she would move heaven, hell, and everything in between to find that child, take that child, and keep it.

If the world wanted to think her a whore, the world could think her a whore. But she would not give her child to any of them, not even to Sister Mary Joseph who had believed her, but who had sent her to the Graingers in the first place.

She knew she was spreading blame everywhere and knew, too, the blame, if there was any, was her own. She was the one who had been caught off-guard. She was the one who had ignored the warnings. She had acted like the chicken, squawking and fluttering, but not removing herself from the yard.

Well, if the world thought her a whore, the world thought her a whore. She walked directly from the boardinghouse to the saloon, went through the door as if she owned the establishment and knew immediately which of the people in the dim and malty-smelling place she wanted to talk to about a job.

"Been half expecting you," Belle said with no hint of a smile on her face at all.

"I need a job," Child Of Her People said, returning her look steadily.

"And isn't that the story of everybody's life?" Belle laughed. "What can you do?"

"Cook. Clean. Do laundry. Ironing. Sewing."

"Anything else?"

"I can read and write," Child Of Her People said desperately. "And do figures, if they aren't too hard."

"Can you keep accounts?"

"I can learn."

"I hope so," Belle sighed, "because I'll go to hell in a handbasket before any pregnant woman is lifting buckets of water in my place!" She heaved her portly body from her chair, made a rude noise with her heavily painted lips. "God damn the decent and honourable of this world! And God save us from the righteous. Come on, I'll show you where you sleep."

She might have learned to enjoy life in the whorehouse; she might have learned to relax and get to know the women who lived and worked there. She might even have found another friend, as she had once, briefly, found Marie-Berthe, but Child Of Her People didn't even try. She learned to keep the books, to carefully mark down the money in and the money out, to prepare the deposit Belle took to the bank every morning, to prepare the little gift given the town constable once a month, to make sure the doctor's stipend was delivered and the mayor's bar bill always paid. She did not realize she never did learn how to keep the books as well as Belle herself had done.

When her time came, she asked for nothing. With no help from any of them, with what she could remember from the conversations and instructions of the women, she gave birth alone on the floor of her room. She cleaned her daughter, held her close, and made all the vows every mother has ever made since First Mother. She examined the tiny body, the creased hands and feet, the flower petal ears and knew whatever names she had been called, it was a small price to pay. Nothing mattered but this promise she held in her arms. Nothing mattered but herself and her child. It didn't even matter about Joseph.

She heard the child's first sounds and wondered, if she had known there would be this joy, would she have resisted Joseph's first advances? If she had known a half-hour of intrusion would result in this miracle, would she have pulled her knife and pressed it against him in the scrub house?

The baby started to cry, and Child Of Her People laughed softly, pulling the tiny body against her own. The crying stopped; the little girl looked at her.

"Hello," Child Of Her People said happily. "Welcome, little woman. Just look at you," she crooned. "Just look at the beauty and wonder of you!"

"You need any help in there, Mary?" a voice asked from the hallway.

"No," she said. But the door opened, and the whores peered in hopefully.

"Get outta my way!" Belle ordered. She came into the room like the empress of the known world, then glared at Child Of Her People. "Self-sufficient is one thing, girl, but there is a difference between scratching your arse and ripping out great bleeding hunks. Nora, get some padding! Gladys, get hot water, soap, and the softest towels you can find. And you," she said firmly, "get up off of that goddamn floor and get into bed with that child!"

Somewhere between the blood-soaked sheets on the floor and the freshly made bed, Child Of Her People realized she had known all along that her life since the attack by the wolf hunters had been a time where the normal rhythms and flows of life were off-balance, a time where all the ups and downs had been squashed.

She had tried so hard to protect herself from pain that she had insulated herself from pleasure. But lying in a bed of clean sheets, tended by a half-dozen whores and a portly madame, holding her daughter to her breast and watching the delicate jawline moving in the first greedy suckling motions, she knew she could never again live as she had been living. She had tried to make everything assume equal importance or equal triviality, and that was impossible now that she had her daughter. Her daughter, her very own daughter, who could never be the least bit trivial.

Had she been living with the Human Beings she could have given her daughter a proper name, but she knew her life among the Crazies would be made difficult if she did that. So she chose the name least offensive to her, a name almost pleasant in sound. A name that did not hurt her ears or come clumsily from her tongue. Rachel.

"Gonna have to find you a different job," Belle said regretfully. "Not right away, maybe, but for sure before that child is old enough to take notice of what's going on around her. A whorehouse," she said flatly, "is no place for a growing girl."

The cattle ranch was located on what had once been the Sarcee hunting lands, where the Red River ran to join the South Saskatchewan. Child Of Her People was working in the cookhouse, trying to stay safely clear of the cowhands and drifters who came and went as the job demanded. She was trying to make some kind of future for herself and Rachel, working as hard ignoring the jibes and laughter as cooking, cleaning, and doing the laundry.

And there he was, riding up with a fresh-killed deer slung over his extra horse, grinning and saying, "I'd gladly swap every speck of it for a proper supper, with pie for dessert."

She was suddenly too shy to speak and could only nod.

He carried the deer into the cold-house, a small, dark structure dug deep into the earth and banked thick with sod to block the heat of summer and the bitter freezing of winter. He laid the deer on the plank table and skinned it expertly.

"What do you want done with the hide?" he asked.

"I don't want it," she managed to reply. He nodded, rolled it carefully and put it to one side while he butchered the meat into roasts, steaks, and stewing chunks. When the messy job was finished and the scraps thrown outside to the dog, the cheerfully whistling stranger took the hide back outside with him and tied it with his gear. Then he walked off, still whistling, leading his horses down to the corral.

Child Of Her People watched from the kitchen window as he unsaddled his horse and put his saddle on the corral fence. From a saddlebag he took a small brush and carefully groomed the animal. He checked the hooves, took snarls from the tail and mane, then held the horse's head in his hands and rubbed firmly. She couldn't see if he blew in its nostrils, but she could tell from the way the horse butted gently against the front of the fringed buckskin shirt that the animal was content.

She cooked an enormous roast for supper, with mashed potatoes and gravy, fresh peas and baby carrots from the garden, and made so many rhubarb pies she was sick of the sight and smell of them. She skimmed the thick cream from the pail of yesterday's milk and whipped it until her elbow was sore and the cream stood in soft peaks.

When she looked back out the window, the horses were standing slack-hipped, heads lowered, and the saddle was gone from the corral fence. There was no sign of the darkly tanned stranger, but clean, freshly washed clothes she had not scrubbed were hanging from the washline, dripping on the dry earth.

"So he does his own washing," she said, the sound of her own voice surprising her.

"Was'?" Rachel echoed.

"Not today," Child Of Her People answered.

"Was' han's?"

"Yes, you can wash your hands." She ladled water into a small basin and took it to the front porch.

"Feet?" Rachel smiled.

"Yes, feet, too, if you want. I wish we lived where there was a safe place for you to play in water." She hunkered, cuddling her treasure. "Some place where you could splash and dribble and laugh all you wanted. But this is the best we can do."

"Was'." Rachel dropped to the porch in that delightfully boneless way children have of sitting, just plunking themselves down by moving their own feet out of the way.

"If I tried to sit the way you do," Child Of Her People laughed, "I'd ram my spine up through the top of my head."

"Was' head?" the baby echoed hopefully.

"Wash head if you want."

The newcomer ate as if he hadn't seen food in days. Child Of Her People watched him as he wielded his knife and fork with unexpected delicacy, chewing slowly, swallowing quietly, nodding appreciatively. He ignored the sideways glances of the other men, the ones who sat at the table with him but kept a noticeable space between themselves and this dark-eyed man with his hair hanging in braids on either side of his face, wearing rider's boots, rider's pants, rider's belt, but a doeskin shirt with fringes and quill-work.

He ignored the coffeepot and the teapot, and filled his enamel mug with fresh milk, drinking thirstily, smiling as he lowered his mug to the table and licked the milk from his lips.

"You a wrangler?" one of the men asked.

"I've done that," the newcomer replied. "Don't much care for it, though."

"What don't you like about it?"

"Knowing it'll be the same thing tomorrow," he grinned.

"You looking for a job?"

"Just a couple of meals in exchange for whatever the boss finds for me to do before I move on again." He reached for the bowl of potatoes. "Sure do get tired of my own cooking after a while," he said. They all nodded, but none of them was satisfied. He talked white, but he was dark. He dressed almost white, but his hair was too deliberately braided and wrapped with soft buckskin strips. They didn't trust him. And he didn't care. His unconcern only added to their distrust.

When Child Of Her People put the rhubarb pies on the table the dark-skinned stranger grinned widely.

"And to think I didn't even feel any pain," he chortled. "Here I've died and gone to heaven and it didn't even hurt!"

"I hope you like rhubarb," she managed, cursing herself for her sudden awkward shyness.

"I like rhubarb," he said firmly. "I like it in pie, I like it in tarts, I like it in pudding, I like it raw. I've hardly ever had it," he admitted, "but I like it!"

After supper the men went back to the bunkhouses to gamble away their wages, but Marcel Cormier took the water buckets from the kitchen counter and went to the well to draw water for her. She thanked him and he grinned at her, nodding cheerfully as he scooped Rachel into the crook of his arm.

"Let's us go have a smoke and get out of the way of busy feet," he suggested. Rachel stared at him, then gurgled with laughter and began to chatter to him in her own special language.

"That so?" he replied, as if he had understood everything she had said. "And then what happened?"

When the dishes were washed, dried, and put away, and the pots and pans scrubbed and stored, when the counter and tabletop were washed and the floor swept, Child Of Her People stepped from the kitchen to the porch. Marcel Cormier was sitting there, half leaning against a support post, smoking a long-stemmed, small-bowled pipe. He was speaking softly to Rachel, and at first Child Of Her People didn't understand what he was saying. Three and a half years of hearing only English had almost trained her to consider Cree a foreign language.

"And so the Transformer changed himself and on the other side of the mountains he is a Raven, and in the North he is a wolf, but he is still who he always was, the one who brings change and understanding, and the one who jokes and plays tricks. It is through his tricks we often see the lie, and because of the lie we can see the truth. If we look for it."

"Where did you learn the language of the Human Beings?" she asked quietly.

"From my mother," he looked up at her and smiled. "Her name was Daughter Of Many Women. And my grandmother, Strong Tempered One."

"With a name like that," Child Of Her People laughed, "she must have been fearsome."

"Hell on wheels," he admitted, in English. He stood, handed Rachel to her mother, and walked toward the barn, where he had spread his bedroll in the loft.

He stayed two days, splitting wood for her and hauling water. He helped the Chinese gardener and odd-jobber clean the barn, shoveled the manure out of the corral, and replaced fence poles cracked by winter cold or the pushing bodies of the wranglers' horses. When he rode off, she thought she had seen the last of him. More than once, Child Of Her People lectured herself for being foolish and daydreaming about someone she did not know.

He was back two weeks later with more fresh meat and a small pair of buckskin slippers for Rachel.

"Do you like working here?" he asked, slipping the little moccasin over Rachel's sun-browned bare foot.

"It's a job," she answered, concentrating on the washtub full of dirty dishes.

"They tell me you were raised by Indians," he said. He watched her intently, studying her face, her eyes, and how the skin around them tightened before she took a deep breath and nodded.

"How did that happen?" he probed.

Quietly, she told him the story as it had been told to her by Woman Walks Softly. Told him everything, right up to the events known to the Crazies as the Cypress Hills Massacre. He listened carefully, listened as did the Good People, his eyes turned politely aside, not invading her privacy, not trying to peer into her own eyes to spy on her soul. He gave her as much time as she needed to choose her words, examine her reactions, re-live, if necessary, events of the past. He nodded several times, and when she had told her story, he grunted, the soft gutteral sound of acceptance, and something inside her relaxed.

"Anything else you want to know?" she asked in the harsh and direct language of the Crazies.

"Why stay here?" he grinned. "Why not just pack your stuff and come with me?"

"You?" she laughed with surprise. "Why would I go with you?"

"Why not?" he shrugged. "I see how these men watch you. I see how the foreman stares when you aren't watching him. These respectable men, these honourable men," he wasn't smiling any more and was looking directly into her face, wordlessly offering her the chance to examine his intentions and sincerity. "Won't even ask you, they'll just take. I'm asking. I'm not respectable or honourable though," he warned, grinning again. "I'm just another dirty breed, and every story you ever heard about us is true." He left the cookhouse abruptly.

She fell asleep thinking of how it had been before the Cypress Hills Massacre, of the smell of sweetgrass and sage, of waking in the winter mornings and feeling the sharp cold air on her skin, snuggling back under the warm robes and whispering her thanks to the One Who Created All Life, giving thanks for life, and warmth and the sound of her own mother's voice, the smell of the morning meal coming from the coals glowing in the firepit.

She rose as usual and started the fire in the big stove in the cookhouse, then she put the coffee on to boil and started slicing hog jowl for breakfast. She set the table and put buns in the oven to bake. She got Rachel out of bed and took her to the outhouse, brought her back and fed her before the men arrived to wolf down the food she had prepared.

Marcel sat at the breakfast table eating slowly, ignoring the men who ignored him. He spread jam on his hot bun, patted his knee, inviting Rachel to climb up. When she did, he gave her some of the bun and moved his coffee mug to where she could sip and dunk. When the other men pushed back their chairs and hurried from the cookhouse, Marcel continued to sit, watching Rachel finish his coffee.

"I have two good horses," he said, "and one who is too old to be called good, but she's pregnant by a strong stud and her foal will be fine. I would let you have your pick of either of the good horses, and then it would be yours. The unborn foal will belong to Rachel when it is born. I know you are a twenty-horse woman," he grinned, "but I would have to owe you the other nineteen. I have two good guns, several knives, and lots of blankets. And I'm asking you one more time."

"Why?" she asked, confused.

He ignored her question. "If at the end of a year you don't want to go on with the bargain, you take your horse, Rachel's foal, and half of everything we have, and no hard feelings. I'll wait until you're out of sight and sound before I'll roll on the ground and gnaw the sod like a poisoned wolf." He tried to smile and couldn't.

"Why?" she insisted.

"I had a vision," he said simply. "There was a woman in it. I couldn't see her face, and so I thought she was a supernatural. And then I saw you and knew you were the woman in my vision." He waited to see if she would laugh at him.

Child Of Her People did not laugh. She remembered her mother coming back from a Vision Quest, gathering her in her arms and telling her a day would come when they would be separated, but not forever. So, no matter what happened, she must not be scared, not be discouraged, but only wait patiently for the proper time.

She packed her few things and rode off with him. The boss, the foreman, and the men stared at her with open contempt. She rode with Rachel in front of her, their few belongings on the pack frame carried by the old mare. When she would have ridden behind him, as the Crazy women often did, he turned, waved his hand, and the horse quickened its gait until she rode beside him.

"My mother," he said conversationally, "was Cree, my father was a mix, half-Cree, with both French and Scot thrown in. One of his parents was a Cree-French breed, the other, Cree-Scot." He laughed suddenly. "I was sent off to school but they never taught me how to add, subtract, multiply, and divide blood."

"How long were you in school?"

"Not long," he admitted cheerfully. "Every time they beat me, I ran away. And every time I ran away, they beat me. As soon as I was big enough to run far enough fast enough that they couldn't catch me, that was it, no more school."

"Your parents?"

"Smallpox," he said briefly.

They rode all day and well into the evening. When Rachel started to fuss, he took her, talked softly to her and gave her pemmican to chew on and water from his canteen. He let her hold the reins, assuring her she was in control of the horse, promising her they would find a nice place to stop where a little girl could run if she wanted, play if she wanted, and make all the noise it was possible for a child to make. She fell asleep in the crook of his arm, wrapped in his jacket, held easily against his chest. When they finally stopped at a small line-shack, he carried Rachel inside and settled her on a blanket on the floor, his movements so casual Child Of Her People knew he had been around children often enough and long enough to be comfortable with them.

He spread their blankets, then went outside to look after the horses. When he came back in, Child Of Her People had food ready, but was sitting nervously, obviously feeling very shy and uncertain.

"Relax," he said softly. "You're safe." He winked at her and she felt her face grow hot. "For tonight," he amended, laughing. "Tonight I'm my savage side. Tomorrow night I might decide to be a white man."

They left the cabin after a cold breakfast and rode until late afternoon, then stopped by a small stream. He watered the horses and turned them loose to graze, laughing at Rachel's struggles to haul off her clothes, get into the water, and pick ground-hugging berries, all at the same time.

"Easy on there, little woman," he said. "One thing at a time, here."

"Was'," she said firmly.

"No," he shook his head. "Not until your mommy is ready."

"Was'!" Rachel insisted stubbornly.

"Wait for your momma," Marcel said firmly. He reached for his bag of necessaries, dug into it and pulled out a clean sock. "Watch," he waved it at Rachel, diverting her attention from the stream. "Look what we can make." He pulled a handful of grass, stuffed it into the toe of the sock, pulled more grass, compacting it into a rough ball. He knotted the leg of the sock, and threw it, the unstuffed material fluttering, the ball wobbling in the air. Rachel laughed, raced after it, picked it up and tried to throw it back at him. It fluttered and fell. She chased after it, picked it up, threw it again, laughing.

Child Of Her People had the cooking fire going, the meat and vegetables simmering together in a black cast-iron stew pot.

"Hey, Momma," Marcel yelled, "what's this about was' in the water?"

He stripped off his buckskin shirt, pulled off his boots and slipped his belt from the loops, then walked into the stream and flopped onto his belly, sending water splashing. Rachel whooped happily, raced to the edge of the bank and just kept on going, in a joyous cross between a fall and a dive. She went under water, then Marcel was lifting her back up in the air, her face shocked, water pouring from her hair and clothes.

"Take a deep breath," he said, "and we'll do it again!"

She gasped, almost frightened, but took a deep breath. He dumped her in the water, then scooped her back up again.

Child Of Her People pulled off her soft moccasins and walked into the water in her pants and shirt. She held out her arms and Rachel reached for her, still wide-eyed and uncertain.

"It's just like a big bath," Child Of Her People said quietly. "Only the water isn't warm, and we aren't going to use any soap." She sat on the rocky bottom, Rachel sitting on her legs. "See, it's just water," Child Of Her People soothed. "It's just water for a wash. Wash hands, wash feet, wash ears, wash nose, just the same as ever."

Rachel looked up and smiled, all evidence of fright gone from her face. "Was'?" she asked.

"Wash," Child Of Her People said firmly. "Rachel do what mommy do." She pinched shut her nostrils and lay back in the stream, the water covering her face. Then she opened her mouth and blew. She could hear her daughter laughing happily, then the dear little face came toward her, snuggling against her under water, and Child Of Her People straightened, bringing them both back into the air.

"Fun?"

"Was'," Rachel assured her.

Marcel went upstream and waited behind a clump of bushes, where he couldn't be seen, giving Child Of Her People some privacy. She stripped off her wet clothes, rinsed them thoroughly to get rid of the smells of horse and human sweat, then draped them on a bush to drip dry.

Rachel was shivering, and Child Of Her People lifted her from the water, stripped off the wet shift, then hurried to the cooking fire to warm them both and find fresh clothes for them.

She heard Marcel come from the stream but didn't turn to look at him. When he reached past her to his possibles bag, his arm was bare and still damp. Then he pulled clean pants from the bag, and she heard the rustle of grass as he stood first on one foot, then on the other, sliding his legs into the pants.

"Coffee or tea?" she managed.

"Tea, please," he said, then coughed nervously. That nervous cough reassured Child Of Her People in ways she couldn't have explained to anybody. She wasn't the only one who was feeling a growing tension.

They ate supper together, each trying to find something to talk about and both failing. Rachel spooned stew into her mouth, chewed, and swallowed hungrily, but neither of the adults had much appetite. When Rachel put down her plate, then yawned, the tension between the adults increased. Child Of Her People put her daughter to bed, simply wrapping her in a blanket on the spongy cushion of prairie grass.

Marcel made them a bed of long-stemmed scented grass, spread a blanket over it, then, watching her with large dark eyes, he stripped off his clean clothes and sat naked, waiting for her.

It was everything her mother and grandmother had told her it would be, and it in no way resembled anything that had happened to her after the wolf hunters had attacked. They slept together on the bed of scented grass, bodies touching, warm skin against warm skin. She wakened once and he was curled against her, his hand cupped around her breast, his breath warm on her back. She pushed against him, snuggling closer, and pulled the blanket up over their shoulders. He muttered something, then kissed her skin, his hand tightening briefly, his arm cuddling her close.

In the morning, she wakened to the smell of fresh coffee, the touch of steam against her skin. He was grinning down at her, holding out a fragrant mug, and she felt her face flush, felt the heat rising from her shoulders, up her throat, until she knew her face was flaming with something that wasn't shame, nor guilt, nor even shyness.

"Look at you," he crooned softly in the gentle cadence of the Good People. "The colour of the dawn is trapped in your flesh."

"Listen to you," she answered easily, "the song of the birds comes from your throat."

They stayed by the stream for several days, playing naked in the water with Rachel, or lying on the grass, bare skin touching bare skin, watching the child as she chased her sock-ball or played by herself in the cool water. Then they moved on, hunting for meat, occasionally fishing when they came upon streams or pools. Rachel tanned, her hair bleaching in the sun, wearing clothes only when the weather changed and the breeze blew cool. Every day she learned more words in English, French, and Cree; every day both Marcel and Child Of Her People taught Rachel something else they had been taught as children. And the pleasure of their coming together increased as they lost their hesitancies and became more comfortable with each other.

"Woman," he said, "you make me happy to be a man."

"Your aunties," she teased, "taught you well. Even if you are as hairy as . . . ."

"Uh uh," he warned, "no tickling."

"The hair on your chest is dark and curly," she traced her fingers slowly, deliberately teasing him. "But on your belly it's as fine as the hair on a newborn baby."

"Play with fire, burn the prairie," he managed, licking his lips and shivering.

The soddy was nestled into the side of a small hill, the visible, projecting part of it made with poles interlaced with willow withes and covered with a thick mix of mud and animal dung on the sides, dirt and sod on the roof. The grass on the roof was as rich as that in the valley, and the willows along the banks of the deep creek were home to singing birds. The entrance to the soddy was marked with two fluttering strips of coloured cloth and a large white tailfeather from an adult eagle. Just in front of the entrance, several sacred stones were set, stones with holes through them. Any bad or evil spirit coming into the valley would be attracted to the stones and would fall through the holes in them; either destroyed or imprisoned by the protective powers of and in the various-sized rocks.

"I hold the papers on it," Marcel said quietly. "It's where I spend the winters."

There was much of the feeling of a winter wickiup camp, but much of a settler's homestead, too. A pole and mud shed, its solid side turned to block the winter wind, a small post and pole corral, a lean-to abutted onto the protected side of the soddy, these were not of the People. Yet they fit in, somehow, and if the People would not have bothered, their cousins, the half-breeds or Metis, were known to live like this.

They rode toward the shack, dismounted; he hurried ahead to open the door and hold it for Child Of Her People and Rachel to enter. It was cool inside, shadowed and dim, the only light coming from the door. She realized she was aware of the lack of windows, and smiled, knowing herself changed by her time with the Newcomers.

"I dug it out over a winter," he explained. "It wasn't really much more'n a natural cave, at first, a place to get out of the wind. But I had a shovel, and I had lots of time, and when I'd gone back a ways, well," he shrugged, "it started to feel like home. Later, I added the cabin to the front."

"It's nice," she smiled. "Nice and cool after the heat."

"Warm in winter," he assured her. "It's the lazy man's answer to the winter wood pile. Bit of a pain in the cabin when it rains," he warned her. "The water seeps through the sod and the ceiling drips, but when it's raining I just move back into the dugout."

There was a stone and mud cooking hearth with a rough chimney where the soddy cabin joined the dugout cave, and room for them all to live without falling over each other. By nightfall there were two beds, with fresh grass for them to lie on, the scent of it pungent and pleasant.

The horse that had been hers since she escaped from the wolf hunters settled in contentedly with Marcel's small string, and Rachel blossomed, as free and happy as any child of the People had been before change followed change and the world turned inside out and became crazy.

Strapped onto the pack horse was a large and awkward canvas bundle and in it Marcel had an assortment of vegetables: beet root, turnip, and some other roots Child Of Her People did not recognize. Their first morning in the valley, he showed her the root cellar, another excavated structure near the soddy. The floor was covered with sand, and into the sand he put the root vegetables he had brought. He watered them, then saw her look of absolute puzzlement.

"This is about all the water they get," he explained. "And now I just leave them here. By springtime, I'll be able to open the door and give them some light. And in no time, we'll have fresh greens."

"Don't you have . . . " she gestured to the valley and he laughed.

"These'll be ready a month before the wild ones," he assured her. "Temperature in here never gets anywhere near freezing, no matter how cold it is outside. We bank up the doorway with sod before the snow flies," he explained.

She showed Rachel how to set snares along the bank of the creek. When they caught small animals, she showed her how to skin them, how to cure and tan the hides, how to store them for the time in the winter when they would have nothing else to do but fashion the hides into blankets and clothing.

She built drying racks and smoking racks for the meat they had no trouble finding in the valley and hills. She wondered at the abundance of game until Marcel showed her the blocks of salt he had set out to tempt the deer.

"I've never shot a female," he said quietly. "I figure one or two randy old bucks can keep the females havin' young, and I'd sooner try to fill the valley with real food than move in those goddamn stupid beef that practically have to be tended like babies all winter long." He grinned at her. "I'm not such a great hand at knittin' that I want to try to make sweater-coats for cows."

Sometimes, at night, she would waken, and get out of bed to check on Rachel, then stand at the door of the soddy cabin staring out at the valley, fixing the stars in her mind, trying to imagine exactly where she was. When she was back in bed again, she snuggled against his warm body, memorizing every curve, imprinting the very shape of him into the memory of her own flesh. They had told her, and she had not known what they had meant, but she remembered now, and it made sense so she knew it was true: the flesh has a memory of its own. When he was gone she would be able to lie on her side like this and recall the comfort of his back against her belly, of his knees curved comfortably against hers, the steady rise and fall of his chest against her hand, the particular smell of him. Often she would stroke his belly until he turned to her, reaching to hold her. His breath warm on her throat or against the side of her face was the answer to questions she could not put into words.

Marcel bundled Rachel in his jacket one night and carried her down to the willows along the creek. He told her to hold the sack open and not to drop it no matter how surprised she was.

"Trust me," he said, his face serious, "and know I will never tell you to do something for no good reason. And don't say anything until after I speak to you."

The fool hens were roosting in the willows. He showed her how to start at the outside, picking them up one at a time, his hand tight around their necks so they made no sound. He dropped them, one at a time, into the sack, and she gripped it tightly. When they returned to the dim light of the lamp in the soddy, he showed her the birds in the sack, dazed and stupid, but starting, now, to struggle and squawk.

"As long as it's dark," he said, closing the sack, "they just sit. And as long as they don't see or hear anything, they think they're safe. Never put your hand or arm in front of their eyes or they'll kick up a fuss. If you shut their throats so they can't make a noise, the one sitting right next to them thinks the fluttering of wings is just getting comfortable. Like you rolling over in bed." He grinned. "You did real good, Rachel." He hugged her gently. "You're a real hunter."

Child Of Her People watched him, and wondered why it seemed so natural to her that he occupy himself so fully with the training of a girl child not of his own blood. Where were his nephews? A man's duty was to teach his nephews, to protect his nephews, and to train them while leaving the education of his own sons to their uncles.

"I had two sisters," he told her when she asked. "One died of sickness, the other was younger than me and was taken to school when I was taken. But the girls had to go to a different school and I don't know what name they gave her or where they sent her, or . . . ." He looked away, his face suddenly hard, his voice carefully controlled. "I asked when I was old enough and on my own, but . . . ." He shook his head. "So many people just got swallowed," he finished.

He turned to her then, allowing her to look into his eyes if she wished, to search his soul and examine his motives. "Not everybody is a threat to Rachel," he managed. "And not everything the Good People did is the best way, or the only sane way to do things. Some of what the settlers do is . . . sensible and . . . good. And she has no aunties . . . ."

"I only asked if you had nephews," she protested.

"I thought I heard something else in what you asked."

"It may have been there," she blurted, "but . . . not directed at you. I very often," she turned her head so he could see into her eyes and her soul, "am not sure if I am sane or not. Some of what I was taught is no longer of any use to me and . . . ." She shook her head, unable to find words.

"Son a bitch, eh?" He took her hand. "Son a bitch." He tugged gently. She sat next to him, leaned her head on his shoulder. She wanted to tell him she trusted him; it was his Newcomer Crazy upbringing she didn't trust. He made no secret of his mixed blood, and she knew it was foolish to distrust his white half when she herself was not born to Human Beings. And how to convey the confusion, the constant need to be on guard, the obsession to protect Rachel even against the man whose smile made her own belly grow warm, who brought to her emotions she couldn't even name?

They went to Evert's Crossing, a comfortable three-day trip, and camped in a grove just beyond the town.

"Why not?" he puzzled, staring at her with troubled dark eyes.

"I don't know," she admitted. "I just feel . . . I would rather stay here and watch the camp."

"You scared someone's going to steal our bedrolls?" he laughed.

"I don't know these people," she flared. "They might steal the fleas off our dog if we had a dog to have fleas!"

"Someone sure taught you to be proddy," he growled.

"Yes," she agreed, "several someones over a period of time!"

He shrugged, climbed on his horse and rode off wordlessly, his back stiff. She sat in the shade watching Rachel playing with a pile of stones, wondering miserably if he was going to stay angry with her. Why did he care if she went into town or not? What difference did it make if one person or three walked into the store to buy a bag of salt and a five-pound tin of tea?

He was gone the rest of the day and still hadn't returned to camp when darkness began to close in on them. She wondered if he had just ridden off, too angry to care what she did or where she went.

He arrived just as Rachel was crawling into her sleeping robe. He dismounted carefully, stood for a moment with his back to her, then turned and waited for her to comment on his blackened eye. She stared, almost said something, then turned away, troubled.

"Got the things we needed," he said with forced casualness. "Got a few other things, too."

"It looks as if you also got a punch in the face."

"Walked into a door," he said flatly. She turned, looked at his eye, then nodded, but not with acceptance.

"Here," he reached under his shirt, "got something for you." She looked at the puppy held in his hands, blinking seriously. "She's not much as dogs go," he admitted, "but she was due to be put away tomorrow."

"Put away?" She wasn't sure she understood. "Put where away?"

"Bang bang," he answered, passing the puppy to her.

Child Of Her People would have wanted the puppy even if Rachel hadn't jumped out of her sleeping robe and rushed over, hands outstretched, laughing happily.

They lay together under the stars, and finally began to speak of the near-quarrel.

"It doesn't matter," he assured her, "except that I was proddy myself."

"And you think you don't have any right to be proddy?"

"Right or wrong didn't enter into it. I thought one thing and when it didn't happen that way . . . I'm not much used to living with other people."

"I don't know why I didn't want to go into town. I thought I was used to having people stare at me, stare at Rachel, and wonder."

"I don't wonder at all why people stare at either of you," he held her close. "You're both so beautiful."

"No," she said quietly, "that isn't why they stare."

"I thought maybe you didn't want to be seen with a breed," he blurted.

"A fool," she said to the stars. "This man is a fool."

But she couldn't tell him what she felt when she thought of him or saw him working to prepare the place for winter. Their agreement was for a year, and her life had conditioned her to expect only the temporary, never the permanent.

Back in the valley they collected firewood and stacked it in the lean-to. They gathered piles of curly buffalo grass and stored it in the pole shed where the horses could shelter from the worst of winter. The sacks of grain brought back from town were stored against the back wall of the dugout, where there was no chance of the horses getting into them and eating all the grain before it was needed.

"The big fault with these town type horses," he told Rachel, "is that because they are bigger, they can't make it through the winter as well as a range pony. The more town horse blood they've got, the less chance they have of toughing it in the hills. On the other hand, the better they can tough it on their own, the less reason they have to need us, so the wilder they are."

The little girl watched his face as if she understood his every word, her puppy clutched against her, its already patient little face turned to watch Rachel as intently as Rachel was watching Marcel.

They made snowshoes and with them tracked across the drifts, checking their snares and the trap line Marcel had in the hills above the valley. They had flour and tea, they had rice and beans, they had smoked meat, jerky, pemmican and the meat of the animals they snared and trapped. The long cold period was a time of comfort, a time to sit warm in the soddy, carefully stitching moccasins and insulating them with dried grass, decorating them with beadwork flowers, the beads from the full pouch Marcel had stored in his possibles box. Child Of Her People stitched cured and softened rabbit skins together, and fashioned him an undershirt, fur side against his skin. He blushed with pleasure.

"If I'd known you were so handy," he teased, "I'd have considered you a forty-horse woman."

And she knew he meant it as the Good People would have meant it, an admission of his awareness of her worth, not a purchase price as if she were a thing, or a slave.

"Twenty horses is sufficient," she said contentedly, "and one dog who thinks she is a person with the right to live in the house and sleep in the same bed as my daughter."

When the snows began to melt and the water dripped from the roof of the soddy, Marcel sorted their gear, then packed it carefully. They set off through the soggy snow,

Rachel warm in her insulated knee-high moccasins, her fur-lined deerskin pants and shirt, her rabbitskin mitts and hat. "They'll be hungry," he explained, "and moving down to the flatlands where they can paw for grass. But they still can't move well in this heavy snow, and that's like having a dozen people with us."

He'd caught wild ponies here before, his chutes and fences were still intact, all they had to do was check every-thing carefully, replace some rawhide lashings gnawed by hungry rodents, and check that there were no sharp points sticking out from the fence to gouge into the milling herd. They trampled the snow, making it look like a game trail, and the unnatural outlines of the fence and gate were hidden by bundles of branches and twigs, bunches of long dry grass.

They moved away from the horse camp, taking with them the scents that might warn the wild ponies. Child Of Her People and Rachel camped in a willow thicket, while Marcel went off by himself for two days. He arrived the third night, grinning and excited, explaining repeatedly to Rachel what it was he would need to do.

"It's a hell of a job by yourself," he laughed, "but this time it's going to be easy!"

Rachel laughed and nodded, and snuggled against him as he demonstrated to her with small sticks and bits of bark what it was they were going to do.

"And you have to sit up in the tree," he told her often, "and watch to see that none of them get away."

He positioned them near the wild horse camp and rode off again, and Child Of Her People waited until Rachel was sound asleep. Then she climbed a tree with her daughter, sat her on a sturdy branch, and lashed her to the bole of the tree. Rachel half roused, blinking, then went back to sleep, safe above the ground, and warmly wrapped against the cold.

Child Of Her People rode to where she had been told to wait, and the half-grown dog padded beside the horse, whin-ing occasionally, looking back to where Rachel was sleeping.

"Ssssh," Child Of Her People warned. "Be quiet, Dog."

She dismounted, patted the dog, and gave it a piece of jerky, then waited patiently in the chill of pre-dawn. The sky lightened, until she could see down into the sheltered valley, see the wild horses starting to move, the stud pacing uneasily, sniffing the wind. She clamped her hand over her horse's muzzle, spoke soothingly, and prayed it would be as well-trained in a strange situation as a pony of the People would be.

The wild stud circled his herd, nipping at the unwilling mares, moving them ahead of him, away from the disturbing scent of man coming to him on the wind. She saw Marcel, on foot, moving against the far ridge, waving his jacket.

The mares surged across the valley, the colts staying close to their mothers, the old stud bringing up the rear to protect his harem. As Marcel whistled, his horse moved to him, and he swung himself up easily; the horse started to move toward the herd. The stud shrilled, the mares quickened their pace, and then they were moving along what they thought was a game trail. The stud was preoccupied with Marcel and his horse's approach, and the lead mare had been to the water hole so many times she accepted the easier footing of the trampled track.

Suddenly Marcel was yelling, his horse charging toward the herd, and the wild ponies were galloping. Child Of Her People waited, calming both horse and dog, until the first shot rang loud in the morning air.

"Haaaaah!" she yelled, swinging herself onto her rested horse's back. "Haaaaah!"

Her own horse was racing after the herd, the dog yapping excitedly. The wild stud screamed defiance; his feet lashed. But the dog, though young, was no fool, and he was well clear of the hooves, barking fiercely.

The entire wild herd plunged down the game trail, herded only by two mounted humans and one sturdy dog. It was wild and terrifying; it was exciting and thrilling. It was the most difficult riding Child Of Her People had done since being taken from the Human Beings, but her horse had fed on rich grass and grain all winter, and the wild ones had known days of hunger. Her horse had been sheltered from the worst of the weather, the wild ones had survived as best they could. Many of the young ones were too weak to be able to keep up with the herd for very long. Child Of Her People and Marcel rode past the stragglers, concentrating on the strongest and best, chasing them into the gully.

Desperate to escape the noisy pursuit, even the crafty old stud kept to the packed snow, following what he thought was a deer trail that would lead them all to safety. Then the main bulk of the herd was in the corral, the stud and several of his older mares were skidding, veering, heading into the willows, avoiding the trap.

"Let 'em go!" Marcel yelled. "Let 'em go!" He was off his horse, racing forward, the dog by his side, yapping and barking. He swung the gate, pushing it shut, then Child Of Her People was off her horse, running to help him.

The stud was shrilling from the willows, screaming for the mares to follow him, and the horses in the enclosure were milling wildly.

"Go away!" Marcel yelled, pleading. "Go! I don't want to have to shoot you! G'wan!" He waved his hand. The dog obeying, raced for the willows, barking. Enraged, the stud whirled and crashed through the willows, the dog following.

Child Of Her People lashed the gate shut, leaned against it, breathing heavily. Marcel whistled, and the dog returned, tongue lolling, body wet with sweat and slush, her breath a cloud around her black bristled face.

"Good dog." He patted her. "Good dog." Then he looked up into the trees, waved and grinned. "Hey, Rachey," he yelled. "You doin' your job?"

They wrestled the extra poles in place, lashing together a second chute, leading away from the corral. Child Of Her People stood on the outer side of it, with a blanket, and waved it at the horses they did not want to set free again. Marcel went into the corral on foot, moving like a cat, waving his arms, separating the ones he did not want to keep.

"Let 'em out!" he called as Child Of Her People pulled the blanket away from the chute entrance.

The unwanted horses flashed past, screaming with rage and fear.

"Stop 'em!" Marcel called, and she dropped the blanket across the opening, waving it, yelling fiercely, sending the dozen or more captives back across the corral to paw the earth and blow clouds of steaming breath.

"Gotta leave 'em calm down," he explained. "Some of 'em's what are called 'hot bloods,' they've got the best of what they need to survive wild. They're the ones that are gone at the first hint of danger, but those tight-strung nerves that keep 'em alive in the wild can kill them when they're up against something like this. If a person can train them, they're the best horses for this country. But I've seen 'em drop dead of heart attack," he added somberly. "Helluva thing."

He went up the tree and unlashed Rachel, carried her down and stood by the corral fence cuddling her. "Some of them are pregnant," he explained, "and we'll let them go. That way they can have their babies the way they're supposed to, and we'll be back for them next year. Now that one and that one over there," he pointed at the nervous horses trapped in the corral, "they're old, and they're set in their ways, no sense trying to break them or sell them. The first time they hear that old stud whistle, they'll be gone and when they go they'll take the others with them. So as soon as things calm down around here, we'll cut 'em out and let 'em go." He grinned ruefully. "I'd 'a let 'em go already," he confessed, "but when things get busy a person sometimes overlooks the finer points."

"Do I hear you making noises suspiciously like humility?" Child Of Her People said drily.

"Humility?" He pretended to be shocked. "Me? Humble?"

"I thought not." She sighed arching her back, trying to ease out the stiffness and fatigue. "Do you intend to sell them all?" she asked.

"See that one with the black stripe down her back and the black stripes on her legs? Well, she's too good for those nosepickers in town! She's got a lot of Spanish blood. We'll let her go, too. Then she can have lots of babies for us to catch. Eh, Rachey?"

"I don't like staying in the tree," Rachel said clearly.

"Somebody has to sit up there and watch to see if any of them are getting away," Child Of Her People said easily.

"Not me," Rachel decided. "You."

They made a small fire, boiled coffee, sweetened it with honey, and drank it gratefully.

"These wild ones," he said softly, "they could teach us a thing or two about how to live in this country. The young studs, they don't even start to get interested until they're almost two years old. So the old one, he lets them stay around, teaches them what they need to know. When they start getting randy, the old mares start driving them off. If they don't go, well, the old one, he gets into it. If he has to, he'll fight them to the death. Mostly he doesn't have to; they take off, maybe hang around in a bunch together. Sooner or later, they find some free-running mares and start their own herd. The young mares, they get driven off when they're just about ready for their first season. And it's the old man drives them off! Who knows, maybe he knows that if they come in season he won't be able to think clearly. The old one who told me about horses said he'd seen an old stud keep young mares that weren't his daughters and drive off others that were, as if he knew which was which. I don't know about that. But I know I never saw a wild herd get inbred like some of the settlers' stock gets inbred! I find that a miracle," he admitted, almost shyly.

The gelding was unpleasant and Rachel cried, but Marcel ignored her and just continued his gory job.

"You want to learn how?" he asked Child Of Her People quietly.

"I know how," she said briefly. He looked at her, a question almost ready, then he swallowed the question and stropped the knife on a whetstone, readying it for the next young stud.

"I didn't mention it," she forced a light tone, "because it just didn't seem anything special. Besides," she shrugged, "you might not have slept easy if you'd known."

"See that spotty-rump?" he grinned, acknowledging her teasing. "Well, him we keep the way I'd dearly like to spend the rest of my life. Whole and entire, with all his parts, portions, and as the Metis would say, his 'morseaux'!"

"My mother would have called him a Chief's horse," she agreed. And suddenly it was welling up in her. She blinked, swallowed, and turned her face aside.

"Easy," he soothed. "Easy, Child, I didn't mean to say the wrong thing."

"You didn't." Her breathing steadied; she swallowed again. "It was just . . . she was so proud of her horses." She blinked rapidly, but the tears would not be stopped. "She fussed over them, she had little bells for their manes and special charms to protect them from danger. When one of her mares had a foal, my mother would stay with her and talk to the newborn so it would know her voice from the very moment of its birth. Sometimes, it was as if the foals thought they had two mothers."

"Oh, Child," he mourned. "It's a son of a bitch of a thing for sure."

They kept the horses captive in the pen for several days, giving them no food or water, then brought the thirsty animals out one by one, securely roped, and gave them water to drink from their own hands. They hand-fed them, too, stroking them and talking softly, getting the animals accustomed to being touched, encouraging them to associate the sound of their voices with the smell and taste of food.

When they could walk among the horses without fear, Marcel started the real training.

"Just lean your weight on her," he advised softly. "Don't try to ride her yet, Rachey. Let her think there's nothing to be scared of."

Nothing to be scared of," Rachel repeated, patting firmly. Marcel held her so she could lean on the horse's back, her face alight with excitement.

"Take your time, now," he almost crooned. "Let her know you're her friend. Let her learn to trust you."

"Nothing to be scared of," Rachel repeated. "I'm getting down," she added hurriedly when the young mare shifted uneasily.

"Atta girl," Marcel approved. "Now stand here in front of her. Hold her head and blow in her nose. That's how they recognize each other. Now let her whuff in your face so she thinks you're a horse same as her. That's it. Oh, Rachie, you're gonna be a horse trainer like there's never been a horse trainer! You've got the hands for it, girl. Just keep touching her."

"Good horse," Rachel said, imitating Marcel's crooning tone. "Good girl. See, nobody wants to hurt you."

"Give her this grass. Hold your hand flat, so she doesn't get some finger in her mouth. That's it. See, she's better already."

"Good horse."

"All you have to do to get along fine with a horse," he squatted beside her, "is just think how you'd feel if all this strange stuff happened to you."

"Scared," Rachel decided. "She was scared." Her eyes welled, she looked at Marcel accusingly. "Why'd we do it?" she demanded.

"Oh, don't cry," he pulled her close, wiping her face with his big tanned hand. "She's gonna have a good life," he promised. "No wolves. No coyotes. No bears. No bein' hungry in the wintertime. She'll have a nice shed to sleep in at night. Grain in the winter."

"She was scared," Rachel insisted.

"Sure she was," he agreed. "Everything new is scary, but that doesn't mean it's bad. Here, see for yourself!" He lifted Rachel onto the young mare's back. "If she doesn't like it," he promised hurriedly, "I'll get you right back down again. Don't be scared," he smiled, "she's not scared. Look, she doesn't mind you sitting there. A little bitty thing like you is nothing to a big strong horse like her. Hey!" he called loudly. "Hey, Child, look at this!"

"Look!" Rachel echoed, her tears forgotten. "Look at me!"

Marcel lifted her down quickly, before either she or the horse could be frightened. "Now what we do," he explained to the awed child, "is tether her to a tree. She don't go back in with the others. She stays here, near us, where she can smell us and hear us. And she depends on you for everything. Food, water, friendship, absolutely everything. By the time we leave here, she'll be your horse and if you've treated her good, you'll be riding on top of her, all by yourself."

Three weeks later, they took the herd back to their valley and the training continued. Without the old stud to lead them away, and with the young stud kept in the corral where he called to them constantly, the mares settled in and began to feed on the grass. Marcel concentrated on the young stud, taming him, training him to the halter and lead rope, even getting him to accept the bridle. But the young horse would not accept the saddle, nor would he allow anyone to ride him.

"Well," Child Of Her People teased, "maybe if you sat Rachel up on his back for a while . . . ."

"Child Of Her People," Marcel said with forced patience, "my arse aches where I keep landing on it, my elbow is bruised, my knee feels like there's a badger inside it chewing to get out and that goddamned stubborn stud still won't let me on his back. I am not," he warned, "in a mood to be teased."

"Really?" she flirted up at him. "That's too bad. I thought you might want to stop rolling in the dirt because of that horse. I thought you might want to soak your bruises in the creek and have a rest. I thought," she grinned, "we might have an early supper, and as soon as Rachel is asleep . . . but if you're in no mood to be teased there's no use in going to bed early."

"I have to tell you," he sighed, "that it sounds a lot more inviting than trying to do anything with that stubborn damned stud!"

"They get like that," she grinned. "Doesn't matter if they've got four legs or two if you don't use the knife on them, they get stubborn."

It was three days steady ride to Evert's Crossing, and Marcel did not ride his spotty-rump stud. He rode his deep-chested roan and led the stud by a halter and tether rope, the other horses, mares and geldings alike, willingly following the prancing young herd leader.

They camped on the outskirts of town, behind a thicket of willows, where there was grass and water for the horses. They didn't even have to go into town to look for buyers; their bedrolls were no more than unpacked than the first buyer was there looking over the stock, making an offer on a young mare. By suppertime the entire herd was sold, and they had more money than even Marcel had expected to get. In the morning, they went into town to do their shopping. It was only their money made them welcome. Nobody wanted anything more to do with them than necessary; a man, a woman, and a child, all dressed in buckskin pants and fringed shirts, looking more savage than savages, even if the little girl did have corn-coloured hair. Not the kind of people anyone normal would want to know. But they had money.

They bought only what they knew they would need, knowing they would come back before winter. Beans and tea, flour and salt, and a new rifle for Child Of Her People. Metal fish-hooks, needles and thread, and some candy for Rachel. Then they went back to their camp, almost painfully aware of the sideways looks the townspeople gave them. Marcel sat brooding at the fire, arms wrapped around his up-thrust knees, watching Child Of Her People clean the rifle and demonstrate to Rachel what it was she was doing.

"Get so it's just part of what you do, like checking your horse for ticks or putting your clothes on an ant's hill to be sure you never have fleas. Keep it clean. Just a little bit of dust and instead of the bullet going out the end, it'll blow up and you'll lose the best part of your face. And Rachey, if anyone ever points a gun at you and means to use it, you put your pointy finger in the barrel and push—you might wind up losing your finger, but whoever he is, he'll pick his teeth out of his asshole. You remember that. Better to lose a finger than your life."

"Do people do that?" Rachel asked. "Shoot people for no reason?"

"Yes," Child Of Her People replied quietly. "Yes, they do."

Marcel pulled a leather pouch from his pocket, opened it, and took out the money from the sale of the horses. He looked at it, chewing his lip almost nervously.

"I figured," he managed, "she did her share as best she could. So I split 'er three ways. Kept yours and hers separate from the shopping money." He passed most of the money to Child Of Her People, not meeting her eyes, staring down at his own hands. "It was a year last week," he managed.

"Oh, I know," she agreed, stuffing the money in her pocket without counting it.

"Well?" he asked.

"Well?" she countered.

"You want to . . . ride off?"

"No," she answered calmly. "No, I don't ever want to ride off. Do you?"

"No," he said quietly. "I like things the way they are."

There was no blackrobed priest, no leatherbound book, no prayers. Just a man, a woman, and the woman's child, standing together by a freshwater pond. No exchange of horses or blankets, no gifts of thanks to the mother who had raised her, no dancing, no drumming, no feasting, no merging of families and clans. But it was a marriage, and was done, and done properly.

They went back into town then, and got axes and a saw, nails and a hammer. They got a measuring stick and shovels, eight hens and a rooster, seeds and trading beads, candle wicks and several lengths of bright-coloured cloth.

"When's Rachel's birthday?" he asked.

"Her birthday?" Child Of Her People stared. "She was born in the springtime."

"What month?"

"Month? Uh, March," she laughed softly, embarrassed. "I have to think about it," she confessed shyly. "It never did make much sense to me."

"March." He put a peppermint candy into his mouth, sucked on it, swallowed. "You never said anything," he frowned.

"I don't understand." She felt confused, almost threatened. "Is it important?"

"She should have a gift for her birthday. It should be a special day for the whole family."

He turned to her, ignoring the people in the store who were trying hard to pretend they were not interested in these two strangely-dressed people who were speaking a language no civilized person could be expected to understand.

"Today should be a special day for us all, too." He tried to sound casual but his voice was intense, his eyes piercing. "I know the Human Beings consider every day important and only religious days are given special importance, but we have to have these things. We have to honour the days of birth and marriage. We have to make them very important to us because we are bereft of family beyond ourselves. We have become our entire family. We are our clan. And if we make these days important, we demonstrate that some of us are still here."

"If this is important to you," she soothed, "we will do it."

"It must be important to us all!" he insisted.

"It will be important to us all," she promised.

"And she will have a birthday present." He laughed. "And we will have a wedding present."

He bought Rachel a mouth harp and demonstrated how to play it. She stared at it, eyes wide with pleasure, then took it and blew softly. The sound made her smile again, and, of course, blow again. She headed out of the store, blowing gleefully, and even the disapproving storekeeper smiled.

They decided their wedding present to themselves would be a set of cooking pots and a cast-iron skillet. Then Marcel decided he would like a beer before they started the ride back to their valley.

Child Of Her People and Rachel waited outside, sucking on peppermint candies, sitting in the shade of the alley, leaning against the wooden wall of the small saloon. They heard noises; they heard thumps and shouts of anger. Then they saw Marcel come headlong out the door. He landed with a thump, stood up and began dusting off his clothes.

Child Of Her People said nothing; she simply tugged Rachel's hand. They moved to their horses and mounted quickly. Marcel rode his horse easily, reaching up from time to time to touch his rapidly swelling eye and cheekbone. Then, finally, he laughed, a harsh, explosive sound, mocking and bitter.

"In my whole entire life," he said, "I have had three glasses of beer. Some men have that every night of their adult lives. I've had split lips, black eyes, and lumps on my head. Once I got thrown in jail for a week, but I keep going back every chance I get. And I keep asking. And they keep saying, 'We don't serve Indians.' And I say, 'well, fine, then, give me half a glass for the white half.' And then they throw me out. You'd think I'd learn better."

They lived in the soddy while they dug their garden and fenced it against deer and horses. One of the hens went broody and Marcel went into the bush for an afternoon, returning with pheasant and quail eggs which he slid under the hen. When a second hen went broody, there were mallard eggs in the reeds, and he took Rachel with him to bring them back. Within two weeks of hatching, the pheasant and quail had learned to fly, and it was obvious there was no way to keep the wild-spirited birds with the chickens. The best anybody could hope for was that the wild birds, accustomed to a handful of grain every morning, would stay in the valley where they could be hunted for food. The ducklings hatched and never knew they were supposed to be wild. They stayed with the hen until finally Child Of Her People had to take them, one and two at a time, into the creek with her, putting them in the water where they moved as easily and naturally as any duck ever did, while their foster mother squawked and screeched on the bank, certain her chicks were going to drown.

They worked hard and steadily, but they did not forget the important things in life; there was always time to go fishing, always time to hunt for birds' nests, always time to ride to the salt lick and watch for young deer. And always time to join hands and dance to the noise Rachel insisted was music.

Marcel knelt in the dirt, pulling weeds from the rows of young vegetables, his strong fingers gentle and sure. "My father told me," he said quietly, "that a long time ago, in the country of his mother's father, there were people called Diggers. Like us, all they wanted was to grow some food. But all the land belonged to rich people. They didn't want the Diggers to use the land for anything, not even for gardens, although the land was there and lying empty. Diggers gathered from all over the land, to walk to the capital city, to protest. The rich people sent out hired killers, and even though the Diggers had no weapons at all, the hired killers cut them down and killed them. My father said that we had to remember and learn from that. He said we had to grow our food, even if we could find food, hunt food, trap food, we had to grow food anyway, otherwise all those Diggers had died for no reason at all."

"Is that why he came to take the land from the Good People?" Child Of Her People asked quietly. Marcel nodded, looking out past the fence around the garden to where the valley stretched toward the brush-covered hills.

"He told me more," he admitted carefully, "but I was young, and he got sick. I don't remember everything he tried to teach me. I forget why he said he came here."

"If the story came from his mother's father," Child Of Her People fumbled, "maybe it wasn't him who came here."

"Maybe not," he agreed, rising and knocking the earth from his bare legs. "The damn of it all is, there's no way to find out."

Child Of Her People and Marcel were working on their cabin, fitting the notched logs together, sweating in the hot dry afternoon sun. Rachel and Dog were playing with a stick, Rachel throwing, Dog chasing and bringing it back. Suddenly, Dog dropped the stick, ran to stand in front of Rachel, barking savagely, facing the grassland and pushing Rachel toward the unfinished cabin.

"Stop pushing me!" Rachel ordered, but Dog just backed into her again, pushing and barking.

"Must be something," Child Of Her People grunted, heaving the notched end in place and turning to scan the valley. "Oh," she gasped, and Marcel reached for the rifle. "Oh. Oh no . . . " she breathed. "Dog!" she called. "Down, Dog!"

The angry animal retreated toward her, growling savagely.

"Name of God," Marcel lowered the rifle. Half a dozen Cree fugitives were moving through the grass, seeming to rise out of it as they approached. The leader raised his hand, palm outward, asking for peace and unmolested passage.

The people who had been the Human Beings, the free riders of the Plains, were bone-thin and half-naked. The children's eyes were huge in skinny faces, and they all looked like old dried leather. There wasn't a gun among them, and the only knife they had was old, the blade broken.

"Start cookin'," Marcel managed. Then he was running toward the people, hurrying to help them, lifting an old woman as easily as if she were still a child.

"Water," Child Of Her People snapped. Rachel ran for the bucket and dipper, raced down to the creek and back in the time it took the desperate people to make it to the cool shelter of the soddy.

Child Of Her People felt as if she needed more arms, more hands, more legs to move quickly, to slice loaves of bread, to put the pot of beans on the firepit to heat, to find the pemmican pouch and open it, to reach for the slab of salted hog jowl and start slicing it to fry.

Then Marcel was putting a haunch of venison on the table, his knife gleaming, slicing strips of meat to drop in the cast-iron skillet with the hog jowl; Rachel was passing out strips of dried jerky to the people. Even before the beans were warm, the people were dipping the bread into the pot, eating the half-cooked meat, nodding their thanks and obviously hoping for more.

"They burn the prairie," a woman explained, "and there is sickness everywhere. They told us they had put aside land for us, but when we went there, we could not stay. There were no animals to hunt, not even any fish. The streams had been blocked by rubble where the prospectors and miners had dug into the body of the Mother. When we tried to leave, they brought in horse police and pony soldiers, to chase us back to the accursed place."

"We got away at night," another woman said. "We slid on our bellies like snakes and followed a gully past the soldiers. We went to the place the Newcomers call Montana, to the dark hills. But the dark hills are over the line nobody can see, and the Long Knives came and sent us back. Then the horse police said they had a place for us and food, but the food was beef, and it had worms in it. Those who ate it got stomach cramps, then they shit and puked and shit and puked—and some died of it. And so we left again."

"Where are you going this time, cousin?" Child Of Her People asked.

They stared at her, their eyes glittering. "We go to die. Better to die free than to die like an animal in a trap," a voice said.

"Better to live," Child Of Her People corrected, "the best way you can."

"If it is meant that we live, we will live," a man agreed. "But if we are meant to die, we will die."

"How is it," an old woman asked, "that a woman of the Crazies speaks the language of the True People?"

"I am Child Of Her People," she replied. "My mother was Woman Walks Softly, her mother was Strong Heart Woman, who was the daughter of Moves With Certainty. We are daughters of the People Of The Wolf, and some of my aunts and other-mothers are healers."

They stared at her, then at Rachel, and some of them nodded.

"I have heard of this," one admitted. "We heard you had been killed."

"Obviously not," Child Of Her People smiled.

"Well," an older man clapped his hands, smiled in spite of his exhaustion. "This is a thing to remember! Not all the dead are dead! I will tell of this," he laughed, "if I do not die myself."

"You will not die today," Marcel promised, "nor tomorrow, either. The cooking here is not so bad as to kill you and we do not eat beef with worms in it."

"And you also speak the language of the First Humans," the man nodded.

"I am bois-brulée." Marcel pulled the coffeepot from the hearth, pouring coffee into the few mugs they had. Hands reached eagerly, mouths sipped, then passed the mug to another, sharing even in their privation. "Some say we are called this because we are as dark as burned wood. But we are not as dark as the Human Beings, so perhaps what others say is the truth, that we are called this because we are the ones who clear the bushland and pile up the roots and burn them, burn the stumps and spread the ash and charcoal on the fields. Others say we smell like burned wood." He sniffed the back of his hand, shrugged. "I have never thought I smelled like burned wood," he said mildly, "although there are times I smell of horse."

"And you?" the old woman smiled at Rachel. "Do you smell of horse?"

Rachel stared at the grandmother, then nodded and moved to sit beside her, sharing the coffee with her.

The Cree refused to sleep inside the soddy, preferring to camp in the willows by the stream. Marcel and Child Of Her

People left Rachel in the care of the women and rode into the hills to hunt. They took anything that moved, rabbit, deer, or bird, and returned to the soddy to cook, smoke, dry, and even salt the meat, although the Human Beings considered salting meat a terrible waste of precious salt.

"We cannot stay here," a young man said carefully. "You are our cousins and have treated us well, but we are not people to live like this. We must try to find our own valley, our own place of safety."

"As you have decided," Marcel agreed. "You must stay here until you are fit to travel. And when you leave, you will have horses and a rifle and shells for hunting. You cannot," he winked, "ride off across the grass no better equipped than a pack of Crazy squatters."

That night he held Child Of Her People while she wept bitterly and cursed the things being done in the hills.

"They rode horses as if they grew from their backs," she sobbed, "and they called God 'cousin.' They even shared water with those bastards who did this to them!"

"Ssssssh," he soothed, unable to find any words at all. "Ssssssh."

When the Cree left, they headed south and west hoping to find refuge among the Nez Perce. They left with food, sharp knives, a good rifle, and plenty of shells. And they left with the extra horses Child Of Her People and Marcel had gentled and trained.

"I thought you were going to give them all our horses," Rachel said. "I thought you were going to give them everything!"

"We still have everything we need," Child Of Her People answered sadly. "We have our original stock; we have the spotty-rump; we have our home, our garden, and each other."

"And we'll have our cabin before long," Marcel assured her, but his eyes were on the departing Cree.

"I don't know if I can stand this," Child Of Her People said in a voice so calm it frightened Marcel more than tears or anger could have. "What did they ever do to deserve to be treated like that?"

Another trip to town, with another punch-up in the saloon, and another bruised face for Marcel. If he still didn't have his glass of beer, they had windows and a proper set of door hinges for the cabin. They had warm blankets and bolts of warm cloth, beans, rice, and lentils; they had dried fruit, tea, and coffee beans. They had salt and sugar, flour and lard, boxes of shells, and even a bag of candy. If they were almost out of money, what did it matter? There were ponies in the hills to be caught and broken, there were buyers in the town willing to pay good money for them, and Child Of Her People was pregnant with their child.

She was sitting in the shade, pounding berries into a mixture of dried meat and rich fat, making pemmican for the winter. Stored in the root cellar soddy with the potatoes, carrots, and cabbage from their garden were other pouches of the rich mixture. Hanging from the rafters of the new cabin were rawhide bags of jerky, more than they could possibly need. They had even traded jerky and pemmican in town, and the cheese they had received in trade was wrapped in sacks, hanging safe from the twitching nose of the dog. Still she felt this compulsion to prepare and store food, as much as possible, the memory of the fleeing Cree seared forever on her mind.

The first frosts had come; the berry bushes were almost bare. The willow leaves were tinged with yellow, some starting to fall. Rachel was gathering eggs and Dog was yapping excitedly at something, when a soft chuckle made Child Of Her People turn, expecting to see Marcel. But it wasn't Marcel, he was standing in the doorway, watching. It was a woman, a skinny wraith, her face lined with pain and deprivation, one hand resting on the head of Dog, the other arm bent awkwardly at the elbow. Her hair was streaked with white, her braids tied with short pieces of thong. Her buckskin clothing was worn thin.

"And so they told me there was a woman who was alive, but who thought her mother was dead," the woman said, voice thick with emotion. "And the mother who thought her daughter was dead wept with joy."

Woman Walks Softly knelt, taking Child Of Her People in her arms, holding her gently, afraid she might disappear.

"They said they thought at first she was a woman of the Crazies, but she spoke the language of the True People and knew the names of her mother, her grandmother, her great-grandmother. She knew how to act and how to be. She knew to feed them and make them welcome, knew to share with them and see them safely on their journey."

"I thought they had killed you!" Child Of Her People gasped.

"I thought so, myself, for a while," Woman Walks Softly agreed. "And this arm will never again bend as it should. But . . . I did not die!"

Child Of Her People clung to her mother, unable to speak, unable to do anything but tremble with joy. And then Rachel was there with the egg basket, and Woman Walks Softly was staring at her.

"Rachel," Child Of Her People said, "Rachel, this is my mother. Your grandmother, whose name is Woman Walks Softly."

"Daughter of my daughter," Woman Walks Softly thrilled. "With hair the colour of the ripe grass and eyes like the summer sky. It is a gift the spirits have given me, to be able to see you."

"I have eggs," Rachel smiled. "Would you like some?"

Marcel made tea and put it on the table for them, with sliced bread and berry jam. He poured their tea, waiting for them to eat, but the older woman was uncomfortable, unable to look at him, unable to answer his questions.

"I know," he said in formal Cree, "that the Good People consider it unwise for a woman to look at or speak to her son-in-law. It was explained to me that a daughter has half the power of her mother, half the power of her father. If a man is attracted to a woman, if he desires to know her, he will be twice attracted to her mother, and will want even more to be intimate, will desire her full power even more strongly than the half power of her daughter. It is known that a mature woman is much more desirable than a young woman for she is also much more skilled in the sexual arts and secrets. Perhaps this holds true for the men of the True People, but I am of mixed blood, and it is not so for me." He grinned, winking at Child Of Her People. "I am not a man of strong passion," he lied, "and this woman is often disappointed."

"I have heard gas rumble in another's belly," Woman Walks Softly smiled, "but I have not often heard it rumble in a man's throat."

"I know I am a very ugly person," he said, "but I did not think myself so ugly that the mother of my wife would prefer to look at the floor."

They laughed, then, and drank tea together. Woman Walks Softly ate, but not much. "I have been without food for so long," she confessed, "that my stomach is too small. Perhaps later, when I can believe this miracle, I will be able to eat properly."

"As you can see," Marcel again spoke formally, "your daughter carries happiness. It is only fitting that you know that I have no other family. My mother and father are dead; one sister is dead and one is lost. We are Metis, bois-brulées, half-breeds, with little connection to the clans of our Human Being cousins."

"There are few Human Beings left for anyone to have much connection," Woman Walks Softly answered. "We are scattered like quail, and every day more of us die."

"But you are home again," Child Of Her People protested. "You are home!"

"There is a sod house," Woman Walks Softly said firmly, "and it seems empty. I would live there."

"You are welcome here," Marcel insisted.

"No," she said. "I am who I am, and I can only bend so far. I can look at you, I can talk to you, I can eat with you, and I can make myself believe that there is no violation of good morals in doing these things. But I cannot live and sleep under the same roof as the husband of my daughter. It is not decent."

Child Of Her People and Woman Walks Softly drank more tea and touched hands often. Woman Walks Softly held Rachel on her lap, stroking her hair and cuddling her.

"They burned the camp of the Crazies," she recounted, "and they stole from their own dead. And then they were gone, and for days I did not know anything. When I returned to my body, my arm was swollen and burning. I was half insane with thirst, and there were carrion birds feasting on the bodies of my people. I could do nothing," she said bitterly, "except crawl to the stream, drink water, and put my ruined arm in the stream to wash the filth from it. In time, the horse police arrived. I was not still lying in the creek by then. Some of our people had managed to hide in the brush that grew on the banks of the ravine. Some had hidden, some had been overlooked, and they came out when it was safe, to look after us and to try to dispose of the dead. But the horse police did not speak our language. They did not believe those of us who knew some words of their language. They said we had attacked the Crazies' outpost. They took us away and locked us in their place they call 'jail'."

"Goddamn them to hell," Marcel swore.

"I do not know what they talked about," Woman Walks Softly said. "And I do not know what they decided. They took some young men to a place and put ropes around their necks and hanged them. Then they made us all sit in wagons and they took us to this place they said was ours. They said we must stay there. That if we left that place we would again be arrested. So I stayed there because my arm was still hurt. I would see it swell up in a bump, and then the bump would ache until I thought I would disgrace myself and scream. Then the bump would break open and bits of broken bone would come out in the gush of puss and blood. In time, I learned to cut open the bumps and release the broken bits that way. I learned to strap my arm to my body, so it would not bounce with each step and ache so badly. And," she looked at Child Of Her People, "I learned to steal from the New-comers."

Child Of Her People nodded, sipping her lukewarm tea calmly. Then she told her mother some of her experiences after the attack.

"And so I stayed with the nuns," she kept her voice calm, but her fingers interlaced each other, her hands white-knuckled.

"I left the place they had told us to stay," her mother continued, "and I made my way to a Crazy town. In their towns they have special places where they leave their horses. When everyone was asleep, I throttled the dog before it could bark, and I stole a horse. And took the dead dog with me," she half smiled. "It was a fat dog, and it fed us all that night. We were not," she admitted, "very many."

"Where did you go?" Marcel asked.

"Wherever we had to," she answered. "And when the Long Knives chased us, I hid. I hid and lived however I could, and then, I met the ones who told me my daughter was still alive."

"The nuns said I was to live with a settler family," Child Of Her People said quietly, and she told a carefully edited version of her life there. Neither her daughter nor her husband knew what Woman Walks Softly sensed, that the story was incomplete and would be finished later, in private.

After supper, after Rachel was asleep, and Marcel was sitting alone with his small-bowled, long-stemmed pipe, Child Of Her People took her mother to the soddy and made her a bed with fresh dried grass and soft sleeping robes. They sat on the bed together, holding each other and weeping together, as she told her mother the rest of what had happened.

"I don't want her to know," she sobbed, speaking the women's language, the soft language, the one with the largest vocabulary for emotions and shades of feeling. "I would rather she think anything at all than think she was the product of shame and hatred."

"One day she will ask," Woman Walks Softly said. "And you must have a story ready for her."

"I will tell her that he was young, and strong, and capable of humour and kindness, and neither of us knew I was carrying joy when I rode away," she offered. "And those things are true. And yet they are a lie."

"And the husband? What story do you have for him?"

"He has never asked," Child Of Her People said quietly. Woman Walks Softly nodded, her opinion of Marcel immediately improved. "He said once that what was important happened when he approached me to trade fresh meat for a supper with fresh bread and dessert."

He was in bed when she returned to the cabin, and he held the sleeping robe up for her. He kissed the tears from her eyes and held her gently, stroking her bare shoulders and making soft comforting noises.

"I wish you could have seen her before," she whispered. "She could ride better than you can. She could move as easily as water flowing over stones and more quietly than anyone else I have ever known. There were no lines in her face and no white in her hair and she had only to smile and everyone around her was happy."

"Everyone around her *is* happy," he laughed softly. "All she needs is fattening up a bit, she'll be her old self again. You'll see."

"No," she corrected gently. "You didn't know her old self. She can never be that person again. None of us can."

Child Of Her People wakened in the morning to soft laughter and the muffled clink of cutlery. She got out of bed and stood at the entrance to the sleeping room, staring at Woman Walks Softly and Rachel, busy at the cooking hearth.

"She was tiny and skinny," Woman Walks Softly was saying, "and covered with flies. I did not think a child in that condition could possibly survive, but she did. And that is how I found your mother, my daughter."

"I found her," Marcel interjected, "working for beef ranchers. She was no longer tiny and skinny, and the flies were gone, but she had a girl with her. Short-legged, short-haired, only a few teeth in her mouth. But I knew I could fatten her up and sell her one day. Maybe trade her for a cooking pot with a hole in the bottom."

"What are you doing?" Child Of Her People asked sleepily.

"I'm making Crazy pie," he said happily. "This is a special day. As important as any birthday or marriage day. This will be the first full day we are all together. And I am making Crazy pie."

She drank sweetened coffee and watched him, flour to his elbows, making his Crazy pie. He had the big cast-iron bean pot and on the bottom of it, a mixture of chopped onion, crushed wild garlic, and venison chunks browning, making their own gravy. When all his chopping and slicing was finished, he added a layer of sliced potato, a layer of chopped carrot, sprinkled with flour, a pinch of salt and some ground peppercorn. Then a layer of sliced meat, and more layers sprinkled and seasoned. When the cast-iron bean pot was almost full he added more crushed garlic and put on the lid.

"There," he nodded, smiling widely. "It will cook slowly all day. When it is almost ready to eat, I'll make a crust for it. Almost like bannock," he explained, obviously satisfied with his life and everything in it. "And when you eat it," he promised Rachel, "it will be so good your toes will curl. The Crazies make it with sheep meat and pig meat and sometimes some beef, but we are not Crazies, and we do not eat such things."

Whistling cheerfully, he started to tidy up the table. Woman Walks Softly watched him, her face expressionless. He grinned at her, and winked.

"No," he said, "I am not an Invert."

"Obviously not," she agreed. "I have known many Inverts, and nothing about them puzzles me the way you puzzle me."

That afternoon, Woman Walks Softly stood outside with Rachel beside her and demonstrated how she had earned her name.

"Have you ever seen the blue heron?" she asked. "Or the sandhill crane?"

Rachel shook her head, and Woman Walks Softly knelt to draw images in the soft dust.

"They can stand as well on one foot as on two," she said. "Balance yourself like this." She straightened, and Rachel copied every move. "Now lift one leg, knee bent, foot hanging. Now lift it higher." She moved her crippled hand slightly, touching Rachel's hand, helping her to balance. "Now straighten out your foot. Careful."

Rachel teetered, and Woman Walks Softly was holding her, smiling at her.

"That was well done. We'll practise and practise and when we can do that as well as the heron and crane can, I'll teach you to kick as fast as a snake can strike. When you can balance and kick, you'll be ready to learn how to walk like the cougar. Have you ever seen a cougar? No? One day you will and you'll see how she walks. She keeps her spine relaxed and knows exactly where she is going to place her feet."

She stood, and Rachel tried again, knowing she would not fall and be hurt. "Your mother might have been called Treads Lightly, or Walks Properly, or even Moves With Certainty, which was the name of my grandmother. But the name I had given her was Child Of Her People, and it was decided she should keep her baby name, rather than leave it behind and get a child's name."

"My mother called me Laughing When Appropriate," Marcel admitted, his face red, "but I never used the name after I was put in their school. This is the Crazy's world, now, and a child should have a name which will not make life more difficult than it is already sure to be." He scooped Rachel up and hugged her, tickling her and making her laugh. "If we were going to go for the names the Good People give their children, you would have a name." He tickled her again, and she laughed until the tears rolled down her cheeks. "You would be Rain On The Face," he teased.

"And you," Woman Walks Softly pretended to mutter angrily, though she was smiling, "would be Man Who Plays Like A Child."

Every day brought its new work; every day brought new satisfactions. The cabin was warm even in the grip of winter. When Tommy was born, it was everything Child Of Her People had not experienced during Rachel's birth. Woman Walks Softly was there, talking and laughing, encouraging and helping. Rachel, wide-eyed and anxious, sponged her mother's face with cool water. Marcel paced nervously, trying to focus his energy on preparing himself for the change that was about to affect his life. He struggled trying to see himself with a newborn, trying to form for himself a self-image he ought to have been helped to form by his uncles, his father and his brothers. Then Tommy was flailing his arms and legs, his eyes open wide with fright.

Woman Walks Softly put the child on his mother's belly where he lay quietly, hearing again the steady beating of the heart under which he had grown. The flailing of his arms became exploratory groping. His wriggling and squirming made him aware of the warmth beneath him, and he snuggled, seeking comfort. His fear seemed to vanish and he rested, watched by his mother, his father, his sister and his grandmother.

"Remember the movements you see him make," Woman Walks Softly told Rachel. "The time will come when you, too, will carry happiness. Then you will feel inside you the movements you see your brother making now. By this time tomorrow, he will have stopped moving this way. See, he moves the way a fish does. He has lived in water for almost a year. Now he must learn how to live surrounded by air."

When Tommy raised his head and peered curiously, Woman Walks Softly nodded, and Child Of Her People lifted her son, holding him close to her, stroking him gently. For a moment, he stiffened, his natural fear of falling surfacing, but then he relaxed and his breathing became regular. He could hear that familiar heartbeat, and the warm bare skin against which he pressed was comforting.

"See?" Woman Walks Softly laughed, "already he has learned to trust his mother. Soon he will learn to trust all of us."

She took the little boy, then, and walked outside with him, holding him up, naked, to the clear stars of the cold winter night.

"This is your world," she told him. "Grow safe in it." Then she carried him back into the house and passed him to the eager hands of his father.

"Child," she said, laughing happily, "this is your father." When Marcel could no longer ignore Rachel's impatience, he handed Tommy back to his grandmother, who in turn handed him to his sister.

"This is your sister," she said formally. Rachel sat on her mother's bed, cradling the newborn.

"There will be plenty of time to hold him," Woman Walks Softly teased. "Give him back to his mother."

"There will never be enough time," Marcel countered, and then he went outside to chant his thanks to all of creation, and to caper madly in the snow, laughing, yelling, and celebrating.

Child Of Her People held her son, watching as he nuzzled her breast, then closed his mouth over her nipple and began to suckle. She wanted to watch him. She wanted to share every moment with her mother and her daughter, but her eyes were closing, the warmth in her body was spreading outward. When Rachel adjusted the pillows, pulled up the blankets, and tucked them both into a warm cocoon, Child Of Her People relaxed and slipped into a deep sound sleep, her son still nursing hungrily.

The warm chinook wind blew early that year, breaking the crisp grip of winter and turning the snow to thick slush. The wind stopped and the snow froze again, but the family knew there would be another wind, and another, until the ground would be bare, and spring would be upon them.

His parents wrapped Tommy warmly, strapped him in the packboard, and rode off to the horse camp site. Rachel was nearly five now, and insulted at the idea of having to stay up in the trees, out of the way.

"And who will explain to the little brother?" Woman Walks Softly asked. "Must he grow up ignorant? Already he is almost bald and without teeth, now must he also be untaught?"

Rachel glared, but finally nodded. When it was time, she was again strapped safely to the trunk of the tree, Tommy strapped beside her, where she could explain to him what was happening.

With three adults and a trained dog to help, they found and brought in two of the wild herds. Their lives revolved around horses for the entire early spring, and to Woman Walks Softly's total puzzlement, Marcel decided to brand the mustangs, even those which he eventually decided to turn lose again.

They built a strong chute with two heavy gates, one of which fell from an overhead frame, blocking the wide-eyed and frightened pony, holding her firmly against the front gate long enough for the branding iron to be slapped against her rump. The smell of burning hair and scorched flesh lingered in the air and both Rachel and Woman Walks Softly glared at Marcel each time a mustang squealed.

"It doesn't hurt," Marcel insisted stubbornly.

"Why do they cry?" Rachel argued.

"It surprises them," he replied. "Look, as soon as they're let back out into the second corral they calm down and stop stamping."

"Why do we have to do it? Would you like it if I did it to you?"

"Nobody's gonna ride in here and claim ME!" he roared. "There's nobody gonna say I belong to them! Nobody's apt to come and try to steal any of us and sell us and keep the money!"

"They aren't *yours!*" Rachel screamed back. "They aren't anybody's!"

"They live on our range," he growled. "We caught 'em." He glared at Woman Walks Softly, then looked at Rachel, then back at the older woman. "And you?" he forced himself to speak politely, to depend on the language of the Good People instead of the more confrontational language of the Newcomers. "Is there a problem in this for you?"

"I am not saying anything," she replied.

"Mother of my wife," he said with obvious patience, "your silence makes more noise than the shouting of this child."

"A child shouts to be heard only when she knows her speaking will not be heard." She reached with her good arm, pulling Rachel to stand beside her, patting the girl's stiff shoulders. "You have made her the sister of our cousins, and now you shout at her for doing what you have taught her to do. I, myself, have heard you say to her in the language of the Decent Hearted People, 'Think how you would feel if you were a horse.' I have heard this. Now she does as she has been taught, and you talk to her as if she were a bug-eating black-robe!"

"Even the Good People mark their horses," he gritted.

"We marked our horses," she agreed. "We braided the mane and tail a certain way, or we painted a mark on them, or we fashioned a braided thong to fit around the neck, but we did not scorch them and scar them. Every horse I ever owned knew who I was and who she was. And these horses may not

believe they live on your land. They may well believe you live
on their land."

"This child does not have as many years as I have fingers
on one hand," Marcel said stubbornly.

"Some people," Woman Walks Softly said proudly, "are
born intelligent. And some people take many years to learn.
There are people who experience every day as a new one,
with new things to learn and remember. And other people
who live the same few days over and over again, learning
nothing at all."

Child Of Her People began to laugh softly, and when
Marcel looked at her with an expression of near betrayal, she
laughed louder.

"What?" he snapped angrily.

"Three people," she managed, "using three partial languages, and no agreement. Rachel trying to use the language
of children, my mother trying to use the language of adults,
my husband using the languages of children and adults and
Newcomers, and no agreement anywhere."

"Four languages," he said. "The Newcomer words are
both English and French. And what good does it do me? I'm
branding them!" He turned back to the fire, pulled out the
branding iron, then cursed and put it down to cool slightly.
He muttered something scuffing the ground with his boot
heel, and muttered again. "Five years old," he shouted suddenly. "Five years old and she bosses me in ways her mother
would never dream of doing!"

"Her mother was properly raised," Woman Walks Softly
replied heatedly. "She was not shouted at, she was not told to
be quiet, she was not ignored and she did not have to shout to
be heard!"

"And the world is not like that any more!" Marcel roared,
forgetting his vow to speak politely to the mother of his wife.
"The whole world has changed and if we don't change with it
we die! Where are the Gentle People?" he challenged.
"Where are the ones who trusted? Where are your herds, now,
and why is your arm ruined? Anyone at all could ride up to our
land and run off the horses, notch their ears and say, 'This is
mine!' Perhaps if the Gentle People had learned to brand their
horses my wife would not lie sweating in her sleep, shaking

her head and protesting something she has never been able to forget!"

Woman Walks Softly stared at him, her body rigid with anger, her face pale. "You blame the Good People for being the Good People?" she asked. "You blame them for not being cruel enough to anticipate the inconceivable?"

"Stop," Child Of Her People said firmly. "Stop this. It has gone beyond any discussion of horses."

The strain lingered for days. Marcel and Woman Walks Softly were so determinedly polite to each other that a full-scale argument would have been preferable. Then Marcel made an attempt to heal the rift.

"I have been told," he said quietly, holding his mug of tea and inhaling the steam, "that there were no horses here before the Spaniards came to the far southern lands. I have been told that the Spaniards' invasion was successful because the People of that place thought them gods who could split in two when they dismounted. I have been told some of those horses escaped and it is from them all horses came. Then settlers came and began to raise horses. The Good People watched, and went at night and stole horses and learned to ride them, and raided for more horses. I have been told the southern People traded horses with the more northern People and the horses spread as the tribes learned to ride them." He looked at Woman Walks Softly, and waited.

"I have been told," she said quietly, "that the horse was always here but we did not ride it any more than we rode the buffalo, the elk, or the deer. I have been told that when the first southern People saw the Spanish riding the horses they were frightened not because they thought those people gods, but because they thought them devils. But an idea had been given. And those who did not learn from the idea and learn to ride were killed or put in chains. And so we learned what we needed to learn to survive. But we never felt easy about taking our cousins from their natural life. So we did not guard our herds very well, and the smartest ones escaped, and went back to the wild herds, to live as they were intended to live."

"Two very different stories," Marcel said to Rachel. "And even in the story your grandmother tells there is conflict. Your grandmother spoke of 'gods.' She spoke of 'devils.' These are words the People learned from the Newcomers." He smiled at the older woman. "Even those People who deliberately avoided the Newcomers learned these words."

"Had anyone told me there was any merit at all in having a man involved in the education of a girl," Woman Walks Softly said quietly, "I would have laughed. Had anyone told me the teachings of the Crazies could have been of use to a child of the People, I would not have believed." She looked at Marcel and smiled. "I still do not believe it is a good thing to burn marks on ponies or to shout at children."

"When I was in the school," he confessed, "they taught me children were to be seen but never heard. It is not easy to hear a child who thinks she is an adult."

Rachel opened her mouth to say something and her mother reached out quickly, putting her fingers over Rachel's mouth, and shook her head. Rachel glared and looked quickly at her grandmother. Woman Walks Softly deliberately pressed her lips together and ignored what she considered to be an insult. Rachel nodded and her grandmother smiled at her.

"One of the Supernaturals was living with her husband in a place that had everything needed for a good life." Woman Walks Softly sat cuddling and rocking Tommy, while Rachel sat beside her, leaning companionably against her.

"They had food, and they had clean water. They had a warm place in winter and cool places in summer, but they had no children. This was because the Supernatural was married to a human and they cannot always have children, just as a donkey and a horse can make a mule but the mule cannot have its own children.

"So the Supernatural decided to make a child. She took mud and fashioned a little girl, with dry grass for hair, little pebbles for eyes and slivers for teeth. And she did magic over it and a little girl stood there, the colour of mud, but very strong and very loving. 'Don't go near the river,' the Supernatural one said, and the mud-girl agreed.

"The Supernatural loved her mud-girl, and the human husband thought she was his daughter and things went well. Then one day when the Supernatural and her husband were hunting, it began to rain. They hurried, but by the time they got home, their mud-girl was gone. She had dissolved in the rain.

"The Supernatural made a second daughter, and this one she made out of sticks. She told stick-girl the same thing she had told mud-girl, 'Don't go near the river.' And stick-girl was obedient, she did not go near the river. The Supernatural had not forgotten what happened to mud-girl, though, and she warned stick-girl 'Don't stand out in the rain.' And stick-girl, who had heard what happened to her sister, did not stand out in the rain, and she always wore the hat and the cape her mother made for her to keep the rain off her.

"So the Supernatural and her husband were hunting and it started to rain and they rushed home. To their horror, they saw that stick-girl had come in out of the rain, as she had been told, but she had stood too close to the fire, and she was gone, all burned to ashes.

"The Supernatural mourned, then went to a special place, and she prayed. She fasted for four days and thought about what had happened and contemplated her dead daughters, and the Voice Which Must Be Obeyed took pity on her. She allowed the ears of the Supernatural one to stretch, and these ears heard the sound of a child weeping bitterly.

"The Supernatural one did magic and her spirit flew to where the child was crying. A little boy, all alone, frightened of the dark, cold and hungry. And the Supernatural one wanted to pick him up and cuddle him. She wanted to hold him close so he would be warm, and she wanted to feed him good food. But she was in her spirit form and she could not do any of this, for she had no body. She knew if she went back to her body and used her body to travel, the boy would die before she got back to him. And so the Supernatural did what she could do. She visited him in his heart, and she visited him inside his head, and she made his eyes work so he could see that there were berries on the bushes. The boy ate the berries and felt better. And the Supernatural one made his eyes see the dry grass and moss all around him. She made his little hands reach out and gather it all together, and pile it under him and around him and on him, so he was warm. And she made the nightbirds talk to him and sing to him, and made the breezes bring him the scent of flowers and the sound of the frogs and toads to reassure him.

"In the morning, his own parents came and found him, and they fed him. And the little boy told them he had been frightened, but then he had heard the toads and then he told of making a bed and of finding berries and his mother said, 'Surely you were helped and protected!' She gave thanks, and made smudge and went back to tell the others how her little baby had been saved.

"The people told their children, and the Supernatural learned that you do not have to be a birth mother to be a mother. She learned that all children are the children of all who love them, and that all good women are Mothers to all children, and all good men are Fathers to all children. Instead of having no children, the Supernatural had many many children.

"And the children learned that there are reasons why people tell them, 'Do not go near the river.' 'Do not stay in the rain.' 'Do not stand near the fire.' 'Do not play with sharp things. Do not . . . do not . . . do not . . . .' "

She lifted Tommy's hand and flapped it, and he giggled up at her. "When you feel alone, or frightened, or think there is no mother or father to be seen . . . you wave your hand. Feel the wind it makes? That wind will go to the Supernatural woman, and she will stretch out her magic ear and poke out her magic eye and she will find you and come to you and then you will be happy."

"Tell him how dogs came to the People," Rachel pleaded, snapping her fingers and calling Dog to her.

"We did not have dogs," Woman Walks Softly smiled, "and there was an emptiness in our lives. And in a certain tribe there was a beautiful young woman who was kind and loyal and loving and all good things. All the young men prayed and dreamed she would honour them by asking them to be her husband, but she was not interested in having a husband. She was not even interested in sharing happiness or meeting the young men at night under the stars.

"She was working one day, preparing skins, using her curved woman's knife to scrape the shaggy fur off a wolf skin and one of the hairs from the skin floated just in front of her mouth. Someone said something funny and she sucked in her breath to laugh, and sucked in the wolf hair too. And she swallowed it.

"When this young woman showed signs that she was carrying happiness, everyone was puzzled. Even the Old Woman did not know how a young woman could carry happiness without ever having known the embrace of a man. And then the young woman went into labour and her babies were born. Not one, not two, not three, not four, but six babies. And they were covered with fur, like the wolves are, but they were not wolves and their fur was shorter, not as thick. They were smaller than wolves and they were very different. When a wolf takes a drink of water he does as we do, bends down and sucks up the water. Our cousins the horses do this, too. But these children of the pure young woman could not do that. They had to lap with their tongues. A wolf can turn her ears so that when she bends her head to drink, one ear listens in front of her, one ear behind her, and her eyes watch the sides. These children could not do that, either.

"The People thought these strange children might be cursed. Or they might be blessed. They did not know what to think. And then they saw that all the human children loved these strange furry four-legged babies! And the furry babies loved the other children. They ran after them and laughed 'huf huf huf' and they played games and even curled up to sleep with them. So the People decided it was a good thing, these first furry dog-babies.

"And the dog-babies at first ate only the food the People gave them, they were too young to find their own food. But when they were bigger, they could find eggs and birds' nests, and chase and catch rabbits.

"And the pure young woman gave thanks for becoming the mother of these dog-children, and she was so happy she breathed in another hair and she had more puppies!

"And that is how we got dogs. Because their First Mother was a woman, dogs are our friends. You can look at their eyes and know they are our friends. More than any other animal, a dog's eyes tell of our connection. There is nothing gives more pleasure and is more worthy of respect than an old dog."

"Why are we allowed to eat dog meat if the dog is born of a woman?" Rachel asked, frowning. "Those who are related to the deer are not allowed to eat venison, and those related to the turtle cannot eat turtle eggs. Are we not all related to the dog?"

"There is no dog clan," Woman Walks Softly smiled. "And we are allowed to eat dog because when the famine arrived, at the time the ice covered the face of the Mother, the children began to starve. And the dogs have always loved children. And so it was the old dog went to the head woman and tried to talk, but all she could do was whine, whine, whine. The head woman said 'Old Dog, I do not understand.' And the dog went to the cooking pit and she slipped off her fur and jumped onto the spit which had known no meat for weeks. And for one brief minute the dog was allowed to speak, and she said 'Save the children, eat my meat,' and the head woman blessed her memory, and the children were fed. The Eye Who Sees Everything was so impressed by the actions of the dog that she did magic, and the meat of that old dog did not vanish so that children could eat their fill and still there would be meat. They could eat a leg and the dog meat would grow a new leg. This continued for four full days and the People knew they were being given a message. After the ice left, the messages that had been received during the famine were given to the People. And they formed clans, to control marriage and childraising. Some who are turtle clan cannot eat turtle meat or turtle eggs, because they are related and cannibalism is disgusting. Those who are of the deer clan never eat deer meat or wear deerskin, again because cannibalism is disgusting. But there was no dog clan because we can all eat dog meat."

"Newcomers eat horse meat," Rachel said, her voice neutral.

"So I have heard."

"We do not eat horse meat," Rachel insisted.

"There is no horse clan," Woman Walks Softly admitted grudgingly. "And some of the Good People have been forced in these past years to eat horse."

Rachel stared, shocked and disbelieving.

"A thing changes," her grandmother said softly, "when it is time to change. Had we not been dying because of ice, we might never have learned that it is allowable to eat dog. Now we die because of the world being turned upside down and inside out, and some People have eaten horse to survive."

"But not us!" Rachel protested.

"I have eaten horse meat," Woman Walks Softly admitted. "I did not like it and I wept while I ate it, but I ate it. If you were starving," she looked down at Rachel and locked glances with her, "if you were dying for lack of food and if a Newcomer chanced by, I would kill and cook that Newcomer and feed that meat to you and never say to you that you were eating Newcomer meat."

"But cannibalism is disgusting!" Rachel paled.

Child Of Her People, who had been listening quietly, joined them and said, "Unnecessary starvation is more disgusting. I did not think I would ever eat pig meat, but salted hog jowl is pig meat and bacon is pig meat and salt pork is pig meat and we have eaten that often."

"My grandfather told me," Marcel said, leaning on the top rail of the corral, watching the half-trained ponies prancing in the soft glow of evening, "that in another land, I do not know which one, there was ownership the way the Newcomers know it, but that a portion of the land, even though it belonged to the landowner, was not his to do with as he wished." He held up his hands, fingers outstretched, so Woman Walks Softly would have some understanding of the numbers he was going to use. "One measure out of ten," he folded down a finger and she nodded, "was there for the poor to grow on it what they wanted. Nine measures was for him to make decisions about but one measure was for those without land or money. And it was an obligation of honour that he ensure the one measure of every ten was not rocky ground, or parched earth, or barren and infertile, but rather the best land he had, so the poor who lived in his area would not be hungry."

"Hmmmm," she said. And he knew she did not understand the concept of private ownership of land, or the concept of that sort of charity.

He sighed. She smiled and patted his shoulder. He looked at her, shrugged, and they both nodded.

"The sunset," she said, "was never like this before the Newcomers came. Sometimes, when the great herds were rolling across the prairie, we would have painted sky, but it is only since the grassland began to be ploughed and the chinook began to blow the dirt into dust that we have seen these fiery skies."

"Your daughter," he said shyly, "carries happiness again."

Woman Walks Softly stared at him, eyes wide, as if she had never seen him before, and was not sure she understood his meaning, even though he had spoken to her in the most formal of Cree.

"Your son," she said carefully, "is not yet three-by-your-numbers. Rachel is not yet seven-by-your-numbers. And my daughter again carries happiness?"

"Yes," he grinned proudly.

"You should ask your wife to find you a second wife," she lectured sternly. "One woman should not have so many children so quickly!"

"I want a dozen children," he blurted.

"Then you had better find several women my daughter likes enough to invite to be her sisters."

"We do not do it that way," he said, frowning, and puzzled. "We have one wife."

"Until she dies," his mother-in-law scorned. "Then you find another one until you kill her, too." She pointed at his dusty work pants. "It has no brain," she warned.

"I do not want a second wife in this house," Child Of Her People said firmly. "I do not wish to even think about it."

"I do not understand," Woman Walks Softly said, shaking her head and frowning. "I have never heard of such a thing except among Crazies."

"When I think of some other woman with him," Child Of Her People admitted, using the language of women and groping for words, "I feel as if there is anger starting to grow in my belly."

"I wish there was an old woman we could visit."

"I didn't feel that way at first, my mother. I felt . . . sane. And then one day we were at the creek and we were swimming. He lifted Rachel over his head, and I knew he was not going to throw her to the rocks and hurt her! I knew! He tossed her into deep water and she went underwater, and he was there, with his hand over her nose, pinching, so she would not inhale the water. She surfaced and he lifted her and said she was a fish. She laughed and I knew she was safe with him forever. And this feeling started inside me. There is no name for it that I know, but he is precious to me, as precious as you, or Rachel, or Tommy, or this one I carry. And my life without him is unimaginable."

"When I think how our lives are now, and then think how I thought our lives would be, there is little similarity." Woman Walks Softly fought against tears. "And I know I am not who I was before my mother was killed and my daughter stolen. I have done things I would never have thought possible and would do them again. And I think what they did to you hurt something in your spirit and in your heart. I think," she said carefully, "that you are quite mad. I also think you control your madness very well. Except in this one part of your life."

Child Of Her People was hoeing the garden, the sun warm on her bare arms. At the edge of the garden the children were playing in the dust, living in and for the moment with no worry about tomorrow and no ghosts left over from yesterday.

"Look, Momma." Rachel spoke in English, because her grandmother was not there and English was a special, private sharing she used only with her parents.

Child Of Her People turned, and the world tipped on its side. She saw Rachel, her hair bleached almost white, smiling up at her, a fluffy chick held in her cupped hands. But she saw Joseph, too, his gentle side exposed to her, the chicks unafraid on his lap, in his large calloused hands.

"She just brought them out from under the shed," Rachel said softly, awed by the perfection of the innocent-eyed chick. "They didn't even try to run away, I just put down some grain for the hen and she came over and clucked chook-chook and they followed, and when I picked this one up . . . it just looked at me. It doesn't know anything at all!" She laughed softly. "Look at its eyes, Momma! Everything is so strange and new and it isn't even afraid."

She said the proper things, obviously, because Rachel smiled and took the peeper back to its anxious mother, and then Child Of Her People was stumbling away from the garden, away from her children, the hot tears scalding down her face. Behind the old shed she sagged against the wall, sliding down to sit in the grass, the mud-wattled poles pressing against her back. Had he died, and his ghost been freed to find her? Was he finally sent crazy by the grim isolation of his life? Was his sterile body even now standing somewhere in that place which had never been her home, standing taut with lunacy and hatred, his mad mind searching for her to remind her of what she wanted so much to forget, what she could never forget for so long as Rachel smiled his smile? What had her anger and vengeance done to him, to his father, his mother, and their world? Had they realized what he had done that had placed her hand on her knife? Did they excuse him, blame her for tempting him, blame her for being there, being female, for not being flattered? Did either of them feel anywhere in their hearts that he had brought on himself that skilled slice? Did they long for grandchildren they could never have?

"And what is this?" Woman Walks Softly asked carefully.

"I did not hear you coming," she answered, evading the question.

"I would worry if you had," her mother smiled. "I am the one who walks silently. If you had heard me over the sound of your breathing, I would feel I was no longer myself. What ghost is blowing cold air down your back?"

She tried to talk to her mother, tried to explain, and could not. She could only tremble and hug herself tightly, staying stiff even in her mother's embrace.

"Something must be done about this," Woman Walks Softly said firmly. "This must not rule our lives!"

"I stared and stared," Child Of Her People recounted, "and there was nothing but broken earth, the rail bed, the cross-ties, and the rails leading into the split in the mountains. Something inside me," she touched her chest, "broke, then, and I knew there was no safe place left anywhere. Rides Proudly and the others left this land and went to find the Elders, but the thing they fled has followed them. And in following them, it has destroyed the Pillar of Promise. Destroyed the Pillar to show to the world that they can destroy anything."

"No," Woman Walks Softly contradicted. "Not everything. The mountains are still there. The pass through them is still there. The Promise is still there."

"No," Child Of Her People mourned stubbornly. "No."

The sun was hot on the dry hill, heat waves shimmered above the hard earth, distorting distance, making everything wavery, altering the outlines of the stark bluffs and broken rocks, making the Mesa dance as if cut loose from the earth, suspended above a strip of shimmering clear space that wasn't really there at all, an illusion of heat and distance.

Child Of Her People had been on top of that Mesa for days, without food or water, praying, and waiting for some explanation for the nightmares that had been gnawing at her sleep for months. Even awake, dread hung over her. She would be doing the most ordinary of tasks and suddenly she would fear for her children, would rush out to call them, hold them close, to reassure herself. Marcel had tried to soothe her. Woman Walks Softly had tried to calm her. Both had tried to reason with her in those times when her pulse raced for no apparent reason, and finally, both had suggested she go on a Dream Search or Vision Quest.

Here she was, cross-legged under the washed-blue arc of the sky, bare-headed under the stark sun, too parched to sweat, watching as bits and pieces of the earth seemed to separate themselves from the ground and float suspended in the middle of nowhere at all. She was settled in as comfortably as anyone could be, with her one blanket, her offerings of sage and tobacco, of cedar and salt, knowing her mother was waiting for her at the base of the Mesa, her husband was waiting for her back on their place with their children.

He was waiting and doing those things she could not properly do any longer because of the terrors that had no more foundation than the idea that rocks could float or even move themselves to another place. He was caring for the children she could not properly care for because of phantoms and irrational fears.

She sat facing the place where the sun would rise the next day and thought of the terror with no face, the terrors with too many faces, the times she knew herself to be awake but unable to move, unable to rise from the bed to seek comfort or help; the times she lay as if dreaming and knew it was no dream, knew she could hear the sounds of the house at night, could see the outline of the furniture, could see and even hear the children sleeping; she could see through walls, hear through floors and ceilings, paralyzed and knowing herself paralyzed, dreaming while awake, seeing herself asleep on the bed while she floated through the rough-hewn log wall, floated outside, wanting to get back into her own body; resisting whatever it was that was trying to take her somewhere, show her something. Finally, when she was drenched with sweat and perishing cold, nearly dead with fear, she would be back in her own body, a body grown stiff and numb. She would fight until the paralysis began to ease enough that she could move her leg those precious few inches until her foot touched his, then she would fall immediately into an exhausted sleep that never refreshed her, and morning always arrived far too soon.

The first night on the Mesa she sat wide awake with her blanket wrapped around her as she prayed and considered the words of her prayers, relived those parts of her past that she could remember, and felt no need for sleep. When the sun rose from its bed, she stood, and greeted it with her arms raised above her head as she offered herself to the spirits and asked for their help. All that day she sat, her hair hanging loose, her body baking in the heat, and before the day was half done she was parched with thirst. That night she fought sleep, fought it with prayer and chant, digging deeper into her own mind, trying to unearth the memories buried by time and years. The second day her lips cracked and she tasted the sharp salt and mineral tang of her own blood. She placed pebbles under her tongue and drew from her own body the moisture she needed, and that day, she had no need to urinate, no feeling of hunger. The third night she swayed and trembled; she thought the rocks were moving and trying to talk to her. A lizard came to her and flicked its tongue up and down her arm, and she was sure the lizard was puzzled, recognizing her for a person, but not recognizing her actions as anything a person ever did. That third night seemed only minutes long, and when she stood to greet the sun, she stumbled and fell. She had to rise a second time, and before she could form her prayers, she was again falling, face down, into the hot red, falling without even putting her hands out to protect herself. She floated, as she had floated from her bed at home, floated above the dry dust and saw herself lying face down, eyes open, so still she thought herself dead. She floated and then flew, over the edges of the Mesa, across the land below, to the river. As she swooped from the skies like a fish-hawk she saw the cabin, saw her own children playing while doing their chores, saw them laughing, saw them pointing at her, pointing at the fish-hawk, the osprey. Then she was swooping into the cold clear water of the river, soaking in the moisture she needed, drinking from the cold depths, filling her feathered form. She felt her talons sink into the body of a fish, grip it tight, and rise from the river, droplets sparkling silver in the hot sun. Then she flew back to the Mesa and perched on her own lifeless body, ate her fish raw, preened her feathers, and sent one wild scream cutting across the sky.

She wakened slowly, her lips bleeding. There were blisters on the backs of her hands and her head ached with a sharp pain that drove like a needle into the back of her eyes. She bit the blisters on her hands and drank the fluid, and waited, swaying with hunger and thirst, fatigue and delirium until the sun died and the bitter cold of night was on the earth. They came to her then, every fear she had ever had, every horror she had ever imagined. She looked at them and knew she could only die, that was all, that was the worst thing anybody or anything could ever do to her. And if she died, so what? She only lived inside her body; she was not her body and her body was not her. If they killed the body, so what; she would become something else, or she would be or become nothing, it didn't matter. The fiends and horrors screeched and gibbered and she turned her face away from them, and lay on her right side, her knees drawn up, the blanket over her. She closed her eyes and invited sleep. And so what could they do to her while she was asleep? Kill her? And so what if they did? She slept, and again left her body behind, but this time there was no hesitation. She went with whoever or whatever was insisting, and she was taken to a place so high the air was thin and it was difficult to breathe. Through a wall of ice and into a place and she could remember only a glimpse of it. Then the image was gone, and she wakened knowing she had been in that place for a long time, knowing she could not remember what had happened there because it was not yet time for her to remember, knowing she would go back again and again, and one day, when it was time, she would remember what had happened in that place.

When she returned to her body there was no warm comfort of his touch, no safety from another, there was just herself in a body as cold as the ice over which she had flown. It was up to her to find the warm things that would revive her. She thought of her children, of their tough little bodies, the two who looked like him, the older one who was his because of the love he had given her. She thought of holding them for the first time, the two youngest with such dark hair; the oldest born almost bald, her head covered with a thin fine film of soft down like a new-hatched chick, her face puckered and frowning, unsure of her welcome. She warmed then, sat up, and was on her feet singing her thanks before the sun came from its sleeping place. She prayed her thanks, sang her thanks, chanted her thanks and made her offerings, then rolled up her blanket and started down the side of the Mesa, following the faint tracks of her ascent. She slipped often and fell several times, skinning her forearm on the sharp rocks. She frowned in concentration. For a moment, she thought she heard him calling her, but, of course, that was impossible, he was miles away, with the children, in the log house they had built together on the banks of the stream. It was only the wind whistling past her sunburned ears, not his voice calling her name, not Rachel wailing.

Then her mother was standing, holding a water jug, waiting. When Child Of Her People stood in front of Woman Walks Softly, the older woman nodded, then passed over the jug of lukewarm water. Child Of Her People wet her lips and waited, counting four times four, then she filled her mouth with water and let the tissues of her inner cheeks and throat absorb what they needed. Finally, she swallowed. So much of the water was soaked up by her throat she was hardly aware any of it reached her stomach. She sat, then, and waited; when there were no cramps, she drank again, and this time drank deeply. Then she capped the jug, and sat, waiting. She would have wept if there had been enough fluid in her body to make tears. She gave thanks to the spirits, and managed to smile at her mother, then uncapped the jug, sipped again and felt better. She wanted to tip the jug and drain it to the last drop but knew if she did she would only heave it back up again, waste it all, and die before she got home again. Home to him, home to the children, home to the house they had built, the furniture they had fashioned.

Woman Walks Softly hunkered in front of her, handing her a strip of cloth. Child Of Her People nodded, soaked the cloth with precious water, and wrapped it around her head, the ends trailing wet down her spine, cooling her body, refreshing and relaxing her. It was a cloth in which they had wrapped food, but before that it had been a cloth for drying dishes, before that a tablecloth, and before that, a sheet for a child's bed. It was worn thin now, and good for very little, so thin it almost wasn't even there. But it held water against her body, and she was grateful for it; tired and poor as it was, it was precious and had use. Another sip of water and then she was chewing the bannock her mother pressed on her, bannock she didn't really want, bannock which sat in her stomach like a piece of earth, like particles of sand, but when she drank again, the bannock soaked up the water and the edge of desperation was gone from her thirst.

Minutes later, she was chewing on dried jerky, and she would have sat there longer. But her mother was gesturing for her to get up, to prepare to return. Just before they mounted the waiting horses, Woman Walks Softly handed her a white feather, which she tied to the string threaded in the neck of her shirt. Then they mounted the horses her mother had cared for all those long hot days, and headed toward home, not finding anything at all strange in the fact that not one word had passed Woman Walks Softly's lips.

The silence continued unremarked and unnoticed, even in those times when they stopped to rest, to sip water and eat, more often than Child Of Her People would have thought necessary, but she said nothing. After all, Woman Walks Softly was no longer a young woman, was a grandmother three times now, was closer to fifty than to thirty, and there were times her arm ached terribly. And Child Of Her People hadn't expected to be so weak herself, hadn't thought she would welcome the chance just to sit chewing jerky and sipping water. You don't think of yourself as getting older when it's your life and you're living it one day at a time, but just when you've ignored the passing days often enough and long enough, something comes along and reminds you that you aren't fifteen, you aren't even twenty anymore, you're almost twenty-eight, and three children have grown in your body, drank of your milk, thickened your waist, and sapped your strength. She almost laughed, but instead drank some more water. He had known. That's why he had sent two canteens instead of just one, why he had packed two days' rations instead of just one. She had been so busy living her life one day at a time, noticing him, not herself, noticing the first traces of gray in his hair, noticing the lines which had once been faint squint lines where the sun darkened only the surface of the pucker and not the skin hidden in the folds, were now cut into his face, and the laugh lines around his mouth showed even when he wasn't laughing or smiling. But she hadn't noticed herself aging with him.

Perhaps if they lived in town, or at least closer to town, where she saw other people and had comparisons forced on her, she might have noticed more, or noticed it more quickly. But there was no place for them in the towns, or even on the outskirts of the towns. Their life was here, and they both said if ever the day came when they could see the smoke from a neighbour's chimney, they would pack their few things in a wagon, hitch the horses, and head north and west, into Alberta, into the untouched land.

There were neighbours now, less than half a day's ride from their place. There was a track where wagon rims had cut so often into the prairie that the grass no longer grew, the start of what might one day even be a road, although it seemed ridiculous to think of roads in the middle of this enormous grassland. They had fences now, and needed to register a brand and burn it onto the rumps of their cattle and horses. Every year it was harder to track and catch wild ponies, to trap the animals they needed for food and fur.

"They sure did a job on us," Marcel had laughed. "I should'a run faster and further when I was younger. Didn't feel at home with the Blackfoot because I was raised Cree and the language isn't the same. I already speak three languages and didn't want to be bothered learnin' a fourth. But I got too much Cree in me to live white, and too much white in me to live Cree. I was with the Blackfoot too long to like the idea of neighbours close enough to smell their smoke from their fire, but I've put so much into this place I hate the idea of leaving. If I'd'a run farther and faster when I was a kid, I might'a got away from the whole shiterooni." And he laughed again, a short hard laugh, almost a snort of self-mockery.

She would have camped for the night, but Woman Walks Softly just pointed her hand, her crippled arm angling like the wing of a bird and grunted, and Child Of Her People nodded. It was getting chilly, now, and Child Of Her People wrapped a blanket around her shoulders, settling herself into the slumped slouch of a rider prepared to sleep on horseback. It was thirst, hunger, and exhaustion that made her feel the cold, she told herself. It had nothing to do with anything else. Certainly nothing to do with the dreams of terror because she had faced those terrors and closed her eyes to them. They were now on their way home again, and would arrive in time to cook breakfast.

She wasn't aware of sleeping, nor of waking, but she was awake, and the sky was streaked with colour, she could feel the cool damp of the river in the air, and she smelled smoke.

She turned, eyes narrowed, and saw only the face of her mother, grim and hard-planed, nodding, then raising her hand, finger against her lips, demanding silence. The wrong kind of smoke smell. Not the clean white of cooking smoke. Hot smoke, and too much of it. Hot black smoke, from a fire nobody had any need of, nobody had any use for, the kind of fire nobody wants to be near.

Woman Walks Softly was off her tired horse, stripping the blanket from its back, dropping the blanket to the ground, freeing the horse. She moved forward, her rifle held easily in her good hand, her horse already moving away from the strong stench of smoke, moving to safety, moving to water. Child Of Her People dismounted, freed her own sweat-lathered horse, and followed her mother, fatigue forgotten, hunger forgotten, thirst forgotten, everything wiped out by the smell of hot smoke, too much hot smoke.

She ran silently, her throat dry and tight, her plain moccasins making no impression on the grass, grass no longer
thin and yellow but thickening, greening as it neared the
water and the stand of trees that encircled the house on three
sides; trees that broke the bitter winter wind, providing the
fuel for their stone and mud-mortar fireplace, giving them
shade in the burning heat of summer.

She didn't have to look to see where Woman Walks Softly
was or what she was doing. She didn't have to worry about the
older woman not being able to take care of herself. Child Of
Her People knew her mother was angling to the trees, angling
to get a different view, a different aim if need be, to hide and
stay hidden and still cover her daughter and protect her. And
Child Of Her People knew she knew exactly where her
mother was, the way she knew where her arms were, and
what her legs were doing, knew without looking.

She moved carefully through the trees, keeping them
between her and the house, and when she could see the
cabin clearly, she flattened herself on the ground and peered
anxiously through the screening of long grass and berry
thicket.

The fire was smoldering in the yard, in front of the door
to the cabin. It didn't make any sense at all. Why would he
throw their chairs outside and light them, why would he toss
their mattresses on the fire? They had spent so many long days
making those mattresses, stuffing them with clover, sweetgrass, and hay, stitching the cloth carefully shut. He had
laughed when she had taught him the small, delicate stitches
the nuns had insisted she learn. He held the needle in his
enormous hands, and tried, clumsily, to duplicate her moves,
but his stitches were not like hers, and even the children
could tell which part of the mattress Dad had sewn, which
part Momma had done. Why would he toss them out onto the
fire?

He wouldn't. So who had? The gate to the corral was
open, the horses scattered. There should have been eight,
including Rachel's young half-Morgan stud. Instead, there
were only two, the ancient mare and the young black mare
that nobody but she and he could approach. She lay belly
down and slithered through the grass, moving only when the

breeze from the river blew and the grass waved. She went up the woodpile, to the overhang of the woodshed roof, swung herself up and lay quiet on her belly, straining her ears. No sound of voices in the cabin. She moved up the slope of the cabin roof and looked over the lip at the stock shed. The door was open, the inside empty.

She looked down, then, and saw him lying on the hard-packed earth in front of the doorway, lying on his belly, one arm under him, the other flung out as if reaching for something. He was wearing his faded blue shirt, but the back of it was dark red, red becoming brown, brown drying to near-black at the edges of the terrible stain. She forgot all about caution, then, and dropped from the roof, landing beside him, moving to roll his body over, to look into those big black eyes. He stared at her, stared past her, stared with eyes that would never see again, had not seen for hours. His face was pale, his limbs already stiffening. When she touched his hand, it was cold, and too pale, too thin, not his hand at all, not the dark, strong hand that had held her and touched her so gently, so firmly.

She cradled his body against her own, rocking him, but she could not cry. She could see the inside of their home, a shambles, everything turned over, spilled out, kicked around, broken. And beside him, poor dead Dog, looking as if she were asleep in the sunshine.

She looked at the earth, at the garden they had toiled so hard to create, the vegetables trampled, uprooted, smashed; the flowers around the border of the garden bright against the trampled dark earth. She laid him down, then, and went into the house, walking around like a poisoned wolf. She sat, finally, on the floor, staring at the mess and rubble, unable to understand anything, unable to believe anything. Then she noticed the woodbox was pushed aside, just an inch or two, as if someone had tried to get it back in place again and not had time, someone too small, too weak to be able to shift it easily.

She moved like a cat, was on her feet and standing in front of the woodbox, pushing it easily aside, reaching down, lifting the concealed trapdoor. As the clatter of its falling dimmed, she heard the terrified whimpers of her six-year-old son.

"Tommy," she said quietly, "it's Momma." He raced to the hole; she reached down, caught his arm and swung him up out of the hole he had called the "just-in-case place." She held the boy tight, felt his body shaking with terror, with sorrow, with relief.

"It's okay, Tommy," she said softly. "It's okay, Momma's here."

"Daddy," he said.

"Never mind," she soothed. "Save it for later. Save it for when there's time. What happened?"

"Danny and Rachel were outside and I was asleep upstairs in the loft. And then I heard men, and they were fighting with Daddy. I ran down and Danny was cryin'. Rachel was yellin', and I went for the gun, but Rachel came runnin' in, and she slammed the door and threw the bolt, like Daddy said to do. She told me to get in the just-in-case place, so I did, and she closed the trap."

He gulped and sniffled, the tears streaming down his face. "And then I heard the woodbox slide, and I was scared." He clung to his mother, his body shaking, and she heard him whisper to her about spiders and maybe rats.

"How many times in one life?" Woman Walks Softly gritted. Child Of Her People looked up into her mother's face and knew finally what it had been like for her after the world went crazy and the wolf hunters had attacked. She knew from the look on her mother's face, from what she could feel mirrored on her own, and from the knot of cold fear and hot rage burning in her belly.

Woman Walks Softly began to move around the cabin, taking note of signs Child Of Her People knew she herself would overlook. Anything that might ever be of any use, the older woman salvaged and kept, until her hands were full and she had to heave the table upright to place objects on it: two sharp knives, a box of rifle shells, the broken pieces of the whetstone.

"Then what, Tommy?" Child Of Her People pulled him from her, wiped his face, fighting to keep her voice calm. "Then what happened?"

"Then Rachey was yellin' and Poppa was roarin' and someone said turn 'im loose and then a rifle started shootin' and Rachey just screamed and screamed and screamed. And then I could hear them bustin' everything up and then I heard 'em leave and Danny was still bawlin' and cryin', and Rachey was cryin' too."

"Did you see them?"

"Just a bit," he sniffed, pulled his shirt from his pants and wiped his nose on its tail. "Just from the peek-crack upstairs."

"How many?"

"Maybe five or maybe six." He was calmer now, his body still trembling, but his eyes no longer wide and glazed with fear.

"Why?" she asked.

"They said Rachey—" he shook his head, puzzled, unsure of what he had heard, what he could remember. "They said Daddy wasn't Rachey's Poppa. They said what's a breed doin' with a white girl? He told 'em to leave, an' they didn't, they jumped him." He grabbed her hand, held it tightly, his little face tight with fear. "I was gonna help him! I was! I had the gun and all, but Rachey said . . . ."

"You did a good thing," she told him, holding him again, stroking his head, rocking him. "If you'd tried anything else, they'd have killed you, and then I wouldn't have known what had happened, and I would have been all alone. You did exactly the right thing, Tommy."

She held him until his weeping stopped, and then she found the candles, and lit one, and took it with her down into the hole under the woodbox, the hole so laboriously dug that first winter, the hole that extended back almost under the woodshed. Marcel had never finished it. He had worked on it when he had time, but how much time is there when everything has to be done from scratch?

If he had been able to finish it, Tommy would have been able to come up out of the hole by himself, come up in the woodshed, hidden by the stacks of wood, able to make his way through the long grass to the trees, instead of being locked up for who knew how long in the blackness, unable to lift the trap because of the woodbox that hid it so well.

There was food down there, dried fruit, jerky, pemmican and smoked fish, and a large skin of water they had been careful to empty out, clean, and refill regularly. Extra clothes. Two almost new Winchester rifles, four boxes of ammunition, and a razor-sharp skinning knife.

Child Of Her People could hear Woman Walks Softly talking to Tommy, her voice matter-of-fact, urging him to salvage what he could, giving him no time for panic, no time for the fear to surface. Talking as if something like this was ordinary, apt to happen at any time, to anybody, as unavoidable as winter snow, unpredictable, but always something you could learn to anticipate, something for which you could prepare yourself, something you could survive.

Child Of Her People lifted supplies from the hidey-hole onto the floor of the cabin and knew her mother and son would sort them, packing them carefully. She went back for more of the emergency food, and when she had what she figured they would need, she hoisted herself up out of the hole, from habit carefully replacing the trap door, and sliding the woodbox into place.

Tommy's face was washed, his hair slicked down; he had on his new boots and was holding his warm jacket. She had never seen him so pale, even when he had been sick with chicken pox he hadn't been this white. She ached to hold him, cradle him, rock him, but there were other things that needed to be done, and too little time to do them. Every minute she was here was one more minute her children were with whoever the animals were who had done this.

She moved to the steps, went down them, crossing the front yard, heading for the pasture, and did not look at him lying there on his back, sightless eyes staring. If she looked at him, now, like that, she would start crying, and if she started crying, nothing that needed to be done would get done. She would cry later. When there was time. Time to do it, do it fully, do it properly. The rest of her life.

Woman Walks Softly had the fat old mare saddled, but the young mare was skittish, would not come close enough even for the rope; she danced away, tossing her head, teasing. It had been funny; it had been almost entertaining. One by one, they had tried coaxing, talking, cajoling, but only Marcel or Child Of Her People could actually catch the mare, and for either of them the young tease would run up, nuzzling, could be ridden with neither saddle nor bridle, would even prance as if to music only she could hear; but now, minutes were lost because of what had once been amusing.

"Hoooo-ah," Child Of Her People crooned, "hoooo-ah, pretty girl." The young mare came to her immediately. "I know," she muttered to the uneasy animal, "I know, it's not your fault."

The sturdy horses they had taken with them when they left for the Vision Quest were somewhere out in the rich grassland, bone-weary and spooked by the smell of smoke. Even if she could find them, they were too tired for any further work.

The raiders hadn't bothered to make much of a mess in the stock shed. The saddle was in its place behind the stall; the bridle still hung from its nail; the chickens were pecking at corn scattered on the floor, spilled from an overturned sack. The nanny goat was in her stall, bag swollen, eyes desperate.

"Later," Child Of Her People promised.

Woman Walks Softly appeared with grain and water for the horses, and then Tommy was sitting behind the nanny, talking softly, his voice surprisingly level, his hands almost steady. In the midst of no matter what, Child Of Her People thought hysterically, there are goats to be milked and chores to be done. Even now.

And another part of her was screaming for haste. Screaming that she should just turn the animals loose, what did it matter any more, just let them go. But the hawks and falcons would make short work of the chickens, and poor patient Nanny would be wolf meat or bear meat before the next dawn.

She pushed down her need for frantic activity. It was six miles to the closest neighbour, a few minutes would not get them there that much more quickly. The necessaries could be done, and done properly. No sense riding off at full-tilt, unprepared. It wasn't each individual moment that counted, it was the use to which you put that time, what you got accomplished in those minutes, in that time before they began trailing the men who had killed her husband and stolen her children.

Or worse. But she didn't want to think about that. Rachel was past eleven, Danny only four. What would they do to them? What would the kind of man who would kill a father on his own doorstep do to an eleven-year-old girl? And why had they taken Danny? If they were afraid he could identify them, why hadn't they just killed him, left him dead beside his dead father? She didn't want to think about it. She couldn't stop thinking about it.

She was running out of things that needed done. She kept thinking as if she were alone in this, forgetting Woman Walks Softly was there, and knew even more clearly than Child Of Her People what needed done. Everything was already piled near the steps, everything they would need or could use.

And then she was eating something, drinking the warm milk, wondering what she had been doing, suspecting she had just been staring into space, trying to get herself prepared for what absolutely needed to be done. She hated to think what might happen to the hens and goats left on their own. If the trail went past the patch-ass squatters, they'd be glad to walk back a few miles and get a free milk goat and free laying hens. Anything they wanted from the stock shed, they could have, but nobody else was going to live in this house, this house he had built, nobody else was going to sit on the chairs or store food on the shelves. He had died here with no help from anyone; he had built here with no help from strangers; they had spent so much of their happy time here without anyone coming to visit, to exchange news and drink tea like civilized people, and nobody was going to take over what he had sweated to build, died to protect. The feather Woman Walks Softly had given her had fallen, somehow, fallen from her shirt and landed in his blood. The end of it was stained, a drab rust colour, not at all like blood. She considered for a moment leaving it with him, then rejected the idea. She pulled a mattress to the middle of the kitchen floor, soaked it with kerosene, then pulled the other mattresses on top, and soaked them, too.

When she went back outside, to bend over and take hold of him under the arms, Woman Walks Softly and Tommy were there to take his feet. She almost screamed when his body bump-bump-bumped on the steps, but she heard Woman Walks Softly say quietly that he was no longer in this bag of meat and bones, he felt nothing, and it was true, so she didn't scream. They laid him on the mattresses, and arranged his arms and legs into some semblance of dignity, not sprawled like a poisoned wolf, but lying on his back, as if asleep. She stroked his hair back from his face, touched the bruises, and kissed his forehead, but the gesture meant nothing to her, once it was done. It wasn't him. Now he was gone, and this cold corpse meant no more to her than a side of beef. Except . . . except those were the hands that had stroked her hair and held their children and chopped wood and carried water and made games out of lengths of string. Turned now into grotesque lumps, bruised, fingers broken where someone had stomped on them with heavy boots.

It wasn't time for the finality of the last act. There were things that had to be done, and they did them. They went to the river, stripped off their clothes, scrubbed themselves clean with the strong bar of yellow soap, even washing and carefully rinsing their hair. Then they dressed in clean clothes, and she stood patiently while her mother braided her hair in that special way, wrapping the braid in rawhide, wrapping until almost no hair showed, just the careful wrapping. Then she braided her mother's hair and wrapped it, forcing her fingers to do what was supposed to be done, forcing her body to respond to her will, not react to her emotions.

And then they went back to the house and stood beside the body on the kerosene-soaked mattresses. They prayed, giving thanks for the days and nights they had known this man, giving thanks for the memories and the many pleasures they had all shared, wishing him happiness in that other place, asking him not to forget them, to wait for the day they would join him. And then Woman Walks Softly used the sharp skinning knife and cut off the long braid hanging down Child Of Her People's back, and they laid it over Marcel's dead hands. She sobbed once, then. But took the knife and cut off her mother's braid, and placed it, too, on Marcel's hands.

Tommy moved to stand in front of her, waiting. His hair wasn't long enough to braid, but she cut it in handfuls, dropping them onto his father's body, cutting until the boy looked as shorn and as wild as she and her mother looked.

Woman Walks Softly took the knife then and cut strips from Marcel's blood-stained shirt. She handed one each to her daughter and grandson, wrapped her own strip around her forehead, nodded once, and moved to the doorway.

Child Of Her People knotted her headband in place and from it hung the blood-stained snow goose feather and knew she had no time to waste, what had to be done had been done, so the soul of her husband would not wander in the night wind, howling, lost, and confused. She picked up the kerosene can, backed toward the door, sloshing the sharp-smelling clear liquid on the body, on the floor, on the walls, on the furniture.

She heard Tommy racing outside, heard Woman Walks Softly speak to him, her tone reasonable and calming. And then she struck a match, dropped it in the thin film on the dry porch. She didn't wait to see what would happen, she didn't want to watch anything burn, she knew she couldn't have endured that. She moved quickly, mounted the young mare, reached down, took Tommy's hand and pulled him up behind her. Woman Walks Softly, mounted on the fat old mare, was already riding away from the cabin, already searching the ground for the easily read sign, already following the people who had taken her granddaughter and grandson.

It was easy to follow the trail. The men hadn't expected to be pursued, had made no effort at all to erase or disguise their tracks. Five men mounted, eight horses trailing loose, three of them shod. Child Of Her People couldn't tell which, if any, were riding double. But she knew some of them had to be, otherwise Rachey and Danny would try to break free, return home. If they could.

The tracks followed the dim trail south and east, toward Evert's Crossing, winding along the bank of the river. They rode in silence, with no need to talk about what they were doing, no need to hear words of reassurance, just the driving need to try to catch up to and free the children.

The patch-ass neighbours stared at them, eyes full of questions, but they put none of their questions into words. Child Of Her People knew without asking they had seen the riders, had probably even seen her children, but they had made no move to ask questions, no move to try to help, no move even to ride to the place and see if there was anything they could do to assist anyone. Neighbours, she thought bitterly.

She told the squatters of the milk goat, of the laying hens, of the feed in the stock shed, and of the tools. They nodded, unable to meet her eyes, and when she, Woman Walks Softly, and Tommy rode on it was without any help, without any sympathy, without even so much as the wish for good luck. What did strangers care what happened to a Cree woman, to a breed child, to the woman who had married a breed, or to the other children of that kind of mongrel match? But she knew the hens and nanny would be safely in the surprisingly well-constructed shed before nightfall.

Woman Walks Softly said nothing, refused to even look at the patch-ass neighbours, but as she rode on she spat in the dust and sucked her teeth contemptuously. Tommy stared at the sullen-faced man, stared accusingly, even turned as they rode off, to fix the man with the knowledge blazing in his exhausted young eyes.

They stopped only to empty their bowels and bladders, then pushed on, moving at a steady pace, not wanting to exhaust the old mare, letting her find her speed. Woman Walks Softly dismounted often and ran easily alongside the willing old tub, talking to her, praising her for what she had already managed to do, saving as much of the old nag's strength as possible.

Twice they passed cold fires, and it was easy to ensure that it was indeed that same group. At both sites they found whiskey bottles and coffee grounds where the men had wastefully emptied their coffeepot into the fire to put it out, and they knew they were gaining, rapidly, but not rapidly enough.

Child Of Her People was certain now, beyond any nig-
gling doubt or residual fear, that they were heading towards
Evert's Crossing. They could guzzle their whiskey and discard
their coffee because they would be able to get more, and
soon. And that meant she could risk night travel, just head
straight for the town, no need to follow the tracks.

Woman Walks Softly knelt at the cold fire, sifted the
ashes, lifted bits of charred wood, smelled them, even tasted
them. She dug in the middle of the fire, digging her fingers
into the ground, feeling the temperature of the sand. Then
she rose and studied the tracks leading away from the camp
site, kneeling, peering to see how much the edges of the
tracks had been softened and blown by the breeze, how
much of the soft dust had drifted down over the harder-
packed imprint of shod hooves.

"One full day," she grunted.

"They are heading for the town," Child Of Her People
said, as certain as if she could hear their voices, read their
minds. "We can ride straight to town."

"No. They might split up," her mother contradicted.

"Every minute the children are with them . . . " she
argued.

"No. We rest this fat old thing. Rest ourselves."

"But . . . ."

"If they haven't killed them by now, they won't kill them
for several days," Woman Walks Softly said flatly, her eyes
glittering.

"How do you know that?"

"Do you think you were the only child stolen from the
People? Some were found dead close to where they were
taken; others were kept for a week or more and then killed.
Many others were taken so far we could not follow, they were
given to the religious and raised to detest their own families.
Of all of them, only you are known to have lived and
returned."

"Mother, I . . . ."

"We rest. Soon. And head out again in first light."

Child Of Her People nodded, unwillingly. Obviously,
her mother had done this too many times to be ignored.

They camped by the river where the grass was thick and lush, and, even so, even with ample forage, she took a double measure of grain from the saddlebags and fed it to the horses. There was water for them to drink, and room to roll and relax, and for the people, food, water, and a chance to lie down and try to rest. She was sure she wouldn't be able to sleep, but she did, almost immediately.

She dreamed of Danny, and in her dream he was lying curled in a ball, eyes wide with pain, and something about the way he was holding himself made her think he had a belly-ache. In some ways, Danny was the toughest of the three, in other ways he was the most fragile. He was the baby, the one who hadn't even tried to talk until he was well past two. Why should he? He had interpreters to get him what he wanted; to tell his parents if he was hungry, or thirsty, or wanted to cuddle, or needed to be cleaned. Everything he saw either of the other two do, Danny tried to do, and when he couldn't, he roared with fury, flung himself to the ground, pounded his fists on the earth, and raged. Then he got up and tried again. He had sucked his thumb until he was three, but would willingly try anything, even if it frightened him.

In her dream, he was frightened, terrified, to the point of nausea. She woke in a sweat, almost insane with her need to be with him, reassure him. She rolled from her blankets, wide awake, began to bring food from the saddlebags for breakfast, then she stopped, wondering why she hadn't dreamed of Rachel, too.

They ate, filled canteens with fresh river water, and were on their way before the sun showed. The old mare was tired, but stubborn, as stubborn as Woman Walks Softly, who walked steadily, explaining to the fat horse why it was neces-sary to impose on her this way. As if she understood every word, the old horse just kept plodding forward, putting one foot down, then another, willingly, bravely.

They saw signs of a campfire, but the tracks they were following led right past it, and Child Of Her People didn't get down to investigate. They rode between the twin ruts laid down by metal-rimmed wagon wheels, following the im-prints of the shod horses. The grass was lower here, and there were bare patches where cooking fires had been, and though it was as rough as a road could be, it encouraged travellers to follow it rather than find their own route.

It was Tommy who saw him. Woman Walks Softly was urging the fat old horse on, and Child Of Her People was following trail, would have ridden right past the tangle of tall grass and brush, intent on the tracks she was following. There were signs of scuffling, several of the riderless horses skittering and shying, and she wondered if it was a snake that had spooked them. She didn't get down to study the sign. Whatever had happened had barely slowed the group, the tracks led off, deeper cut in the dirt, closer together, as if the horses had been spurred or rein-slapped.

"Mom!" Tommy blurted, and then he was sliding off the young mare, racing toward the tangle. Woman Walks Softly moved quickly, followed behind her grandson, and then Child Of Her People saw the dark head of her youngest son, flopping against the struggling arm of his older brother, and she was off her horse and racing to the thicket.

Danny didn't seem to see them. He stared, mouth halfopen, lips dry with thirst. When she spoke to him he did not respond, and he was almost naked, his shirt torn, his legs bare and filthy, there was blood on his scrawny babybum and welts on his arms and legs. One side of his face was puffed and bruised, and he was scratched and scabbed from the sharp branches and thorns of the bushes.

"Danny," she held him gently, more gently than she wanted to, and talked softly to him. "It's okay, sweetheart. Momma's here. NaiNai is here. Tommy's here. It's all okay." But he didn't seem to hear.

"What's wrong with him?" Tommy asked, sobbing.

"I don't know," she answered honestly.

Woman Walks Softly carried Danny, talking softly all the time, down the bank to the river, where they washed him from head to foot, and he responded to nothing. They dressed him in clothes from Tommy's pack, pulling pants and shirt onto the unresponsive body, rolling up sleeves and cuffs, and still he just sat, his body wracked with tremors at irregular intervals.

"What did they do to him?" Tommy asked.

"I don't know," she lied. But she knew what they had done. Knew, and her fears for Rachel trebled.

They put Tommy and Danny up on the young mare together, and both Child Of Her People and Woman Walks Softly ran, one on either side of the horse, just in case Danny slid off and fell to the ground. But while he seemed unable to focus his eyes, hear, speak, or focus his attention on anything, he sat on the horse as well as ever, his hands gripping the horse's mane.

An hour from Evert's Crossing, the group had split. Two riders and four riderless horses heading north, three riders and the other four horses continuing toward town. Child Of Her People followed the ones going to town only because the young half-Morgan was with that group, and it was the only link she had with Rachel. When the old mare had foaled, Marcel had given the filly to Rachel, as he had promised. And it was a joke, see one, see the other. Sometimes, when the filly was hungry and needed to nurse milk from the mare, Rachel would stand, waiting, or sit, patient and waiting, until the necessities were taken care of, and the filly could again accompany her. Two years later, the filly was a mother herself, and her fixation on Rachel was transferred to her colt. Rachel pined, Rachel fretted, Rachel was angry, and jealous. She willingly sold the colt as soon as it was old enough, but, of course, the mare was pregnant again, and when the next foal arrived, it too, displaced Rachel. And then two years ago, as part of a herd of wild ponies, they caught the young stud. What a go-round that had kicked off, Rachel defying Marcel, threatening to use the gelding knife on Marcel's pride and joy, the spotty-rump stud.

"They won't fight!" she had screeched irrationally. "And anyway, why does everything have to be done your way? He's a better horse! Yours is just pretty, is all! He's *mine*, and it isn't up to you!"

Marcel roared back, "I've been catching and judging horseflesh before you were even born, don't you tell *me* which is better than the other!" stamping his foot as if stamping would win the argument.

It might have gone on forever, because neither would back down, although Child Of Her People had never understood why Marcel hadn't just taken his knife out at night, when Rachel was asleep, and done what he said was the only sensible thing to do. And then, instead, he came back one day from a solitary ride, opened the pasture gate, whistled, and rode off again with the stud and several mares following willingly. He came back alone, walked over to Rachel, bent over, kissed her forehead and grinned.

"He's got himself two valleys full of grass," he said softly, "and he'll find himself other mares out there. Might even be less of a backache rounding them up in the springtime. But," he frowned, "you'd better get yourself ready to help me take hay out there in the wintertime. Don't see any reason for me to freeze my ass just because you got some kind of dumb idea about bringing in new blood." He had tried to pretend to glower, but Rachel was hugging him, telling him he was the nicest person she knew, and his grin spread until Child Of Her People thought his face would split. "I won't say you were right," he managed, "but maybe with all these damn squatters moving in, maybe we need some sturdy-bodied stock, too. Spot-rump," he admitted, "is more what you might call pretty."

Rachel had her stud saddle-broke and hand-trained so quickly even Woman Walks Softly shook her head and whistled softly.

Late afternoon, and Danny was riding in front of Tommy, his small scratched hands gripping the mare's mane, his face white, eyes round and glassy. He hadn't said a word from the time they had found him, hadn't eaten a bite of food, had swallowed water only because she had tipped his head back, pried open his mouth, and Woman Walks Softly had stroked his throat while dribbling water into his mouth. He didn't look to be as stiff-bodied as he had been, but maybe it was desperate maternal hope that made Child Of Her People think he was relaxing. Maybe he was just falling asleep.

What use to talk to him about returning to the body? What use to tell him she herself had sent her spirit elsewhere and came back only when it was safe to come back? Danny was too young to have learned what she prayed Rachel had learned. And Danny hadn't sent his spirit anywhere, it was inside him, hurt and cowering, bruised and hiding. Besides, there were no words she could force past the red-hot band choking her throat. What good are words? She couldn't even think of the words to say how grateful she was to have him back, and yet having him back was nothing compared to the horror of not having Rachel.

It was like that night when she had finally got herself loose, and had moved to garrote the pissing wolf hunter. What had been done was nothing compared to what had to be done. And when he was dead, it was nothing, because there was more to do, and so she did that; lifting a rifle and doing with it what she had seen others do; doing what she had never practised, because all her hunting had been done the traditional way and the only guns the People had belonged to the most skilled, who needed them least. And when that was done, still it was nothing, because there were other things still to be done. So she did them, then she was riding away, trailing the other two women, and knew they would not wait for her; she knew their duty, because their duty was the same as her duty; their duty was not to wait for her, or help her, or look after her, or do anything except survive. To do what needed to be done, nothing else could be given importance. The two women had ridden as fast as they could. If it was too fast for Child Of Her People, that was not important.

She would have found them, eventually. She would have stayed by the water and recuperated enough to be able to think. She would have gone by the stars, or by the sun, or by the moon, and found food and then, as she mended, she would have been able to think and plan properly. Time would have become her friend, as it would become Danny's friend, when there was time and things did not need to be done. But the horse police had intervened. And she had been in that time the way Danny was now, with her spirit in her body, but not connected to it. Nothing anybody had said to her then had made any sense, it had only confused her. Even if it had been comforting to Danny, or would have made sense to him, she could not speak. There was more to do, much more.

Evert's Crossing was nothing in the way of a town. A general store, a saloon with a whorehouse on the second floor, a livery and smithy combined. Most of it owned or run by George Evert or one of his sons. Ten years ago there had been no whorehouse but three women had arrived shortly after the ranchers and squatters had begun to move into the region, and the women must have had enough customers, they had not moved on to some other town. A preacher came through every few months, but there was no church, he gave his sermons in the general store. There was no school, but there were hardly any children.

The family had been there at least twice a year for ten years, camping on the outskirts of town, where the horses they had brought to sell could graze and the prospective buyers could come to study them. Nobody would think it unusual if she showed up with the boys, especially if she bought a few things at the store and just listened. Asking questions might only warn the people she was looking to find, and she didn't want them warned. She didn't want anybody wondering what it was she really wanted, because if they wondered that, they might wonder why her head was shorn, why both boys looked exhausted and frightened.

And she didn't want the prey to see the horses. The fat old mare would give them away immediately. The young mare might have simply run away, might not have been noticed, hardly even been seen, but the old mare had been left behind because they thought her useless. And yet, fat as she was, old as she was, she had managed, on heart and courage, to keep up with them even though they had made a three-day journey in two days.

"Danny must not be seen," Woman Walks Softly said quietly. "We do not go by the street. Use the alley."

They came in from behind the buildings, dismounted in the dark shadowed alley, and looked carefully up and down the hard-packed dirt track that was the main and only street.

"Jack!" Danny blurted, cowering against her.

She looked at her son, then in the direction he was staring. A heavyset man was walking toward the saloon, and from his gait she knew he had already spent hours there, drinking.

She wondered where he had been. The whorehouse was above the saloon, so he hadn't been there. And he hadn't been to the livery because there, in front of the saloon, tied to the hitching rail, was the young Morgan cross and one other horse from their own herd.

The heavyset man entered the saloon, and she waited long agonizing moments; then, when he didn't reappear, she relaxed, slumped against the side of the building, patting Danny's shoulder approvingly.

"Good boy," she whispered. "Now we know what he looks like!"

"Camp?" he stared, stupidly.

"The boys are exhausted," the older woman stroked their heads gently. "The horses need to be fed, they need water. We need rest."

"Rachel . . . ."

"They don't take Rachey in that place," Woman Walks Softly said reasonably. "Maybe they have hidden her. Maybe . . . " she shrugged. "We just wait some."

"I can't wait!"

"Wait. They can't live in that place forever." The smile burned on her weathered face. "We got 'em," she grunted in the Crazy language. "Got 'em good."

Danny was hanging onto Tommy now, watching her with wide, frantic eyes.

"Danny," Child Of Her People said firmly, "you have got to settle down."

He blinked. Every time he'd had a tantrum, she'd told him to settle down, and now the familiarity of the words and tone registered, he nodded, sighed deeply, as if consoled, and reached for her hand.

They walked back behind the buildings, to that place out of town where the thicket screened them from casual passers-by, where there was grass and water for the horses, where she could spread out bedrolls and feed her sons, try to calm and reassure them, maybe even get them to go to sleep.

Woman Walks Softly fussed over the horses, cleaning their hooves, wiping them with bunches of grass, praising them and giving them double measures of grain. She took the boys to the stream and bathed them in cool water, talking softly to them in Cree, bending Danny over her knee and carefully pouring water on his sore and swollen backside. He said something to her then, but Child Of Her People could not hear his words. She heard her mother say something in an agreeable tone of voice, a tone of voice too matter-of-fact to be upsetting, and yet Child Of Her People was upset.

She forced it down, there would be time later, time to shout and roar with rage and grief. But there was no time for that now.

She didn't light a fire and their food was cold but Danny ate; not much but some, and then she forced herself to talk calmly to them.

"You don't have to worry," she said. "Nothing bad is going to happen to you. NaiNai will be here when I'm not." She tried to force a smile and knew it was a total failure. "You know we have to find Rachey," she said, and both boys nodded. "I know you both want to help but right now the most help you can be is to just lie down and sleep. If you sleep," she patted Tommy's head, saw his eyes well with tears and realized how lonely he was feeling, even with what was left of his family surrounding him. "If you sleep, that poor fat old mare will think everything is safe, and then *she'll* sleep . . . and she's just about ready to fall over with being tired." Danny looked over at the exhausted old mare, and his mouth twitched briefly in what a few days ago would have been the start of a smile.

"Dog," Tommy blurted. "Dog got shot!"

"Yes," she said. "She got shot, and she died."

He nodded, sighed deeply, then leaned against her, stroking her arm, taking and giving comfort.

She held them, forcing herself to take the time to cuddle them, to rock them, knowing there was nothing else she could do anyway, knowing it was the best thing she could do for them and for herself. Calm down, she lectured herself. Calm down. Your breathing is wrong. Your muscles are too tight, too stiff. You have to remember what it was like, what you were taught. It's just like hunting wolf, or any other predator. Forget your fear. Turn it into something else, turn it into hate.

Woman Walks Softly approached, sat beside the boys' bedroll, and nodded. Child Of Her People tried to speak, then rose, and walked to where the young mare was waiting, looking as rested as if she had been given hours to recuperate. She mounted, looked back once at her mother and sons, then rode slowly and quietly back behind the buildings, back to the alley where she dismounted, and waited.

Two men came from the saloon, laughing and obviously drunk. The bottles they stuffed into their saddlebags glittered in the last rays of light. Their voices were loud in the first evening hush, but she let them ride off unchallenged; neither of them was the man Danny had identified as Jack. The Morgan cross was still in front of the saloon, with another horse she did not recognize, a strong-looking but quite ugly mud-coloured gelding. Jack was her link to whatever it was had happened to Danny, and the Morgan was her link to Rachel.

She moved quickly then, to the store, and went inside, pretending to be interested in cloth, pretending to be absorbed in the buttons and strips of lace and ribbon. None of the gossip had any bearing on what she wanted to know— that had to mean nobody had any idea at all that *anything* had happened, not the slightest hint that she was here for any reason except to look at the stock, plan her purchases. She bought a few peppermint candies, then went back to the shadowed alley, and hunkered against the wall, the young mare whoofing eagerly, nudging her insistently. She gave the horse a peppermint, popped one in her own mouth, and sat, waiting, as darkness crept from between the buildings, rising from the earth to the sky, blotting out the wild sunset colours and merging with the overhead clouds.

After a while she pulled a piece of the broken whetstone from her pocket, slid her sharp skinning knife from its sheath, spit peppermint-flavoured saliva onto the whetstone, and began to sharpen the already razor-sharp blade.

Woman Walks Softly appeared briefly, nodded twice, held up her hand, open palm facing Child Of Her People; then she vanished briefly, reappearing in front of the saloon, looking like any other travel-weary Cree stunned by the strangeness of a civilized town. She patted the Morgan cross, looked with interest at the mud-coloured gelding, then walked off, flat-footed, with apparent weariness, head bowed, just an aging woman shuffling her last days on the periphery of life.

Child Of Her People grinned mirthlessly. The boys were asleep, settled for the entire night. And by now, Woman Walks Softly knew everything she needed to know about the men she was following. She would recognize those prints anywhere. Years from now, if she saw the prints she would remember she had followed them, remember why.

Men were drifting into the saloon. Noise was spilling from the brightly lit place each time the door opened. The lights were on upstairs, too. In some of the windows women were standing, outlined in the lamplight, quietly advertising their presence in a town that was aware at all times that most of the commerce that kept the livery, the store, even the smithy in existence, came from or revolved around the whores who drew lonely men from the surrounding country the way honey draws flies and bees.

A burst of laughter, sound of voices raised in bawdy song, and then Jack was moving toward the horses, a bottle in each hand. He stuffed the bottles in a saddlebag, patted the Morgan heavily, put his foot in the stirrup, and swung himself up awkwardly, plumping drunkenly into the saddle. He leaned over, nearly losing his balance, untied the lead rope of the mud-coloured gelding and fastened it clumsily to the Morgan's saddle. Then, weaving noticeably, shook loose the Morgan's reins, freeing them from the hitch-rail, and rode off slowly down the packed trail that served as a street in Evert's Crossing.

Child Of Her People moved quickly, swung herself up on the young mare, slipping her knife into its sheath, the whetstone back in her pocket. With her knees and hands she turned the young mare around, moved down the alleyway and, riding behind the few buildings, followed Jack's passage out of town.

Clear of the buildings, she slowed the mare, trailing well back of the weaving figure on the Morgan cross, riding on the grassy strip growing alongside the bare earth track. She breathed deeply, flexed her fingers to release the strain building in her taut body, and, face hard, eyes slanting with a growing rage and hate, quietly followed the man who had so terrified her son.

He sang to himself and hiccuped; he swayed in the saddle and twice nearly fell from it. She kept her distance, watching him, ready to stop the second he showed any sign of stopping, any sign of turning to check his back trail. When he finally pulled up under a large tree, she dismounted before he did, putting her hand over the muzzle of the young mare to silence her. He didn't bother with a fire; he didn't bother with much of anything; he didn't even bother to remove the Morgan's bridle, or to lengthen the mud-coloured gelding's tether rope. He pulled his bedroll from behind the saddle, dropped it on the ground, unrolled it, then got one of the bottles and flopped with it to the ground. She waited. He didn't even have time to uncap the bottle and drink, he was out like a wind-blown candle, snoring.

She waited. Waited with a cold fury until she heard his snores. Then she moved, quickly and silently. The mud-coloured gelding nickered softly, but the Morgan wasn't bothered by her presence so the gelding didn't try to run. And Jack continued snoring.

Child Of Her People patted the Morgan, spoke in a whisper to the gelding, rubbed her hand along his neck and blew in his nostrils. Then she took Jack's rifle from its scabbard, and, gripping it by the barrel, swung it the way she had so often swung an axe, and crashed the butt against the sleeping drunk's head. Not hard enough to crush his skull. Just hard enough to ensure he would sleep for hours.

It wasn't easy to haul him from his bedroll and sling him bellydown across his own saddle, but she did it. Then she rolled the blankets up, strapped them in place, put the rifle back in its scabbard, mounted the young mare and rode back quickly, leading the Morgan cross and the mud-coloured gelding.

She detoured the town altogether, not wanting to risk being seen by anyone, aiming for the slow-moving river, riding among the trees dark along the bank. When she heard the old mare nicker, she felt herself relax. Then Woman Walks Softly was there, stepping from between the trees, nodding.

"It's me," she said softly. "It's Momma." Tommy was sitting up, reaching for the rifle his grandmother had left beside him. "It's okay," she said, and he sobbed, once. "Open your mouth," she crooned. "Open your mouth and close your eyes and you will get a big surprise." Obediently, trustingly, he did, and she gently placed a peppermint on his tongue.

"Me," Danny said, his voice trembling, and she turned to her youngest, her baby. He was sitting up, a knife clutched in his small hands, but his face was lifted, his eyes shut, his mouth open, waiting, like a baby bird. She gave him his candy, and then she was hugging them both, wanting just to sit down and cry, wanting to wail, to protest that it wasn't right, children shouldn't have to live like this, sleeping with guns, sleeping with knives, sleeping ready to try to defend themselves against people three times their size, ten times their strength.

"We're moving out," she said instead, and they nodded, reaching for their clothes.

They moved more quickly with the extra horses. Woman Walks Softly swung up on the Morgan cross, riding behind the belly down form of the unconscious Jack. Tommy and Danny sat on the mud-coloured gelding, holding their bedrolls, yawning. And the fat old mare followed as best she could, grumbling and grunting her disgust at having to move on so many hours before daylight.

They moved away from the river, away from the town, Woman Walks Softly leading the way, following the trail she had already followed once. They could have moved faster without the children, but they knew the children needed to be with them, needed to be part of whatever it was that was going to happen. They could have moved faster than they did, but they wanted to move quietly, and so they took their time, careful, determined.

Jack was still unconscious when they stopped in a rubble of rock fallen from the crest of a low bluff outlined against the pre-dawn sky.

"Another hour," Woman Walks Softly grunted.

"I want some answers," Child Of Her People replied, dismounting quickly. "And I'm hungry."

"Good," the older woman smiled. "We know where to go. Now we look after us."

As the boys moved to gather firewood, Woman Walks Softly stripped all the gear from the horses, turning them loose to roll, and to crop the rich grass. The horses weren't going to go anywhere; the stud would stay close to the young mare, the gelding would stick close to the stud, and the young mare wasn't going far from the person with the peppermint-scented pocket.

Child Of Her People pulled Jack's limp form to where a small stunted tree grew from the rough rocky soil. She tied his hands together, stretching his arms above his head, and tying them to the trunk of the sturdy tree. She tied one booted foot to a rock, the other to a thorny bush, then went to his gear and rummaged through it to see what there might be to add to their food supply. He had a slab of bacon; she grinned, took it, and moved to the small fire, picking up the frying pan from the tidy heap of gear.

She was so hungry her hands were shaking. But she took her time and made it a proper meal, johnnycake in a pan greased with the bacon fat, and when the johnnycake was done, she turned it from the pan onto her clean slicker, put the hot pan back on the fire and dropped in slices of bacon. While the johnnycake cooled and the bacon fried, they all drank coffee, sharing Marcel's enamel mug, drinking the brew black and bitter.

She heard Jack groan, turned to watch him try to sit up, groggy, unable to understand or believe he was tied securely. She grinned at the thought of how his head must feel, hangover combined with the pain of her solid whack. When she turned back to watch the bacon, she saw Woman Walks Softly reaching for a piece of pitchwood. The tanned, strong fingers turned the wood this way and that, the graying head nodded once, and then her mother was shaving regular thick pieces of dark pitchwood from the irregular broken hunk. It peeled easily, and when she flicked an unsatisfactory piece into the fire, it flared, blazing briefly. Woman Walks Softly peeled another strip, tested the end of it against the palm of her hand, and nodded, satisfied; the wood was as sharp as wood, as hard as rock, neither one nor the other, but almost both.

Jack sagged again, unable to rouse himself from his stupour. Child Of Her People took the cooked bacon from the frying pan, set the slices on the johnnycake, draining the fat from the frying pan onto the brown crust of the cornbread. Then they ate, slowly, happily, cornbread and bacon fat, with crunchy strips of jowl.

Jack was stirring again, trying to thrash his arms and legs, still not realizing he was securely tied. Child Of Her People rose from her place by the small fire, and moved toward the captive. He stirred, grumbled, opened his eyes and looked into Danny's expressionless little face.

Jack's eyes widened, he paled, his glance darting around frantically, a mouse looking for escape, and they watched as the realization hit him, the realization he was tied hand and foot, surrounded by vengeful people, people he considered uncivilized savages. Tommy moved to hunker down next to Danny, staring at Jack with the same intent look he wore when watching ants swarming in and out of their grass and dirt nests. Jack stared at him, then at Danny, at two faces so much alike they had to be brothers. He turned to her then, licking his lips, shaking his head, babbling with fear.

"I didn't do it," he vowed, and she knew he was lying. She knew he knew she did not believe him. He turned his gaze again to the child he had violated. "You tell 'er, kid," he babbled. "I was good to you, right? I gave you water to drink, right? It was that crazy bastard Kruger threw you in the bushes, not me!"

Danny stared at Jack, then lifted his small hand, put a piece of cold bacon in his mouth, and chewed, his eyes wide, accusing wordlessly.

Woman Walks Softly moved to where Jack's tightly bound hands were stretched toward the stunted tree, swollen, dark red with congested blood.

"Where is my granddaughter?" she asked quietly.

He stared at her, shaking his head, terrified. Woman Walks Softly carved a sharp splinter from the pitchwood, and Jack watched her shining knife blade, the colour leaving even his lips.

"Where?" she asked carefully, in the language she had never even tried to learn until she had heard her darling

Rachel speaking it. "Where is my granddaughter?"

"I'm not the one!" he blurted. "It was Pete Wade! Him and Kruger!"

"Where is she?" the older woman insisted, her face stony, voice cold.

"With Kruger. Kruger took her."

"Tell me," she invited.

And so he did, babbling, spilling his guts, describing Kruger in detail, describing his horse, babbling the names of towns he had heard Kruger mention. With words and throat, with tongue and voice he tried desperately to save his own life.

"Is he alone or travelling with someone?" Child Of Her People asked.

"I don't know," he said and she knew, again, that he lied.

She nodded and Woman Walks Softly reached out, holding one of the splinters carefully and inserting it firmly under the nail of his thumb; she rapped it with the handle of her knife, and drove it down a half-inch deep into the tender flesh under his nail. He screamed, jerked, and begged. Woman Walks Softly took a second splinter, and placed it under the nail of his index finger.

"Him 'n' Wade are riding together," he screeched. "They've got the girl."

"Who are the two who were in town with you yesterday?" Child Of Her People asked.

"I don't know them," he lied.

"Why is it," she smiled at him, her voice deceptively soft, "every time you speak to me you tell a lie, but when you speak to my mother, you tell the truth? Do you think because I am younger I will hesitate? The two who were with you in town yesterday have our horses."

Woman Walks Softly drove a third sliver in, hitting it decisively with her knife handle, ramming it under his other thumb nail.

"Walters," he screamed, "and Riley!"

"Why did they leave?" she asked. He looked at her and knew there was no mercy in her eyes.

"Supplies," he gasped. "They got the supplies. They're catching up to them. Not me," he assured her, "I had enough of them crazy bastards. I've had it! No more of that. Honest. I told 'em, but . . . " he started to weep then, begging forgiveness, making vows.

Woman Walks Softly leaned sideways, reached for a piece of blazing twig from the fire and lit the pitchwood slivers dispassionately. Jack fought the ropes, he pitched and heaved, his voice raw, face contorted with agony. Tommy moved away, back to the campfire, and stared into it, face pale, hands shaking. Danny watched every move, heard every plea.

"Who hurt my son?" Child Of Her People asked calmly.

"Kruger," he insisted, "and Wade. Not me. I never done that to him. Nor to her, neither. Lady, I never hurt a kid in my life." She might have believed him, but she remembered how Danny had stiffened with fear, how he had blurted Jack's name.

"I told 'em," he babbled, "I told 'em it isn't right. But they were drunk. Mean drunk. If I'd said or done more they'd a turned on me. So I . . . " and then he began to sob, again, and to pray, "Hail Mary full of grace . . . ."

Woman Walks Softly looked over at her, and Child Of Her People shrugged. She tapped Danny on the shoulder, he rose immediately and moved toward the fire where Tommy was weeping. Woman Walks Softly slit Jack's throat and walked away, wiping her knife on her leggings. Who did what and who watched while it was done was of no interest to her; the Cree have always known what you do not stop from happening you allow to happen.

Child Of Her People left him there, to bleed to death, as he had left Marcel to bleed to death, and moved to extinguish the campfire. Danny was still chewing bacon, eyes hooded, face blank, but Tommy was trembling, almost ready to heave back his breakfast. Let him learn, she thought, smothering back her pity, let him learn. Danny knows. Danny understands. Let Tommy learn, too, and learn now. The soft ones die. The hard survive. The People had learned this, and learned it the hard way. Let Tommy learn now, before he refuses to learn. The Inverts had never been made to feel it was their obligation to go to war, and most of them had traditionally stayed away from war, had helped look after the children, the old, the pregnant, the helpless. And the Inverts had been slaughtered just as cruelly as the ones they had tried to assist. Holy people, who refused to kill and who honoured all life, had died at the hands of the insane and conscienceless. Let Tommy learn now, that one does what one has to do to stop obscenities, or one becomes what one does not resist.

They packed then and prepared to leave, and she heard their names over and over inside her head. Riley. Walters. Kruger. Wade. Rachel was with Kruger and Wade. Riley and Walters had been in Evert's Crossing yesterday, so Kruger and Wade were the ones who had turned off because they didn't want anyone to see them with a little girl. She could go after them, now, but Riley and Walters were closer, and you do not leave an enemy at your back, you do not ride past those who would do you harm.

She went through Jack's pockets, taking what she thought they might need. In a leather belt around his waist he had money, more money than she had ever seen at one time in her life, and she knew he hadn't gotten it honestly. But she didn't care how he'd gotten it. He had taken from her everything that had been her life, it didn't bother her to take from him anything she wanted. His spirit had no power over her, she had defeated him in life, and there was nothing to fear from him.

Child Of Her People and Woman Walks Softly untied him and stripped him of everything, left him for the buzzards and coyotes, for the slithering worms and creeping death beetles. He had a six-gun and holster on a belt and she put that around her waist, tying the holster thong around her upper leg. Boxes of shells. Food. Everything one man would need for a month's travel. Child Of Her People appropriated it all, then they cleaned up the camp, erased all sign they had ever been there, and rode off, without a backward glance. If anybody ever did stumble on the place and find the bones, there would be no hint of any answers to any questions.

Three good horses, used to the weight of adult men and their gear, were burdened now with the lighter weight of women and children, and though they had all been ridden hard, they had been fed grain, lots of it, and had rested. The miles slipped under them, and the old mare was left so far behind they almost forgot about her. If only they moved fast enough, if they had any kind of luck except bad luck, they could do it.

She found Riley and Walters before the afternoon sun began its dip toward the evening sky. It was smoke from their fire that betrayed them. She slid from the mare, and pulled Jack's rifle from its saddle scabbard, checked the rifle with the skill of years of training, and dug in the saddlebag for extra shells.

"Stay here," she grunted, and both boys nodded.

She moved on foot, knowing without having to check that Woman Walks Softly was moving with her, angling to one side, blocking at least part of any possible escape routes.

Moving from rock to rock, hiding in the grass, staying below the lip of the ridge, taking as much time as she needed, silent as a snake, remembering everything she had learned from Woman Walks Softly, everything she had learned from Strong Heart Woman who was the daughter of Moves With Certainty, remembering everything she had been taught by her Marcel, known also as Laughing When Appropriate.

They were sprawled on the ground, half drunk, laughing at a joke one of them had told. Four horses were hobbled and grazing on yellow grass. Two saddles and two bedrolls beside a fire too large for cooking, a fire none of the People would ever have thought to make so big. Pots and pans, a large bean kettle—they had been here a long time and had settled themselves in for a while, possibly waiting for Jack.

She lay on her belly, tucked the rifle to her shoulder, feeling the wood warm on her cheek. She had no idea which was Riley, which was Walters, and she didn't care a rat's ass. She took the one closest to her, closest to the rifles still in the saddle scabbards. Marcel had told her if you ever have to shoot a man, aim for the biggest part of him, don't try for a nice neat head-shot, just hit what you can, slow him down, stop him, get fancy when there's the time for it.

She sighted for the middle of his chest, her finger squeezed the trigger, gently, the rifle kicked against her shoulder and from her left there was a second shot, almost an echo. Her target jerked backwards, his chest blossoming red, and then the other target sprawled, kicking reflexively. She aimed again, taking her time; neither of them was going anywhere, she could take all the time she wanted, get as fancy as she wanted, get her head shots if she wanted.

She fired twice, then went back for her sons, knowing Woman Walks Softly would ensure that what needed to be finished, if anything, would be properly finished. There was no need to even think about it, her mother was there, and knew better than she did what had to be done and how to do it.

Tommy didn't want to get down from the Morgan, but Danny did, and he walked over, his bare feet padding silently, and looked at the faces of the dead men. Then he nodded. Nodded, and turned away, totally disinterested.

"Take everything," Woman Walks Softly instructed. "Leave no sign, no gear, nothing. Waste is a sin. Besides, the animals will take care of these ones, and nobody will know. But if you leave horses wandering around, or leave saddles lying behind, someone will start looking for the reason such valuables have been abandoned. Bones . . . " she shrugged. "The face of the earth is thick with bones, and the Crazies cannot tell which are dog, which are wolf."

They had rested horses, now, and saddles, too. They could let their own animals rest, relieve them of the weight of even so small a form as Danny's. Both dead targets had had moneybelts, and she took them, stuffed them in the saddlebags on Danny's horse. It was almost like counting coup, almost like the stories of the days the Human Beings had ridden free in a land not yet streaked with innocent blood.

Woman Walks Softly even took the warm bean pot, wrapping it several times with blankets, holding it in front of her, pressed against her body, held by her arm which had healed crookedly. They headed north, moving quickly, putting distance between the carrion and themselves, moving to cut the trail of Kruger and Wade. Moving towards Rachel.

It was all part of something larger, and she knew it, but didn't know how to interpret what she knew. Since before she had been born there had been bandits and outlaws in the Montana badlands. Everyone knew that. Even before the Metis had been slaughtered at Batoche, there had been whiskey runners and thieves moving back and forth across the border, hiding from the Queen's Law in Montana; hiding from the Long Knife law in the shadow of the Queen's flag, raiding and stealing from the People and from the settlers.

How many times had they heard stories of bands of angry people from both sides of the border riding into the badlands and lynching anyone they thought might even begin to answer the description of a wanted man?

And the People had shrugged it off. What business was it of theirs? They owed allegiance to neither the Queen nor the Long Knives, and if the bandits shot a horse police, what did they care? The horse police were no friends of theirs. If the Long Knives were caught in a trap and slaughtered, what did it matter to her? The Long Knives had killed the People and the less of those Crazy pony soldiers there were, the better she felt.

Marcel had told her about Batoche, the walled city of the Metis, and how the federals had come, riding on the train as far as they could, then riding overland dragging the huge gun. A gun from below the border nobody could see, a gun designed for the Long Knives. They had tested it, and knew it would shoot a hole in a one-inch thick spruce board but they had no idea what it would do to the human body. They loaned it to the general the Queen had sent, and the general used it at Batoche, used it against women and children. What did she care what happened to those soldiers? All she wanted, all any of them wanted, was to be left alone, to live the life they'd always known and catch their ponies, take them to town, and sell them for the cash money they needed to buy supplies to build up their places, their homes.

She had been a fool to believe that if she left the world alone, the world would leave her alone. It never had before! Sister Mary Joseph had left the world, had cloistered herself, dedicating her life to her idea of God, and the world had not left even her alone, but sent to her the terrified children, the lost and abandoned, the orphaned and kidnapped.

When there are poisonous snakes in the world a person is a fool to walk barefoot, an idiot to expect the snake to distinguish between those who would do it harm and those who only want to walk the earth in peace.

That was part of what she wanted to explain to Tommy, some day soon, when there was time, when he was reassured and calm again, could listen and understand. She had not tried to stop certain kinds of things from happening, nor had Marcel, they had turned their backs and tried to live isolated in their own little world. But what you do not stop from happening, you allow to happen. One way of life had been turned upside-down and inside-out and none of the innocent had understood why they had to die. The survivors should all have learned, and some of them had, but some had tried to build an island of safety in a sea of danger.

She looked over at her mother, riding steadily, her face calm. And Child Of Her People knew that the doubts and the turmoil in her mind were hers alone. Her mother was focused; she was at peace with the spirits and the circumstances. Woman Walks Softly had grown up safe in a time when there were still Old Women to teach endurance and survival and the ultimate balancing of all forces.

They camped in the cool of the evening, and while she tethered the horses for the night, Tommy started a small fire. She added wood to it, spread the coals, and put the bean kettle in the coals to heat. She made bannock and fried bacon, and they ate hugely, then sucked on peppermints for dessert. Tommy was pale with fatigue and there were dark circles under his eyes; when she suggested he go to sleep, he nodded gratefully, moved to his bedroll and crawled in. She heard him sobbing softly to himself, but she did not go to him. She sat, staring at the small fire, remembering Rachel, how her hair had grown in so slowly, almost white, how every winter it would darken slightly, but as soon as the sun shown again, it would begin to bleach out, streaking, at first every shade of blonde until it was all the same pale yellow. Child Of Her People sat remembering the big blue eyes, the face that was so serious until she smiled, remembering her voice, the sound of her laughter. Concentrating on not remembering how she sounded when she was sad, or frightened.

"You should sleep," Woman Walks Softly said quietly.

"I will, Momma," she promised.

"Tomorrow we must start early, ride hard, and make only short stops."

"Yes," she nodded. One good night's rest, one proper breakfast, and then their time had to count, every second of it. She heard Woman Walks Softly settle herself for the night and wanted to lie down herself, but her body wasn't ready yet.

Danny moved from the fire, stood peeing on the ground. Then, when his bladder was drained, he moved to crawl into bed with Tommy. She heard their voices, soft, Tommy weeping again, Danny making gentle comforting noises, and she thought it strange that the one who had been most hurt, most frightened, most lost, should comfort the one who had been spared so much. But then she thought of how it must have been for Tommy all those hours alone in a hole under the house, unable to lift the trap, not knowing if anyone would come for him, imagining spiders and rats all around him in the blackness. She rose, then, and moved to the bedroll, dug candies from her pocket, and placed them in the mouths of her sons.

"We're safe," she told them. "Go to sleep. Everything will seem better in the morning." She sat by them until they both fell asleep, then she wrapped herself in a warm woolen blanket, curled up by the fire with the Winchester beside her, and let herself fall asleep. If she dreamed, she did not remember her dream when she wakened.

They breakfasted on reheated beans and cold bannock, drank bitter reheated coffee and broke camp in the chill of first dawn. She gave the boys raisins to chew, and jerky to carry in their pockets, mounted them on the calmest of the horses, and carefully explained to them that there would be no unnecessary stops.

"We have to get Rachel back," she repeated.

Tommy nodded, and Danny gave her his new version of a smile, the quick twitch at the corner of his mouth, the smile that was no smile at all, and certainly not what ought to be seen on the face of a child.

They headed in a direct line toward where the group of men had split up, back to where Kruger and Wade had headed north, avoiding the town because they didn't want anyone to see they had Rachel. They probably had her riding in front of one of them, her hands tied to the saddle horn, held firm by a strong and unyielding arm. Hard to explain why a child is trussed like a pony ready for branding.

There was no need to try to avoid leaving a trail. Nobody was following them. There was no reason two women and two children shouldn't ride across country. And anyway, how do you hide the trail made by eight horses? Nine, if you counted the fat old mare who had found them some time during the night and now limped behind, losing ground with every step. Some of the eight horses were just ordinary, everyday, run-of-the-mill riding stock, but at least two of them were better than average, better even than the young mare and the part Morgan stud. Both mares, and both of them what Woman Walks Softly called war horses, Chiefs' horses; they would travel fast and far, and Child Of Her People was glad of that, because, if she had to, she would ride them both into the ground.

The little band stopped in the heat of the day to rest the horses and switch mounts. Child Of Her People threw her saddle on one of the war horses, a gray mare with a dark mane and tail. She fed them all grain from the supply in Jack's gear, watered them freely, and switched the boys' saddles to alternate mounts. They rested and ate, they drank more water than any Good Person would have, but there was no shortage of water, and they would come across fresh before nightfall.

"Let's go," she said.

"Already?" Tommy protested.

"If you think you aren't enjoying this," she said coldly, "think how Rachel must feel about it."

He nodded. She held his horse's head for him and he climbed on a large rock, grabbed the saddle and pulled himself upright without any help from her. He managed to grin down at her when she passed him the reins, and she patted his leg.

"You're going to be," she told him, "as good a man as your father when you're grown." And his face brightened.

She went to her own horse, swung up, and grinned over at Danny, already perched in the saddle, helped up by his grandmother.

"Ready?" she asked softly.

Danny nodded, dug his heels into the horse's girth, and moved off first, bouncing slightly. She was afraid she might start to weep but swallowed and urged her horse to follow him. Better than any of them he knew why they were in a hurry.

She pushed them all that long afternoon, pressing on in a distance-devouring canter, and when Danny began to bob and jiggle with fatigue, she pulled up beside him, leaned over, put her arm around his small body, and lifted him to ride in front of her. Woman Walks Softly leaned easily to one side, grabbed the reins as Danny's horse moved beside her.

Danny leaned against her gratefully, sighing with relief, and they moved on again, Tommy clinging grimly to the reins of the dark sweating horse that moved so steadily beside the gray she rode.

They cut the trail of Kruger and Wade in the evening, on the south side of the river. She stopped long enough to transfer saddles again, saving the riding horses as much as she could, knowing she wanted to get as far as she could before she had to start making decisions she didn't really want to have to make. There was the chance that eight horses would raise too much dust to be able to track Kruger and Wade as stealthily as she wanted to track them. They mustn't have any reason at all to become uneasy, to begin to think of dumping Rachel in a grave.

Tommy's face was pale and she wished she dared stop; he was, after all, just a little boy. But Rachel was just a little girl, moving from eleven to twelve, too young for what had undoubtedly been done to her, and she was sure neither Kruger nor Wade would stop simply because Rachel was exhausted. She reached over and patted her son gently on the shoulder; he looked at her and nodded, his face caked with dust, his eyes dull.

There was a smudge of darker green on the horizon, the promise of a waterhole or stream. She pointed at it, but Tommy didn't understand.

"Another hour," she said quietly, "maybe two. Then we can stop."

"I'm sorry, Momma," he said sadly.

"Sorry we'll be stopping?" she teased, deliberately pre-tending to misunderstand. "I'm not sorry." His eyes welled with tears, he shook his head, denying her attempt to cheer him. "It's okay, Tommy," she said clearly. He nodded, but turned his face to the front, eyes downcast. "Not long, now," she insisted. "Not long, now."

The cool water of the river refreshed them all, washing more than just the dirt and dust from their bodies and clothes. It gave them energy enough to set up camp properly, in the protection of the willow thicket on the north bank.

There were hot beans and fresh bannock, there was pemmican made into broth with boiling water. There was dried fruit and fresh coffee sweetened with sugar only slightly dusty, and they all stuffed themselves. The boys were asleep as soon as they slid into their bedrolls, and Woman Walks Softly took her coffee to the river bank and hunkered, watching the water, sipping coffee, waiting, her face as unyielding as the granite rocks in the water.

She knew without having to look that Child Of Her People was lying with her sons, cuddling them, comforting and soothing them to sleep. And she knew that her daughter was feeling guilt for not having been able to protect them. Well, when this was done, and done properly, when it was done and finished, she would make Kinnickinick tea, and sit her daughter down to drink it. She would smudge and she would bathe, and she would build a sweat lodge and take her daughter inside, and when the sweat lodge had done its work, when the spirits had come and visited them, she would talk to her daughter about the stupidity and uselessness of guilt.

A person can only anticipate what is supposed to happen; a person cannot anticipate what is never supposed to be part of life. And even if a mistake had been made, what use to feel guilt? No mistake had been made. Until the guilt. Guilt was a mistake.

Her daughter was exhausted. A Vision Quest is a trial, and every fibre of the body, mind, soul, and spirit is tested. Difficult enough to come back from a Vision Quest and pick up the threads of a normal life. To come back, after days and nights of ordeal, and find the unthinkable has happened is more than one person should be asked to endure.

She knew about guilt and the uselessness of guilt. How often had she cursed herself for not ensuring Child Of Her People was on her way out of camp before the firing started? How often had she hated herself for not having been as quick as the Old Woman, for not racing with her daughter and her mother at the first raised voice, the first mention of stolen ponies?

Even now, she did not know how long she had been halfway to where the dead go when they leave this world. And when she knew she would live, she had wanted to die. Hated herself for not dying as her mother had died, and her teacher, and her lovers, and all her dear ones. When she could walk again, and ride again, she had tried to find Child Of Her People but there were horse police everywhere and who would believe her story? She had tried to talk to the People at the fort who spoke the language of the Crazies, but they looked away, those who had been of her own nation looked away and told her they had no news for her and no desire to approach the ones in charge with such a story.

And now her own daughter was feeling that sense of loss and anguish, that gnawing blame and self-hatred. No good would come of talking to her yet. She would only say, "But . . . but . . . but . . . " and meet each word with argument. The time would come when words could be heard.

She sipped her coffee and watched the night close in, the moon pale and distant in the sky. Father moon, look down on me, I am Woman Walks Softly, and I ask you to bring peace to my daughter.

Child Of Her People fell asleep quickly and dreamed she was running after Rachel, running and running, getting no closer, running frantically, arms outstretched, knowing all she was doing was not losing ground, knowing she was not gaining, not so much as one inch. And then she was back on the high Mesa again, seeing her own form lying on the ground, watching the osprey flying, flying free and fast, swooping and riding the air currents, unencumbered. The osprey swooped lower, lower, and then she was skimming just above the grassland, her hunting cry piercing sharply, skree skrrreeee. She wakened with the first hint of morning light touching her eyelids, almost trembling with the need to hurry, to join the osprey and speed across the land.

Both boys were still asleep, curled together, and she knew if she left them alone they would sleep hours more. She walked away from camp, away from the river, and went behind some bushes to relieve herself, then started back to the camp. Woman Walks Softly had a small fire going, water heating for coffee, and the last of the beans in the pot pushed close enough to the heat to warm gradually.

"Get clean," she grunted, "it's as good as sleep."

Child Of Her People took the piece of strong yellow soap her mother handed her, took it without asking where it came from, went to the river and stripped off her clothes. She scrubbed her body, washed and rinsed her hair, even washed her clothes, then walked, naked, back to camp and spread her wet clothes on the thicket. She knew what she had to do. And she knew that her mother knew and agreed.

She pulled on clean clothes, faded clean pants once worn by Marcel, then slid her feet into her knee-high moccasins and adjusted the thongs. She put on a faded brown shirt, the too-long sleeves rolled above her elbows, and the sweat-soaked headband with the blood-stained feather fastened to it. Then she strapped on the revolver she had taken from Jack, tied down the holster thong, and finally, all excuses gone, moved to her sleeping sons.

"Hey," she said softly, "you going to sleep all day?"

They stirred and opened their eyes, blinking, and she waited, talking to them, explaining over and over again, trying to reassure them, trying to let them know everyone had run out of choices.

"We're going to set you up for a spirit search," she told them. "Gonna leave you lots of food, lots of everything. But you'll be alone. Except for each other. You'll have a knife each, you'll have the axe, and I'll leave a gun hanging from a tree branch. Don't touch it unless you *have* to! I mean it. If I come back and it's been moved just to play a game or pretend you're hunting, I'm going to be real mad. It's just-in-case. And if you're good, and if you remember what you've been taught, you won't even have to look at it."

"No bears here," Tommy assured her.

"No bears," Woman Walks Softly agreed. "No berry bushes. Bears want berries. And no wolves, either, because this isn't a place the animals come to drink. All you got to do is eat, and sleep, and catch fish, and wait, and remember what I've taught you."

"When you coming back?" Tommy gulped.

"Soon as we can," Child Of Her People told him. "Now why don't you just lie down and go back to sleep? You're too tired," she explained. "We can't wait or go slow."

"Stand under the sky," Woman Walks Softly told them. "Stand and think of all the time you have known me. In that time I have not lied to you, and in that time I have done only good to you and for you."

She sliced a strip from the hem of her rawhide shirt, cut it in two, and tied one piece around Tommy's throat, the other around Danny's; they were loose and sagged slightly. She smiled, and cut her shirt hem again, then cut smaller strips from the band. She tied these small strips around their ankles and wrists, and when she had finished, they were smiling, and waiting for the explanation they knew would come.

"These tie me to you," she said gently. "Wear them until they wear thin and fall off by themselves. And any time you feel them, or see them, or think of them, know that I am not gone from you; I am tied to you. And if it should happen that I am sent from this broken old body to another place, know that even in that place, I am tied to you. If you never again see me, I am tied to you. For your entire life, I am tied to you. When you are old men with grandchildren and no teeth, when your hair is white or your head is bald, I am tied to you. And while I am tied to you, there is no reason for fear, and no reason for tears."

Tommy didn't cry, and there had never been any fear that Danny would. They lay back down, and even their confusion and uncertainty about being left alone couldn't keep them awake. How long had it been since they'd been able to have a full rest? Woman Walks Softly looked down at them and thanked all her spirits that Marcel and Child Of Her People had agreed with her and insisted almost from the time the children were born that they had to learn what every Cree child had always had to know—how to be alone without being their own worst threat.

Still, they were young. Too young to be left alone like this. But there comes a time when even the hardest of decisions has to be made.

They ate jerky and bannock, drank two cups each of scalding coffee, and then it was time to leave. Child Of Her People moved to the big gray war horse, knowing all she had to do, now, was swing herself up and head out, knowing there had never been anything in her life harder to do than ride away from her sleeping sons.

She knew she would have a difficult time following the sign. It was days old, now, and the wind had blown almost steadily the whole time. But Child Of Her People didn't have to read the sign, Woman Walks Softly was doing that, and even Marcel hadn't been able to fool the older woman. She could track a flea across bare rock if she had to, and she was not tracking fleas this time, she was tracking large, heavy-bodied adult men who had most of the stolen ponies with them.

Child Of Her People wanted Rachel and she wanted her now. Her dream haunted her, she was convinced that if she didn't hurry, didn't get to Rachel soon, it would be too late; there would be no reason to continue looking. Was it six days? Five? How many days had Rachel been with them? She tried to think about their days of search, tried to separate one day from another, and couldn't.

She remembered Woman Walks Softly saying that some of the stolen ones were kept a week or so then killed. She remembered the wolf hunters, the fanaticism of the first few days, and then the sudden swing of emotion, to a kind of boredom, the thrill gone in the unrewarding chore of dragging an unwilling victim with them, having to force the captive even to drink water.

Were Kruger and Wade tiring of the burden of an exhausted little girl? An exhausted captive who had to be watched every waking minute, who had to be tied at night? Would they make sure she ate? Make sure she had enough water? What if she refused to eat or drink? What if she was too hurt, too sick to be able to keep food and water in her stomach?

Child Of Her People pushed the obsessive worries to the back of her mind, forcing herself to concentrate on finding and following the sign her mother seemed to find so easily. There were flat, open places where Woman Walks Softly moved so surely and Child Of Her People could only hope and trust. Flat open places where the wind had blown the dust and dirt, where you would think nothing had passed since the first moment of Time. She wished she could do now what she had been able to do during her Vision Quest, ride with the wind like a hawk, fly high enough to be able to see with ten-power eyes, see Rachel, know she was moving in the right direction, and moving quickly enough.

She didn't think to drink until Woman Walks Softly handed her the canteen; she would have forgotten to eat if her mother hadn't pressed food into her hand. When it was time to change horses, she didn't even bother stopping to change the saddle, heaving her leg over the gray's back and swinging herself onto the bare back of the black gelding with white stockings, guiding him with knees and the shift of her body weight.

A hawk circled above them, and something small and furry scuttled away from the grass the horses were flattening. If they were simply riding somewhere, she would stop, gather pebbles, fashion a sling, and when the rabbits and prairie dogs ran from them, she would bring them down, skin them and clean them, leaving the offal for the hawks and ants. But there was no time for the usual.

"You are too pushed," her mother said. "You will be empty when you are needed if you don't start paying more attention. Look," she pointed, "see, one of their horses is limping. That slows them. It also shows they have no idea at all that there is anyone to follow them. Otherwise, they would turn their limping horse free and ride on as fast as they can."

"Yes," Child Of Her People said, impatiently.

"That means," Woman Walks Softly insisted, reaching for the water canteen, "that means Rachel has not told them of us." She smiled proudly, her eyes more fierce than the eyes of any hawk or eagle. "I am honoured," she blurted, her calm slipping, "I am honoured that our family has been given a child wise enough not to waste her time and our chances by threatening her captors with what will happen when her mother arrives!"

"How long?" Child Of Her People asked, gesturing at the tracks.

"We stop," Woman Walks Softly said firmly. "We rest these beasts. There is shade, there, by the bushes."

"There isn't time!" she argued.

"We have time," her mother said stubbornly, "but if these horses flounder, we will have squandered their lives and our time."

Unwillingly, she followed her mother to the sparse shade of the few drought-dwarfed bushes. The horses were sweaty under the saddles, salt encrusted on their chests and flanks where the heat and the breeze had dried the sweat as fast as it formed. She pulled dry grass and rubbed them dry and clean, checking their hooves. Then Woman Walks Softly slit open one of her bladderskins, holding it carefully, giving each of the horses a fair share of the water inside. When the bladderskin was empty, she slid it under her tattered shirt, smiling as the damp inner side of the skin touched her belly. She reached for the second bladderskin, and slit it too.

"That leaves us only the canteens," Child Of Her People observed carefully, not criticizing her mother, but puzzled at the generous use of precious water.

"These animals are big-boned," her mother said softly. "They are not mustangs or the tough ponies of the Good People. They need more food, more water, more care. It is why," she smiled sadly, "they were never the animals we needed for our day-to-day living, but the animals we saved for special times, for war, and for showing our wealth and status. They were the first to suffer when we no longer had wealth or even food and water."

Child Of Her People nodded, impatiently. Her mother finished fussing over the horses, then squatted, pulling jerky from her pouch and handing some of it to her daughter.

"How long?" Child Of Her People asked, gesturing with her hand at the wide expanse of grassland.

"Not far," her mother assured her. She looked up at the sun, frowned, chewing stolidly, and looked at the horses. "I cannot say how well these animals will continue. I do not know these horses as Rachey does." A sob escaped her, startling Child Of Her People as nothing else could have. "So much of my being is in pain," her mother admitted, "that I am like half a woman. I do not know what it takes from a horse to wear a saddle. I do not know how much time is stolen by the weight of leather, the food in the saddlebags, the grain and . . . Rachey would know. She could look at a horse and tell who had ridden its grandmother."

Child Of Her People sat rigid, her ears buzzing, her head suddenly prickling. She rose, her face pale, and moved to the big gray mare, leaned her forehead against the mare's broad head, tears welling in her eyes. She thought of Rachel walking unafraid to a nervous horse, hugging its front leg, making a soft wordless sound in her throat, and calming the horse. She thought of Rachel with a bucket of warm water and a bar of soap, scrubbing the skin of an animal capable of crushing her, and of how the girl could coax the horse to lie down and allow her to wash its broad back; how it would stay down while Rachel emptied bucket after bucket of clear water over it, rinsing it of soap, and of fly eggs. She thought of her own time with the wolf hunters, then of Rachel, captive and frightened.

She dared to leave her body briefly, then. It was almost like being in love, that feeling of just letting things happen, of relinquishing everything and allowing whatever was unwinding to unwind, of trusting totally that whatever the price to be paid, it would be worth it. If they found Rachel too late, there would be nothing left of Child Of Her People, nothing left for the two boys waiting in the middle of nowhere. Either she had all her children or she had none!

Woman Walks Softly watched, her heart pounding. She had heard of this, but had never experienced it. Her own mother, Strong Heart Woman had told her of it, and had experienced it twice in battle. She had said it was a giving over of control, a matter of depending entirely on faith and on the spirits who had gone before you, a belief that there is balance, if only we dare trust it.

She heard the piercing skree of a hunting hawk and looked up, but saw no hawk, just the hot sky.

Child Of Her People heard the hawk, and looked up, expecting to see the bird plummeting after a mouse or a prairie dog. Intead, she saw a hawk flying in a flat straight line, screaming she had sighted her prey, but making no move to drop to it. Suddenly the hawk was rising, rising, arching her wings and doubling herself, plummeting, then, but not to the ground, rising again and dropping, rising in a way no hawk Woman Walks Softly had ever seen would do.

Child Of Her People smiled then, and her eyes focused on this world. "I have two sons alone in the middle of nowhere," she said calmly. "Any one of a hundred things could happen, and then what would we do? And if we all die, what does that matter?" She almost laughed, shook her head. "This is not the only world, nor the only reality, nor the only future, and the Newcomer priests may fear death, but we are The People Who Fear Nothing."

She stripped off the saddle and dropped it to the ground, leaving on the saddlebags with the grain and food. She tied the straps of the water canteens together and laid them across the gray's shoulders, patting her and talking softly. Then she checked the horses carefully, even checking their flaring pink nostrils, pouring water from the canteen onto her fingers, swabbing the dust from nostrils and eyes.

"Hoooo, beast," she crooned. "What can I tell you? It is urgent, or I would not treat you this way."

She made herself stop thinking. If she thought about the gamble she was about to take, she would burst into tears and be totally useless. She could almost smell the men. She knew she couldn't, but it felt as if she could. She made herself relax, made herself loosen her clothing, hunker, and drain her bladder, wipe herself dry with grass, then refasten her clothing and breathe deeply.

"Hoooo," she called, and the big gray moved to her, tossing her great head, snorting. Child Of Her People was on its back, then, with the rifle in her hand.

"Fool," her mother laughed.

"Fool," she agreed.

The horses moved willingly, even eagerly, and Woman Walks Softly shook her head, marvelling at their reserves of strength. There was no need for words, no need for anything but the growing calm, the growing focus.

It was a commitment they were making; however it ended she was not merely following, she was chasing; she was not being moved and turned by circumstance, she was causing things to happen in the way she wanted them to happen, and there was no need or room to berate herself. Guilt is a waste of time. What has happened has happened and from it we can learn something. If only that we exist only in the dreams of the Supernaturals, and even they can sometimes have nightmares which trap us in events nobody can predict.

Child Of Her People pushed the horses to a steady trot, following the course the hawk had marked, depending totally on faith, ignoring the sign on the ground, ignoring everything but the growing excitement that approached elation.

It was late evening, the sun burning its way over the ridge of hills, and she smelled their smoke before she saw them or heard the sound of their voices. Child Of Her People stopped her heaving horse, then, and slid from its back, her hand on its nose, patting steadily. She hauled the saddlebag free and dumped it on the ground, emptying all the grain on the grass. She could feel a cool breeze, knew there was water nearby, and she didn't want any of the horses moving toward it, betraying their presence.

Woman Walks Softly hauled the bladderskin from under her shirt, emptied the canteen of water into it, and moved from horse to horse, giving them drink. Either they would refill all their canteens at the stream nearby, or they would never need water again.

Child Of Her People stripped the horses of bridles and halters, and patted them, whispering thanks. An unfettered horse could survive easily in this wild country, and if the horses were to be left alone, better they live free than become wolf meat.

She filled her pockets with shells, bit off a hunk of jerky, and chewed slowly, passing the strip to her mother. Woman Walks Softly took it and passed over a half-filled canteen. Child Of Her People nodded thanks, drank deeply, then drank again, and passed it back.

"I love you," she said. Their glances locked, held briefly. "And I you," her mother answered.

Then Child Of Her People was moving, bent low to the ground, hidden from sight by the hill, moving toward the top, where a hawk circled high in the sky above, circling and gliding. She moved as silently as Woman Walks Softly had taught her to move, as controlled as Strong Heart Woman had told her to be. There was no sign of numb grief, now. No sign of guilt chewing her and being chewed by her.

Woman Walks Softly watched her daughter and felt her body thrill with a fierce and intense joy. This was a woman of the People, and this was the warrior woman she had always known her daughter could be. This, the taut-bodied woman dropping to her belly and wriggling foward, her rifle held across her arms, moving like a snake, moving like a lizard.

Child Of Her People knew her mother was moving up the hill, but she didn't turn to see where she was or how she was doing. She didn't have to, she knew as she had always known; there was no need to worry or doubt, she could feel the warmth at her throat, her wrists, her ankles, she could feel the ties that bound them to each other and bound them both to the child on the other side of the hill.

As she approached the very top of the hill she stopped, checking the muzzle of her rifle, checking her revolver for dust in the barrel. Everything she had ever been taught was helping her.

The two men were cooking meat; she could smell it and her mouth watered. She swallowed her own saliva, licked her lips, swallowing again, her throat no longer dry and tight, her breathing even and soft. She parted the fronds of grass slowly, and peeked over the top of the hill.

Kruger and Wade were sitting facing the fire, their backs to her; she could have leaped to her feet and capered openly and they would not have noticed. Two men in boots, filthy pants and sweat-stained greasy shirts, with dusty, battered black hats on their heads. She couldn't see their faces, but knew they were dirty, thick with whisker stubble and dust. Horses grazed around the lip of the small pool, cropping the curly buffalo grass, seemingly unaware of the hidden observers peering from the top of the hill, down-wind from the camp.

Two saddles, bedrolls spread nearby, were on the ground, between the fire and the two nerve-tight women. Child Of Her People nodded. The bedrolls were down-wind, the smoke from the fire would discourage mosquitos and black flies while the men slept, although this close to the placid pool there would be more of the bloodthirsty little biters than if the men had camped above the pool, where the water ran more quickly.

Then one of the men rose, walked to the clutter of gear dumped beside a thatch of brush, bent over, reached out, and grabbed a small bundle of filthy cloth. He hauled it upright and she bit down on her forearm to stifle her cry of protest. Rachel. Stumbling and weary, unresisting and resigned, Rachel tried to hurry, to keep up with the man pulling her by one arm.

Child Of Her People damned the last rays of sun, slanting directly into her eyes! She could see outlines, she could see clearly the clutter of stuff on the ground, but she dared not take aim and fire. She wanted to jump up and yell, distract them, charge down the hill praying Rachel would get free, but they would react by using the child as a shield to hide behind, or, worse, would simply snap her neck.

She made herself breathe slowly and deeply, made herself wait in spite of the screaming need to do something. From her right she heard the low croak of a sand toad, and knew Woman Walks Softly was trying to reassure her, urging her to imitate the toad, who can wait for years for the proper weather conditions; who can actually crawl into a hole for half a human lifetime and neither eat nor move, waiting patiently until enough rain falls to provide her with conditions ideal for breeding.

The man dropped Rachel to the ground, offered her the water canteen, and when the child shook her head, he grabbed her by the hair, forced her head back, put the canteen to her bruised lips and poured water recklessly.

She wanted a clear shot. Two clear shots. She didn't want any risk at all of hitting Rachel. It had taken too long to find her. Rachel had survived so far, survived worse than this rough handling, this brutal forced drinking.

The angle of the sun was changing, the direct glare was gone from her eyes. The man with the canteen pushed rudely, and Rachel fell flat on the ground; the man stood upright, and Child Of Her People knew it was Time.

She fired, then, the bullet hitting the man between the shoulder blades, knocking him into the hot campfire. Before the second man could react, Woman Walks Softly had fired, then both fired again, and it was over, just like that, over and almost finished.

"*Rachel!*" she screamed, leaping to her feet and charging blindly down the hill, dropping her rifle, totally unaware of the revolver weighting her hip, her blood-tipped snow goose feather flapping behind her.

She gathered her daughter in her arms, and then it was safe, finally, to weep, to cling to her little girl and sob helplessly.

"It's okay, Momma," Rachel said, her voice a hoarse, cracked imitation of what it should be. "Don't cry, Momma."

"Yes," Child Of Her People sobbed. "Yes."

And then Woman Walks Softly was holding both of them, her face wet with tears, and Rachel turned to her grandmother and clung to her desperately.

It was safe, then, to take the time needed to get all the crying done, get all the shaking and trembling done and finished, to let the harsh sobs tear from her the fear that had sat on her heart from that first moment she had smelled the smoke back at their home, their home that no longer existed. Time to clear it all away before she rode back to where her sons waited, alone, in the middle of nowhere at all.

ANNE CAMERON

We live on seven acres of rain forest, in which we have managed to clear a small meadow which we have planted to wild flowers and sweet clover for the honey bees who live in two hives just far enough from the house to allow me a feeling of safety; I'm allergic to stings, and thus am terrified of bees. My Sweetie tells me the bees have other things on their minds and are too busy working to be bothered wasting their time and their lives chasing after me. She must be right, the bees and I have co-existed for five years and while I have been chased (at speeds up to, I'm sure, 45 miles per hour), I have not yet been stung. We have chickens, turkeys, rabbits, cats, and dogs. Every year there are more toads, frogs, and butterflies, every year the gardens are better. This year we had saved up enough money to buy kayaks; they are wonderful. No gas fumes, no motor noise, we have been able to come up on a small deer frolicking in the waves on a hot day, an otter sunning herself on a large rock in the sea, an eagle feasting on a fish on the beach; in each case the wild one thought we were just logs floating on the waves, and ignored us. It was wild! We were so close to the eagle we could hear the fish bones crunching.

I am researching the myths and poetry of the Celtic peoples, with a view to doing a book focusing on the female figures, too many of which have been patriarchalized or ignored since the christianization of the Celtic areas.

Completion of this novel was made possible by a grant from the Canada Council. My sincere thanks to the Council and the tax payers of Canada for their financial support and their encouragement. *Meegwetch!*

Photo: Eleanor Miller

▥spinsters | *aunt lute*▤

Spinsters/Aunt Lute Book Company was founded in 1986 through the merger of two successful feminist publishing businesses, Aunt Lute Book Company, formerly of Iowa City (founded 1982) and Spinsters Ink of San Francisco (founded 1978). A consolidation in the best sense of the word, this merger has strengthened our ability to produce vital books for diverse women's communities in the years to come.

Our commitment is to publishing works that are beyond the scope of mainstream commercial publishers: books that don't just name crucial issues in women's lives, but go on to encourage change and growth, to make all of our lives more possible.

Though Spinsters/Aunt Lute is a growing, energetic company, there is little margin in publishing to meet overhead and production expenses. We survive only through the generosity of our readers. So, we want to thank those of you who have further supported Spinsters/Aunt Lute—with donations, with subscriber monies, or with low and high interest loans. It is that additional economic support that helps us bring out exciting new books.

Please write to us for information about our unique investment and contribution opportunities.

If you would like further information about the books, notecards and journals we produce, write for a free catalogue.

Spinsters/Aunt Lute
P. O. Box 410687
San Francisco, CA 94141